WILLIAM THROUGH TIME

WILLIAM THROUGH TIME

A Magical Bookshop Novel

HARMKE BUURSMA

ISBN 978-17374033-5-7 (hardcover dustjacket)
ISBN 978-17374033-6-4 (ebook)
ISBN 978-17374033-2-6 (paperback)

Edited by Megan Sanders
Author photo by Patterson Photography
Cover design by Getcovers.com

Published by Illusive Press
info@illusivepress.com
www.illusivepress.com

For more information about Harmke Buursma and her books, visit
www.harmkebuursma.com

First Edition, 2022

To anyone who thought they couldn't, then did it anyway.

Contents

Contents ~ ix

'Wake ye from your sleep of death,
Minstrels and bard of other days!
For the midnight wind is on the Heath,
And the midnight meteors dimly blaze:
The Spectre with the Bloody Hand,
Is wandering through the wild woodland;
The owl and the raven are mute for dread,
And the time is meet to awake the dead!

- Part of 'The Bards incantation'
by Sir Walter Scott

Correspondence From William Chambers To John Easton

February 1811

Dear John,

My father purchased a spot in the infantry for me. I shall start as an ensign and am leaving for Europe any day now. How exciting it is to be sent out on my first mission. As you know, it will be the first time I'll leave England. My regiment is being sent to Spain. I do hope, even with the war going on, that I'll be able to taste some local cuisine. Once I have arrived, I shall write to you. However, I've been told that the mail service could be slow at the front. I hope you wish me well on my military endeavors. Our lieutenant-colonel has informed us we are supposed to reinforce the troops and hopefully break the siege in Cadiz.

Forever yours, William

* * *

March 1811

Dear John,

I hope my letter receives you in excellent health. Word may have reached your ears about the battle of Barossa on the 5th of March. My regiment managed to pull through with only a few casualties, though the same cannot be said for the others. Our battalion, under leadership of commander Thomas Graham, managed to defeat two French divisions. Unfortunately, because of the lack of support from our Spanish allies the remaining French forces managed to regroup and continue to occupy the siege lines. I've been very fortunate with the men fighting beside me, though it's been challenging to be thrown in to the fray. James, a fellow officer, has been a great comrade so far. His family hails from Lancashire. His father, a Mr. Tyndall, runs Lynton Hall near Blackpool. Perhaps, once I return to England, we can all visit and enjoy the beaches there. It may be presumptuous, but I believe you and James will get along well. For now, I shall do my best to stay safe on foreign soil.

Forever yours, William

* * *

Dear John,

I apologize for not having written in a while, though I was glad to see your letter arrive. It must have been wonderful to see our old school mates up at London. Too bad Bickerton wasn't there. Last I heard, he joined the navy. I believe he serves as a naval officer. Do you remember that gaff he pulled with our mathematics teacher? Poor, old Mr. Welles never entered a classroom without checking every corner ever again. Oh, John. I wish I could have been there. I have found that military life takes some getting used to. Thankfully, I've got James to keep me sane since I haven't got you here to keep me out of trouble. By now, you must have heard about the Duke of Wellington's victory at Salamanca. The siege at Cadiz finally ended. We've pushed the French forces out of Spain. Despite our losses, this victory made me hopeful that a greater victory over Napoleon's army may be imminent. Commander Thomas Graham got into some hot water for speaking out about the lack of help from the Spaniards during the battle of Barossa. He claims the siege would've ended much sooner if the Spanish troops had joined us, so we could have all swiftly moved in on the remaining troops at the siege line. I find it difficult to speculate on what could have been. From our position between the pine trees on the ridge, we could hardly see what was going on below. But Commander Graham's opinion is unpopular with the Spanish, so he's been sent to join up with the Duke of Wellington's forces, and us with it. I do hope you don't find my talk of war too bothersome.

Forever yours, William

* * *

June 1813

Dear John,

Let me start off with saying that I am well. I was so glad to hear that Beth liked the trinkets I picked up during our marches. I miss you both greatly. At least I am grateful I have James to keep my spirits up on this side of the world. The newspapers shall have reported that we had a great victory over Napoleon, but all I can see is the tremendous amounts of men we lost. I do my best to keep the men under me safe, but it is a task that often proves too great. If I would never hear the sound of a gun firing again, it would still be too soon. However, one must commend Duke Wellington for the battle of Vitoria; he is a great strategist. My hope is for this war to end in the near future and for us to rejoin society. James and I have been talking about moving to London. Something about the hubbub of the city sounds appealing. There is always time to live in the country when one is old.

Forever yours, William

* * *

June 1815

Dear John,

I have a feeling the war is coming to an end soon. Perhaps it is only my own wishful thinking, though I cannot deny that Napoleon's armies are retreating and that we are giving chase. We are following them into the Kingdom of The Netherlands. Under Wellington's orders, my regiments will be sent to support the Prussian troops under Field Marshall Blücher's lead. Once this is all over, I hope you'll let James and I come visit Hawthorne. I would so very much like for you both to meet.

Forever yours, William

* * *

July 1815

Dear John,

My superior ordered me to write a letter to my family. Since my own parents hardly count as family, I could only write to you. I'm at the field hospital and will be transferred soon to England for further treatment. I'm alive, though my face will never be the same. James, however, is dead. So, we have won, and I have lost.

Sincerely, William

I

The Waddling Duck

A stiff October breeze blew across the London streets; digging its icy teeth into my skin. I pulled up the collar of my jacket as I crossed the street, my face hardly recognizable in the dark. But I remained vigilant.

Last night, I had one of my nightmares. It felt so real it left me reeling; its after effects haunting me my entire day. So much so, that I needed to be in the company of others. The place I was headed—The Waddling Duck— was a bit of a refuge. A place you could go to be around like-minded people, to be yourself even if polite society wouldn't accept those parts of yourself.

I was flirting with danger every time I visited this place. There was no doubt about it. But the same went for the other patrons. We all risked getting caught whenever we visited. Only last week, the London constabulary raided a different "disorderly" house.

It seemed only a matter of time before they came knocking down the doors of Mary Duck's safe haven for anyone who was different. Being caught meant I risked exposing myself, my truth, to everyone in England. I could be thrown in jail or strapped to a pillory for the masses to mock, eschewed by my peers.

Mary did have a few fail safes; runners—young street urchins who kept an eye out on the streets— that would alert Mary and the rest of the clientèle that constables were on their way. This could provide everyone inside precious minutes to flee the scene. Thankfully, that had never happened the entire time I frequented the establishment.

My hand skimmed the slight bump beneath my coat. James' ring. We'd exchanged our family rings in private one night while the other men in our battalion were fast asleep. His bore his family's crest while mine had been an embossed C for my surname. That's when we had made the promise to each other—to live together, to love together. They were tokens of a future for the both of us. Ever since, I carried it in my breast pocket. However, instead of a symbol of what was to come, it was now a reminder of what I'd lost.

Reaching the unassuming house, I raised my hand automatically and knocked five times; three fast and two slow. A plump woman dressed in menswear opened the door and ushered me in.

I felt guilty sometimes for even going. I'd promised my friend John that I'd be careful, that I'd be safe. I kept part of that promise; I no longer lost myself in gambling. But this was one part of myself that I couldn't give up or deny. I craved connection, not necessarily of the flesh, more like a sense of belonging. And that was what The Waddling Duck provided. That's why I kept coming. But perhaps it was also the sense of danger that permeated every moment, the thrill of doing something deemed forbidden.

Shrugging out of my jacket, I surveyed the room for a spot to sit. Two cross dressers, regular visitors at The Waddling Duck, lifted their glasses to me as I entered the main room before returning to their animated conversation. Grabbing a glass of whiskey from a tray, I slumped down into one of the tufted chairs, then raised my glass as well. A barely dressed young man sang in a high-pitched voice while another accompanied him on a piano.

This room was used for socializing, but for men and women looking to go somewhere more private, there were rooms available. In the case that you arrived alone, you could also find someone that suited your tastes. Mary Duck, the proprietress, would make sure of that. I rarely took her up on her offer to find someone to warm my bed, though she couldn't complain; I paid handsomely to simply sit in a chair and savor a glass of whiskey.

She'd asked me before why, if all I wanted to do was to sit and drink, I wouldn't just go to any regular gentlemen's club. I suppose she had a point. Mary had said it bluntly in her broad accent that revealed humbler origins than the satin dresses she wore would have you believe. This ability to create a place where you could be seen how you wanted to be seen was exactly what made me admire the proprietress. I joked that it was her friendly service that kept me coming back. She raised her eyebrows, let out a loud boisterous laugh, and left to order one of her "boys" to service a client.

I lazily swirled the glass of amber liquid in my right hand, raised it to my mouth, and threw it back. Luxurious velvet furniture, colorful drapes, and men and women of all ages filled the room. A slender man, dressed in a too short silk gown, with feathery scarfs draped across his neck, approached me.

"Anything you are looking for, handsome?" he said, using the tail end of one of his scarfs to brush my cheek. The soft plumes tickling the short stubble on my face. "I can keep you company tonight." I flinched a little, which he noticed. "Or we can just talk. I've been told I'm a great listener."

"Some company sounds enjoyable," I said. He had expressive brown eyes and a gentle demeanor. Perhaps spending some time in the company of another man wouldn't hurt.

"Follow me," he said, winking, as he held out his hand. I slid my hand into his. "Let's go somewhere a little more private."

I followed him up the stairs and into one of the small rooms. Then I plopped down on a bed covered in a lilac bedspread. The space was empty besides the bed and a single wooden chair. But I supposed the private rooms didn't really need much more than that. The Waddling Duck had other rooms for different types of entertainment— rooms filled with wardrobes of all styles and lounges to host private parties. Choice was key.

"Now," the slender man said, as he perched himself beside me and trailed a finger along my bicep. "What would you like to talk about?"

I let myself fall back in to the mattress, which was slightly springy, and stretched my arms behind my head. "I'm not sure." And I wasn't. The sole reason I was here this evening was because I didn't want to be alone.

"You must be full of stories," the man said, leaning back and sliding his palm up from my arm to my chest. "What are you doing here?"

"The same as the other patrons, I assume."

The slender man draped in scarfs didn't know how to reply to my brusque answer. I felt a bit sorry; it wasn't his fault that I wasn't feeling very social. I already regretted following him up the stairs. From the start, I had been in a sour mood, since my nightmares had woken me up. As they frequently did.

I was at war with myself. I wanted to make a connection with someone, anyone. Just so I knew I could. I needed to know that that part of me hadn't died with James. But when it came to it, I wasn't able to. I'd push everyone away. I was tired of feeling numb, of walking through life in a haze.

The man rolled onto his stomach, supporting his chin with his palms. "Why don't you tell me a little bit about yourself?" he continued, changing his tactic. "How come a gentleman such as yourself is spending his night alone at The Waddling Duck? Surely, there are many other social opportunities for such a man to go to."

"Surely, such a gentleman isn't alone since he is in fact currently spending his time with you."

"Touché, Monsieur," he said in a put-on French accent. "Well, then such a gentleman might be in a mood to entertain his companion with a tale?" The man raised himself to his knees and lifted the plumes of his scarfs, letting them fall around me. With the back of his hand, he brushed the feathers along my skin. "What happened here?" he said, as he reached the scar that marred the side of my face.

"It's nothing," I said. He brushed my temple again. I pulled my cheek away.

"Scars give a man character," he said with a wink. "I'd love to learn more."

"I don't want to talk about it." He reached out his hand again, but I grabbed a hold of his wrist before he could touch my cheek. "I said no."

"I'm only trying to make light conversation," the man sputtered. I pushed him aside and got off the bed.

"I don't think I'm feeling up to light conversation," I said, crossing the space between the bed and the door.

"Wait, what about my fee? I did lead you to a private room." I bit my lip and fished a coin out of my pocket. Throwing it to the man now sitting on the edge of the bed, I turned and strode out of the room.

What had I been thinking, following a stranger into a private room? I was in no mood to swap stories. And even if I had wanted to be entertained for a while, as soon as he touched my scar, I got pulled out of the moment. I didn't blame the man, even if he couldn't take a hint. Shaking off the incident, I found myself more liquor, then returned to the chair in the main room.

A while later, the man dressed in feather scarfs returned. His eyes flashed to me before turning to other men sitting by themselves. He quickly found another potential customer which he led back to another private room. I emptied my glass and set it down on a table.

"Another drink?" one of Mary's "boys" offered. Usually, I would stay longer, enjoying the sense of belonging, but today the noise of people laughing and singing together didn't feel like freedom. It grated my nerves. The heat from the fireplace and the swig of cheap whiskey mingled and made me lightheaded.

"I've had enough," I said to him.

"Something else perhaps?" He jutted out his hip and let his eyes glide over me.

I shook my head. "Not tonight." Then, I stood and retrieved my jacket. My hand lingering on the round metal object I kept in my breast pocket.

The brisk air felt refreshing against my heated cheeks when I exited Mary's establishment. I tightened my jacket around myself and pressed my hands into its pockets. Only a few blocks to go before I could order a carriage to take me back to my apartments.

I was being unusually melancholy this evening. I knew the reason. However, knowing why I was feeling a certain way didn't stop the feelings from happening. Weeks could pass where I hardly thought of James except for a random memory here and there. Then there were days when everything reminded me of him, where I felt his loss so acutely, it felt like a punch to my gut—my grief so overwhelming that I couldn't breathe. The aftermath would leave me feeling empty and alone. But I hated the idea of finding someone else to fill that space, to distract me from James.

Once, I wanted nothing more than to share my entire life with James. We had planned to live together in London as two bachelors. That plan now echoed across the empty rooms in my apartments, ridiculing the naïve ideas of two officers in the midst of war. James' death felt like a punishment. How dare we be happy when all across Belgium and France, men were laying on battlefields—hurt and dying.

A few prostitutes whistled and cajoled as I passed them by. I buried my chin deeper into my jacket and picked up my pace. I needed to stop lingering on James. He might be gone, but I wasn't. I still relived what happened to him in my nightmares, but perhaps, when I was awake, I could choose to forget. Start over. Perhaps, someday, I'd find someone else.

It hurt every time I thought of James, but I hoped John was right; that with time, James' memory would hurt less and less, until I could think of him with fondness. Appreciating what we had for such a brief time. Though, I doubted it would ever happen.

Winding my way back into more populated and illuminated streets, I pushed aside my thoughts of James. I signaled a carriage that was making its way down the road. The driver stopped so I could get seated.

"To Albany, please," I told the man.

"Right away, sir."

Once we arrived outside my apartments, I paid the driver and walked up the steps to my home. Inside, I threw my jacket across the banister and made my way to the sitting room, where I stretched out in my reading chair.

My butler scraped his throat as he entered the sitting room.

"What is it, Parsons?" I asked.

"Sir, a footman delivered a letter for you this evening while you were out."

"Did it say who from?"

"Mr. Easton, sir."

Parsons handed me the cream-colored letter and a small letter opener on a tray.

"Is there anything else I can do for you, sir?"

"No, that will be all for tonight," I said, then I remembered the late hour and softened my voice. "Thank you for staying up and handing me the letter. It is late and anything else can wait until tomorrow."

"My pleasure, sir," the butler said with a nod of his head. Then he left me by myself to read John's letter.

I wondered what my friend's letter was about. It had only been a couple of months since I visited him and his wife Rose. I slid the sharp point of the letter opener into the edge of the envelope and with a swift move, cut the paper to reveal the folded letter inside. Dropping the letter opener on the side table, I slid the paper out and unfolded it.

Dear William,

We have missed you these past months. Beth has been begging us to make the trip to London, and I must confess I would have liked to, if it wasn't for a small matter that has arisen. I'm afraid I won't be able to divulge much about the small matter, in fear of this letter falling into the wrong hands.

Wrong hands? I didn't think John could be more cryptic if he tried. Riddles had never been my strong suit. I didn't know what the "small matter" was, but it seemed he was reaching out for help. I straightened out the paper and continued reading.

Whose hands, I don't know. I am more than likely being silly and paranoid, but nonetheless, it behooves me to be apprehensive. Once you know the nature behind this letter, I am sure you will agree with me. Let me get to the point before I either bore you to death or before you assume I am part of some criminal underground scandal. The small matter has to do with my wife. I hope you understand the delicacy of my letter which leads me to invite you to stay at Hawthorne while I sort the matter. Your help might come in handy.
Yours faithfully, John Easton.

P.S. Rose urged me to tell you she misses you too, and that she is looking forward to seeing you. We all hope to see you soon.

I racked my brain for any inkling on what the problem could be. Rose was from the future—a mind bogglingly strange idea that I still hadn't fully processed. To be frank, I generally chose to forget that bit of information. However, the only people that knew of Rose were John, Beth, and I. It didn't seem like the thing to share with others, and I wouldn't know how someone else could find out about it unless they stumbled upon a conversation where Rose and John were discussing the matter. No, someone finding out about Rose was unlikely. Which made me wonder what it was that John needed me for and how it did involve Rose. I didn't detect any sadness in his letter, and surely, she wouldn't return to her own time? Not after marrying John, I wouldn't think.

I sighed and stood from my chair. Grabbing the envelope from the side table, I dropped both the letter and the envelope into my hearth. Using the fire poker, I made sure that John's letter disappeared into ashes. Returning the fire poke to its stand, I made sure to leave the room tidy and left a note for my butler on the hallway table. It had been a long day and I needed to sleep. I would have Parsons pack my things in the morning and leave for Hawthorne as soon as I was awake and dressed.

2

Hawthorne

"William!" Beth shouted as I exited the carriage. She raced down the steps of Hawthorne and enveloped me in a hug. I grinned and patted her head. "Missed me?"

"Of course, I did; although, I would've preferred to come to you."

"Oh, you wound me," I said in a dramatic voice, clutching my hand to my chest. "It isn't me you missed; it is the shopping." Beth swatted me playfully. I gave her a little pinch and she yelped.

"Fine," she said, turning up her nose. "I did miss the shopping." She returned to her bright smile. "But I sure am glad you are here."

"So am I. However, we can always check with John and perhaps organize a trip to London. Rose would probably love to visit the theater again, and we can go to Bond Street for your fashion."

"Perhaps," Beth said, thoughtful.

The driver lifted my luggage from the back of the carriage. I traveled light, with only two suitcases. I waved at John and Rose, who had appeared in front of the double entry doors, before grabbing my luggage with both hands.

"Thanks," I told the driver before walking towards the stately house I had spent my formative years to meet my other friends, Beth in tow. Another man joined Rose and John at the entrance to Hawthorne.

"Who's that?" I whispered to Beth.

"You'll see," she said, her voice lowered for suspense.

"That's it?"

"John can explain better than I can," she said.

"Now you are making me worried."

Beth grinned again. "There's nothing to worry about, I promise."

"I suppose I shall take your word for it." My eyes drifted to the man now settling beside Rose. His hairstyle was odd— clipped short on the sides with a longer sweep of brown hair on top. Or was it red? The watery October sun gave his dark hair a deep ginger glow. I thought the color was a striking match with his vivid green eyes.

"William, I'm so glad to see you," John said as I walked up the steps.

"Let me introduce you to our other guest." John pointed at the green-eyed man. I set down my luggage and held out my hand as he stepped forward. I noted the clothing he wore; they belonged to John. This man was smaller than my friend, so the clothing was ill-fitting— extra fabric bunching at his ankles and wrists.

"Hi, I'm Austin Miller," he said as he shook my hand. He spoke in a similar accent as Rose. Not an exact match, but it was close; they both rounded their vowels in the same distinctive way.

"Well met," I said. "My name is William Raphe Chambers." My gaze lingered a tad too long on his green eyes. I pulled myself together, let go of his hand, and greeted John with a friendly pat on his back.

"It's wonderful to see you again," Rose said as she drew me into a hug, once I stepped away from John.

"It's lovely to see you, too," I said. "But perhaps we can retreat to a private room to discuss the letter you sent to me?" I gave John a pointed look.

"Come, let's go inside," John said. He grabbed one of my suitcases. We all followed him into the warmth of his home. He set my suitcase down by the staircase and turned to me. "Don't worry, William. We can all speak freely here." My eyes flitted to the handsome stranger.

"Are you sure?"

"Austin is the reason I sent the letter," John said.

The green-eyed man hesitated before he spoke. "I'm like Rose," he said.

"Like Rose? You mean..." My voice trailed off. Austin nodded.

"Yes, I'm from the future." I was sure my mouth went slack jawed. I turned to Rose.

"So, did you and Austin meet each other before you, well," I stumbled. "Before you came here?"

"We didn't," she said as she grabbed my arm. "America is a pretty big place. But, before we go into details, let's first get you settled and find somewhere comfortable to sit down for refreshments. I'm sure you'd like to stretch and eat a bite of food after your long journey."

"I wouldn't turn down one of Mrs. Avery's apple cakes."

"I'll send for some tea and food," Rose said. John squeezed her hand.

"Thank you, dear." Rose winked to John before heading towards the kitchen. "Well, how about we withdraw to the sitting room? We can all eagerly await our refreshments there." John led the way.

Entering the room, I could tell Rose had left her mark. The new pastel-colored floral wallpaper had to be her design choice. It didn't seem like something John would pick. The lighter colors softened the room, making it inviting and feminine. I settled on the settee while John and Beth leaned back in chairs. Austin joined me, so Rose could take the empty seat beside her husband.

"I think Austin can probably explain better than I can, since it is his story," John said.

Austin angled his body towards me. "Honestly, Rose is probably the person who knows most. I'm still reeling from everything. One moment, I'm standing in a bookshop, the next I find myself standing in the middle of a street, a carriage heading straight for me."

"What happened?" I asked.

"I jumped out of the way just in time, thankfully. Don't know how I did it, especially when I had never been more confused. I had to pinch myself to make sure it was real and not a dream. The carriage steered away from me and screeched to a halt. Then John and Rose stepped out."

"And I asked if you were from America," Rose said, as she entered the sitting room with Mrs. Avery and refreshments in tow. "The jeans kind of gave it away," she shrugged. Jeans? Sometimes when I listened to Rose speak, I swore she made up words.

Mrs. Avery carried a tray with apple cakes, crust-less sandwiches, cookies, a tea kettle, and cups and saucers. She set the tray down on the side table. Rose poured tea and handed a cup to Austin.

"We've missed having you around, Mr. Chambers," Mrs. Avery said. She thrust a sandwich into my hands. "Eat up," she ordered. "You look famished. We need to put some meat back on your bones."

"I will," I said. "Thank you. Your cooking is always satisfying." My stomach rumbled as the waft of cinnamon coming from the apple cake reached my nostrils. It had been hours since I had eaten. I took a big bite of the sandwich; crispy, fresh, cucumber crunching between my teeth.

"It was the strangest thing that ever happened to me. Or I guess is still happening to me," Austin continued after accepting the cup of tea from Rose. "Seeing Rose walk towards me in those old-timey clothes was a bit of a shock. Especially, when she spoke in a normal accent." At this, Austin stammered. "Umm, I mean. Not that John's, Beth's, or your accent for that matter..." he said, looking at me. "Are not normal. I guess Rose and I are the ones who are abnormal. Your English is the original, after all." Austin flashed me a crooked smile. "I'm glad Rose and John were the ones who almost hit me with their carriage. I don't know what I would've done if they weren't the ones to run into me. They've been incredibly kind and accommodating to let me stay with them while I figure out how I can return to my own time."

"That must be challenging," I offered. Austin nodded and took a sip of tea. I finished my cucumber sandwich and reached for a piece of apple cake.

"Yes, I'm worried about my sister and my work. However, Rose said that when she returned to her own place, time hadn't continued. I hope that will be true for me as well."

"As I said before, you are welcome to stay here as long as it takes for you to figure out a way to return to your own time," John said. Austin glanced at John, his face softening.

"Thank you."

"Does that mean you have a plan to return?" I asked Austin. Mrs. Avery handed me a cup of tea balanced on a saucer.

Rose pursed her lips before answering. "As far as I understand it, there isn't a way to return on your own. I only managed to travel back because the bookshop owner, Melinda, came looking for me," Rose said, apologetic as she directed her words at Austin. "I'm not sure what her plan for you is or why she decides to check in. I wish I knew more."

Austin shrugged. "I guess I'll be stuck here for now."

"In great company at least," Rose added. "When I showed up here, I had no clue what to do. And John—" she gave her husband a loving glance, "was incredibly suspicious of me. If I didn't have my friendship with Beth, I don't know how I would've lasted."

"And you chose to stay," Austin stated, curious. Rose nodded.

"Beth and John had become my family; there was no other choice for me. It was such a relief once they knew everything.

When there was no need to keep my secret all to myself." John reached out to Rose's hand and caressed her skin. They were so happy and in love. While I was glad my best friend had found his soul mate, I couldn't help a twinge of envy from slithering through my heart. Seeing them so in tune with each other and planning a long life together made me wish I had someone to call my own. However, that possibility passed me by. I had loved, but he was gone now. The Earl Grey tea had turned bitter in my mouth, and I swallowed thickly.

"I hate imposing on you and Rose. I asked before, but is there anything I can do to help?" Austin turned to John, waiting.

"You are welcome as my guest. But, perhaps William and yourself can keep each other company? It was one of the reasons I invited him."

"I wouldn't be opposed to that," I said. "While I am here."

"Actually," Rose cut in. "There is something I could use your help with, Austin. And perhaps yours as well?" she said to me.

"Which is?" I lifted my brow.

"Well, John and I have been talking about how I miss my job back home."

"And?"

"It hit me there was no reason I couldn't do the same thing here."

"I remember you mentioning you used to teach children?"

"Exactly," Rose said, excitedly.

"How were you planning on doing that here?" I quirked my brow at John. "You aren't letting her move away to some school, are you?"

John lifted his arms. "You met my wife, if she sets her mind to something..."

"Stubborn," I laughed.

"Hey now," she said, jokingly. "I'm not planning to abandon Hawthorne or Westbridge. "You know that as well," she said, swatting John's shoulder. "No, I was thinking about John's tenants and how marvelous it would be if we started a small school right here for the children. If we have our own little building on the estate, I can teach the boys and girls."

"And Rose said I could help as well." Beth grinned.

"Lord help us," I said.

"I think it is a marvelous idea," Beth added. "Teaching the children of our tenants gives us a purpose as well."

"It sounds like a good plan," Austin agreed.

I nodded. "Where do we come in?" Teaching wasn't my thing, and I couldn't commit to something that would have me stay at Hawthorne indefinitely.

Rose's eyes narrowed conspiratorially. "So, how are both of your building skills?"

"Building skills?" I raised my brows even more.

"Don't worry," Rose said, waving her hand. "It shouldn't be too difficult. I think." I caught John's eye and he smirked. "Yeah, to build the school. It only needs to be big enough for a maximum of ten kids."

"Right." I never built a thing in my life. Rose noticed my uncertain expression because she quickly continued.

"Of course, you and Austin wouldn't be the only two building the school. John and I plan on hiring our tenants to give them a chance at earning extra income. I thought perhaps you both could assist and act as our overseers."

Austin let out a sigh. "Overseeing? I never held a hammer, let alone built something from the ground up."

Rose snorted. "You never fixed anything in your own place, hung up a picture?"

"Eh, my sister helped in a few places. For bigger projects, I hired people. I did put some Ikea furniture together."

Rose's eyes crinkled as she laughed. "Ikea would've come in handy for furniture," she said. "But John and I spoke with Robert McCreary, one of our tenants; he has experience building houses from before he started renting from John. He'll be the one in charge. I figured this might be something to do to pass the time. You can check in every once in a while or stay and help if you are interested in learning anything."

"Where is this school going to be built?" I asked.

"Near the pond where I first found Rose," John said. He glanced fondly at Rose.

"Alright. I can't promise I'll get my hands dirty, but I'll keep an eye on the progress. When is construction supposed to start?" William said.

"Next week," Rose said. "I wanted to start sooner, but we were waiting on materials. Hopefully, the exterior can be done before the holidays. It would be wonderful to start classes after Christmas and before all the activities in London begin."

"My brother agreed to let me attend my first season in London!" Beth sat at the edge of her seat, bouncing her toes, a huge grin plastered on her face.

"Good luck," I told Beth. And good luck John, I thought but didn't say. He was going to need it. John seemed to shiver at Beth's announcement. Rose must have had a hand in persuading him on Beth's behalf. I knew he'd been hesitant to let Beth join the marriage mart. The situation with that crook Danby this past summer hadn't helped things.

3

An Invitation

Gossip spread fast in Westbridge. After only a few days at Hawthorne, the local gentry was coming to call. Nothing was more valuable in society than having information someone else didn't.

Mrs. Avery kept herself busy bringing out treats and tea for guests all day long until supper. Even Mrs. Ashbrook—Rose's chosen great aunt— had dropped by to meet myself and John's new house guest.

Some visitors showed interested in me because, as John had warned me, now that John and Rose had married, I became the next eligible bachelor to snare. Thankfully, most of their interest eventually turned to John's house guest, Austin. Mystery always fueled gossip. Finally, the company had dwindled down to one middle-aged woman.

"Are you and Mrs. Easton related?" Mrs. Brocklehurst asked

Austin. "Cousins, perhaps?" She was sipping tea sweet enough to match the sugary ribbons and frills in her graying hair.

"No, not at all." Austin started.

"We are childhood friends," Rose cut in.

Mrs. Brocklehurst pursed her lips. I understood why she was asking; if Austin turned out to be a cousin, perhaps he would have some claim to Mrs. Ashbrook's estate. Mrs. Brocklehurst had two daughters out for marriage and a third entering society in a year, if her matchmaking went well. Her head turned to me. "Mr. Chambers, how wonderful to encounter you in Westbridge. This town doesn't get to see nearly enough of you. I dare say, we are starved for entertainment. Are you only visiting or are you planning on staying here long term?"

"I wouldn't dare impose on Mr. Easton any longer than necessary," I said.

"Nonetheless, you must come over for dinner soon. My girls would love a chance to entertain."

"Certainly." There was no option to decline a direct offer.

"Of course, Mr. Miller, you are invited as well," she said, looking down her nose at Austin. Her tone and body language told me she only extended the invite because she didn't want to appear rude.

"Thank you," Austin said. I got the impression he was entirely uninterested in Mrs. Brocklehurst's invite but pretended to be pleasant.

Mrs. Brocklehurst inclined her head slightly and returned her calculating gaze to me. "There are some lovely apartments available to let near the river, so I've heard. It must be terribly lonely up in London without friendly company. We'd all be delighted if you returned to Westbridge."

"I can't say that I am. I quite enjoy my apartment in Albany," I replied. I had no plans to move and be scrutinized even more. Life in London suited my purpose.

For the rest of Mrs. Brocklehurst's visit, we discussed the weather— which was cold and mostly overcast— the lack of parties, and if I knew whether Rose's great aunt, Mrs. Ashbrook, visited often.

I was glad when she finally stood and bid us farewell.

"What can I expect?" Austin asked once Mrs. Brocklehurst left.

"Mrs. Brocklehurst will probably parade all three of her daughters before us during dinner to make sure we have a chance to realize what a catch they are. Then, after dinner, we'll be expected to sit through a recital where the girls can butcher some poor tunes to try to impress us."

"That sounds awful." Austin shuddered. "And you go to these dinners often?"

I laughed. "Well, I try to avoid invitations to dinners as much as I can. They are one of the reasons why I have my own apartments in London."

"What are the other reasons?"

"The people that make up the beau monde are a tight-knit group."

"-like you and John?"

"And Mrs. Brocklehurst, and Mrs. Ashbrook, yes. It's difficult to avoid the social engagements and peers, even in London, but, at least, there are so many people, it makes it easier to disappear. To maintain a sliver of anonymity."

Austin frowned. "You need that?"

I paused, thinking. "Sometimes..."

"It does sound stifling, everyone always knowing what you are up to, where you are."

"That's why I like living on my own in London."

"Yeah, that does sound like a better plan." Austin shook his head. "I think it's crazy that every interaction here comes with an expectation." He held my gaze. "So, because you aren't married yet, every mom around here expects you to choose one of their daughters?"

I considered his question. "Yes. Well, mostly. I can't blame the mothers; all they are doing is trying to make sure their children will be safe and secure. However, because I understand why doesn't mean I want to marry one of their daughters."

Austin paused, glancing up at me with his gentle green eyes, "You never want to marry?"

Such a direct question. I swallowed. "I'm not sure... I don't think marriage is for me." His question pried into a subject I preferred to not contemplate. Something like concern flashed across his features, but he said nothing. I wondered what he was thinking, the silence uncomfortable. I squirmed, unsure of how to answer. So, instead, I deflected, hoping to lighten the moment. "Why? You want to marry one of Mrs. Brocklehurst's daughters.

Austin grinned. "Nah, I'm good. I'll focus on getting through my time here safely, without marriage proposals."

Beth ran into the room. "Did Mrs. Brocklehurst leave?

"About a half hour ago," I said.

"Thank god," she said, dropping herself into one of the

chairs, a bundle of thread and cloth in her hands. "I was tired of being up in my room. Thank you for keeping her entertained."

"Just wait until you join society," I said. "I'll make sure every puffed-up dandy comes and visit you!"

"You wouldn't!" Beth gasped. I winked.

"I think it is only fair. Don't you?"

Beth picked up a needle loaded with a pale pink thread. As she started her stitches on an embroidery piece, she said, "We both know you wouldn't. What would John say." Beth acted pleased with herself as she shaped the outline of a dahlia. Austin was badly disguising his laugh. I shot him a glare. I stood and snatched the embroidery work from Beth's hands.

"What are you working on?" I asked, holding the cloth up to my face.

"Give it back." Beth sprang out of her chair and reached for her needlework. I raised my hand above my head, keeping the cloth out of her reach.

"Why should I do that?" I teased. My mouth stretched into a grin. "Are you making something to catch a suitor's eye?"

Beth gave me a small shove. "It isn't for me." She glanced at Austin for assistance. "Can you help me?"

Austin laughed. "This is between you both. I am playing Switzerland."

Austin's comment was strange, but I let it slide, writing the phrase off as another example of his modern colloquialisms. Beth was insistent on getting her handy work back. Raised onto her tiptoes, she was trying to smack my hand. I only meant to tease her lightheartedly, but she was getting peeved.

"Oh alright. Here you go, Beth." I lowered my arm, and she snatched her work. "Your embroidery is nicely done," I added.

"Thank you," she said, as she returned to the padded chair. The compliment seemed to appease her.

John's valet scraped his throat as he walked into the tea-room. "Sir, some mail arrived," he said.

"For me?"

"And Mr. Miller," he said as he handed a letter to both Austin and myself.

"Thank you, George," I told the man. He had been the valet at Hawthorne even when John's father was still alive.

The letter I held in my hand was exactly the same as Austin's, down to the thick cream envelope and the loopy script. I didn't want to search for a letter opener. Instead, I pried a corner of the envelope open, and used my little finger to rip the rest of the paper. Inside was a thick card.

The letter read:

The company of Mr. Chambers is requested at Granhope Manor on New Year's Eve, at 6 o'clock, to partake in a masquerade. RSVPs are required and the wearing of masks are highly encouraged.

Returning a favor, Beth snatched the letter out of my hands. "What did you receive? That looks like Mrs. Ashbrook's handwriting." She scanned the writing. "Oh, a masquerade? That sounds like so much fun. Do you think I'll be able to go too?"

"I'm not sure," I said, taking the card back. "It depends on if you got invited as a part of John's party or not. When do John and Rose return?"

Beth pursed her lips. "They should be soon. John said they'd be back in time for dinner."

"You'll find out at dinner then."

Beth rolled her eyes at me before squeaking, "A masquerade sounds like so much fun. I hope I can go. We'd have to travel into town to find masks." Beth's voice turned dreamy. I could tell her attentions were heading towards fashion and shopping.

"Let's first find out if you are going."

"I'll make sure of it." Her face was determined and hopeful.

"But don't worry about our masks. Austin and I can purchase our own in town."

"You have to let me help you choose," Beth pleaded. "Have you even thought of ideas for what you like to go as? You could go as anything." Beth tapped her fingers against her chin. "I already thought of what you could go as, William. How about a squirrel?"

"And what would you be?" I smirked. "A butterfly?"

"No, I'd be a rabbit. Or perhaps a peacock," Beth said, filling in the dahlia petals.

"A rabbit indeed," I told her. "The perfect animal since you'd be prey at a masquerade. I doubt John will acquiesce."

"We'll see about that." Beth frowned and pretended to be focused on her handiwork.

"I think I'm going to head out, catch some fresh air," Austin said. He stretched his arms out in front of him and left the decorative chair.

"Would you like some company? I wouldn't mind stretching my legs for a bit." I peered at him questioningly.

"Yeah, you can come along."

I turned to Beth. "I'll put in a good word to John."

Her face brightened. "Thank you."

"Of course. You know I merely like to tease you," I said, giving Beth a pat on her head. "Well, we'll be off."

John and Beth were like family. And in a sense, they were my real brother and sister. Growing up, I spent more time with them than I did with my parents. John's parents had been so unlike my own mother and father; they made me feel like I belonged, like I was worth getting to know. All my parents ever did was make me doubt myself. Nothing I did was ever good enough. The kindest thing they ever did for me was to leave me with the Eastons when they moved up north.

"What are you thinking about," Austin said, as we walked the path leading past the stables.

"I apologize if I wasn't paying attention. I was just thinking about John and Beth, and my parents."

"Are they still around?"

I nodded. "Yes, but I rarely ever visit them. In fact, I believe the last time I saw my father was five years ago."

Austin stuck his hands in his pockets and kicked a small rock on the path. "They don't live close?"

"No, they moved to Harrogate." Austin's face remained blank at my answer. "You have no clue where Harrogate is, do you?" I laughed.

He snickered. "Yeah, I don't. But I doubt you could name many places in America either," Austin pointed out, rightly so.

I tipped my head. "I'd wager you are right." I flashed a smile. "Harrogate is in northern England, near York. The place is quite famous for its healing waters."

"Healing waters?"

"People travel from all over to bathe in the mineral waters.

Supposedly, it can cure all manners of illness, including gout and digestive issues. My mother has a touch of rheumatism, so father relocated to Harrogate. Living there lets her use the spa facilities whenever she needs them. She sends me a letter every once in a while, usually detailing her aches and pains."

"It must be difficult to live so far away from your family." I couldn't explain why but something about Austin made me want to be honest and open with him. There was no pretense with him, no scheming. I barely knew him but despite that, I had the sense I could trust him to listen without judgment.

"I wish it were different sometimes, but John and Beth's parents have been more of a mother and father to me than my own parents ever were." We left the main path and started to walk the outskirts of the Hawthorne estate. "What are your parents like?" I asked.

Austin gazed at the ground. "My parents passed away when I was very young."

"My condolences. Can I ask how it happened? I don't want to intrude; we can change topics."

"I don't mind," Austin said. "I was the one asking about your family first." He sighed. "My parents died in a car crash when I was seven."

"A car crash?"

"A car is a kind of carriage that you drive but it doesn't need horses."

I nodded as if I fully understood what he was saying. I would need to ask Rose for a further explanation later. "Where were you?

"I was in the car with them." Austin had stopped walking. "I was playing a game in the backseat. My mom turned towards me, handing me a snack. My dad was talking to my mom. He must've only averted his gaze from the road for a second when bright lights lit up the interior of the car." Austin's face lowered, his eyes turning away from me. "And the impact. I can still remember the pressure of the seat belt locking against my chest so tightly it felt like it cut into my skin." Austin's fingers trailed the upper left side of his chest. "I hardly remember anything from back then, except for that moment, only a few seconds really." Austin swallowed and set off again. I picked up my pace to keep up with him. "I'm sorry I ruined our walk with depressing stories."

"Not at all," I said sincerely. "Thank you for sharing such a personal story with me."

"Normally, you start with what's your favorite color when you want to get to know someone," Austin said.

"Well, mine's yellow, like the color of daffodils.

His face brightened. "That was not the answer I would've expected."

I shrugged. "I always thought it was a cheerful color."

"I like navy blue." Austin's eyes crinkled when he smiled. I knew I said yellow but, in the future, it was possible I might change my answer to green; when the pale October sun hit Austin's pupils, they shimmered like the most precious emerald jewels. Their color was hypnotic.

"Navy is a fine color as well," I said, staring ahead again. I peered in the distance. A carriage was heading towards the turn into Hawthorne. "It appears John and Rose have returned."

"We should probably return then," Austin said. "The walk was nice though."

"It was an enjoyable change to have a conversation with someone that didn't need something from me," I said.

"Does that happen a lot?"

"Often." I frowned. "What I mean is, most of the time you have to censor yourself because everyone you meet has an agenda. They want to use you or your knowledge to their advantage. You have been refreshing."

"Who knows. Maybe I am plotting something, and you just don't know it yet."

I chuckled. "Let's hope not."

4

A Candy Bar

John and Rose opened their own letters from Mrs. Ashbrook at the dining table. We were waiting for the courses to be set out on the table. Beth looked so hopeful when George, the valet, handed John and Rose their cards, only to look crushed when there was no letter for her.

"A masquerade?" Rose said, reading the thick stock card. "Mrs. Ashbrook is asking me, as her heir, to be the one to kick the party off."

"That's quite the honor," John said. "Mrs. Ashbrook's masquerades are one of the most anticipated social events of the year. Everyone in and around Westbridge waits for an invitation. She is incredibly selective with her invites."

"I've never been to a masquerade. I guess we'll need to go back into town to order costumes." Rose returned her gaze to the swirly script. "Looks like we'll have some time. The masquerade isn't until New Year's Eve, which gives us well over two months to prepare."

"Can I come too?" Beth spoke.

"You haven't received an invitation," John said flatly.

"But if Rose is kicking the masquerade off—"

"No," John cut in. "You aren't out in society yet. Besides, masquerades tend to get wild. Something about identities being obscured loosens inhibitions." Beth looked distraught.

"Brother, what does it matter? I'm already joining the season in London next year."

John sighed. "Don't get me started. We both know letting you go wasn't my idea."

"John, perhaps we can make an exception." Rose squeezed her husband's hand. "Although, I'll need to persuade Mrs. Ashbrook to let me off the hook. I've never been to a masquerade, and I'd prefer to attend as a guest somewhere at the periphery—with you."

"I don't want Beth there when I may not be able to keep an eye on her." He shot Rose a dark look. "I know what happens there."

I scratched my head. I promised Beth I would put in a good word for her, and I didn't go back on my promises. "John, Beth is on the older side to not be out in society yet. Besides, you are introducing her this coming season. Why not let her have fun and experience a masquerade?"

"Don't you trust me?" Beth added.

"It's not that I don't trust you," John said as he put down the invitation. "I don't trust the other people invited."

"I'm sure I'll be fine. I'll have you and William to look out for me. And Austin as well," she said, pointing at him.

"We'll all be incognito. I'm saying no. And that is final."

"Fine," Beth said in a huff.

"Fine," John replied. Beth crossed her arms and stared at the empty plate in front of her with a frown.

"What if," I said, drawing out the words, "we reach out to Anne Blakeley? I'm sure the Blakeley family is invited. Perhaps Beth and Anne can go together, that way they are chaperoning each other."

"Please, Brother. I can send out a letter to Anne and her mother right away," Beth pleaded, her face in a pout.

"Besides, what could go wrong with Mrs. Blakeley as their eagle-eyed chaperon." Beth seemed a bit less enthusiastic with the idea of Mrs. Blakeley sticking by her side the whole night.

John remained silent. Rose nudged him in the ribs. "Oh, fine. I'll think about it," he spat. He shot Rose a glare that said he felt betrayed and ganged up on. I kept my smirk to myself. John had a handful running a household with two stubborn and willful women. Austin must have thought the same thing because he was doing a bad job at keeping a straight face. Beth at least appeared mollified by John's non answer, most likely because she knew that she'd get him to say yes by morning.

The arrival of dinner broke up the lull in our lively conversation. I worked my way through a roasted pigeon with a side of browned fork-tender parsnips. Mrs. Avery had even prepared a sturgeon that a delivery man had brought from the docks earlier that day. I couldn't say that boiled white-fleshed fish was my favorite, but it was a popular choice for its tenderness and mild flavor.

"Do you not like your dinner?" I asked Austin. He was

moving his fork across his plate, pushing meat from one side to the other, but not taking any bites.

"I don't want to offend anyone," he said lowering his fork. "I'm just not used to this kind of food." His face was apologetic as he said it.

Rose patted her mouth with a napkin. "You don't have to eat it if you don't like it. I know this is completely different from the food we are used to in America."

"Yeah, they'd probably be confused if they saw what we eat." Austin grinned. Then he sobered. "No, I should try a bite."

"You don't like the pigeon?" I asked. He nodded.

"We don't eat pigeon where I'm from. I suppose it's a silly mental thing that stops me from trying."

"You don't have to. I can ask Mrs. Avery to prepare something else," Rose said. "Or you can take it slow. The meat may not be as bad as you imagine. I enjoy roasted pigeon quite a bit."

"I'll try." Austin speared a small piece of meat and lifted the fork to his lips. He closed his eyes as he tentatively chewed the piece of roasted pigeon. "Huh," he exclaimed. "The meat really isn't bad."

"High praise," I laughed. Beth snorted.

"Yeah, pigeon kinda tastes like chicken," Austin continued. "You know, the dark meat, like a chicken thigh. Not bad." He ate another piece.

"Would you also like to try some sturgeon?" Rose asked.

"No, I think one new thing is more than enough. I'll save strange fish for another day."

After dinner, I decided to retreat to the library. I'd been too preoccupied with other things that day that I'd never read the newspaper. I could use a moment to catch up on current affairs. There was a Typhoid outbreak in Glasgow and Edinburgh, and in the lifestyle section, I read that the Parthenon Marbles were on display at the British Museum. That exhibition might warrant a trip whenever I got back to London. Austin found me leaning back on a settee, leafing through the paper, with my feet propped up on a stool. He sank down next to me.

"Would you like some dessert?" he said, raising his brow and flashing a smile.

"Dessert?" I glanced up from the newspaper, the pages crinkled as I turned them.

"I've been waiting to eat this," he said, fishing something rectangular and covered in a bright yellow wrapper out of his pocket. "I had this on me when I traveled to this time. It's a candy bar." He held the candy bar up for me to see. "I figured since you were one of the reasons I went ahead and tried the pigeon that you might like to try something from the future."

I folded the paper and laid it down on the side table. "Well, I reckon I'll never get the chance again. What does the... candy bar..." I practiced the new word, "taste like?"

Austin's smile was coy. "It's difficult to describe. This candy bar is called a Butterfinger. It tastes like chocolate and peanut butter." I assume he realized that I had no point of reference for what he was explaining. He glanced at me and scratched his chin. "Try it." He opened the wrapper and broke the candy bar in half, handing me a piece. I sniffed the treat before biting down. The texture crunched beneath my teeth.

"It's very sweet." I tried to pay attention to the burst of flavors swirling on my tongue.

"It is," Austin agreed. "But this candy bar is one of my favorites. I would always have some on hand."

"And now we are eating your last one," I said, turning the chocolate confectionery in my hand. Next to me, Austin stiffened. I cursed myself for saying what I did. My comment must have hit Austin hard. Immediately, his expression changed. He was still chewing on his bar, then he swallowed deeply.

"Hopefully, not forever." Austin's lips formed a thin line, and he stared off into the distance, his face despondent.

"Here," I said, trying to press the rest of my half of the candy bar into his hand, partly to make up for my callous comment and to cheer him back up. "It's yours; you can finish the last piece. Thank you for letting me try."

He brushed my hand away and shot me a wistful smile. "No, I wanted you to try and enjoy a Butterfinger. Please." I pulled my hand back.

"I apologize if I said something wrong."

"Not at all. I wanted to share this with you, to introduce you to something from my home. Doing so just brought up certain feelings for me. Hanging out with you is easy, but I'm still in such a foreign situation. I miss my home, my own things."

I nodded. "I may not understand everything you are going through, but I do know what it is like to pretend in front of others."

Austin seemed surprised. He caught my eye questioningly. "Why would you need to pretend? Well, besides with that woman from earlier. That, I get. However, you seem to fit in everywhere else."

"You'd be surprised," I said darkly.

"You can tell me, if you want." Austin placed his hand on my arm.

"Perhaps another time." I took a bite of the candy bar.

Austin had been so excited to show me something new. It should have been a fun experience; instead, we were now both sullen and sitting together in silence.

He didn't deserve to be in this situation, taken away from his own time. Whoever the woman was that sent him here, she couldn't be doing this because she was trying to be kind. Perhaps she was a witch or some kind of fairy; they were known to be capricious.

Before, I would have never believed in the supernatural, but now, with Austin sitting next to me while I tasted a treat from the future? I could believe anything. If a fire breathing dragon flapped its giant wings as it flew over Hawthorne, I would say it was just another regular day. I shook my head.

Surprised, Austin turned to me. "What are you thinking?"

"I think it's catching up with me how strange this is." I snickered. "You are from the future. The future! How does that even happen?"

"Yeah, I'm still trying to figure that out."

Tears of laughter were welling in my eyes. "I can't think of anything more ridiculous."

"It is. It genuinely is." Austin joined in laughing.

"What if you've met my descendants?"

"Who knows, perhaps they've been at my workplace. Or they're my neighbors." Austin snickered.

"I was just thinking how after meeting you and Rose, I could believe in anything. Are you sure that Rose and you aren't witches?"

"Wouldn't I be a warlock in that case."

I laughed. "I'm not sure. I suppose a witch is a witch. Regardless, this whole situation has turned everything I know upside down. I can't even imagine what it must have been like for you."

"About the same, I'd wager." Austin sighed. "I'm questioning everything I thought I knew."

"I don't think I've asked yet. Was there someone you were courting back home?"

"I had someone, but I broke it off a few months ago."

"I suppose that is a relief. At least, if time did pass when you returned, you wouldn't have someone worried about where you were. That could've been challenging for her."

Austin was silent for a moment. "Yeah, challenging for her." His voice sounded odd as he said it. "You know, I'm feeling a bit tired. I think I'm going to go to my room," Austin said, out of nowhere.

"Oh, of course, if you are tired." I wondered if I said something wrong again. Nothing I said came out the way I meant it. I wanted to thank him again for sharing his candy bar. I wondered why he decided to share it with me, but I appreciated it. "Thank you for dessert," I told Austin. I wanted to ask him to stay longer, but I didn't.

"You are welcome." Austin stood and walked away.

I leaned back again. The newspaper was still laying on the side table. But I didn't feel like reading it any longer. I knew I said something to offend Austin, but I had no clue as to what. I racked my brain for what it could have been.

What was it about Austin that turned my every thought and remark into an incoherent jumble? I generally knew what to say around other people. Perhaps it was his lack of guile. Austin's straightforwardness was disarming in a society built around the deception of having it together. John tended to be brusque while I was supposed to be charming. I had put a lot of effort into being charming. Then why couldn't I be charming when it concerned Austin?

I gave up. I hadn't shared this much with another person in a long time. Time would have to decide whether or not that was a good thing.

5

A Carriage Ride

Austin spent a few days seemingly avoiding me. Whenever I entered a room, he had an excuse to leave. If our eyes crossed, he hurriedly glanced away.

I wondered what I had said wrong the night he shared the candy bar with me. I couldn't think of anything that I said that would make him avoid me. Now, after a few days, I was even more unsure. I decided I was going to have to speak with him. John wanted me to help him out as long as he stayed at Hawthorne, and I wasn't going to let my friend down. And I had to admit, I was intrigued by Austin.

I found Austin in his room on the second floor, engrossed in putting away some clothing. I rapped my knuckles against the door post.

"Hey," he said, as he noticed me.

I swallowed. "I was wondering if we could speak." He moved a stack of clothing to the desk.

"What's up?" Austin folded his arms and sat down at the edge of the bed.

"Did I say something wrong?" I shot out.

Austin glanced at the floor. "What do you mean?"

"I think you understand what I mean," I said calmly. "The night when you shared your treat with me. Something I said must have offended you. You ran out so fast and ever since, you've barely spoken a word to me. Hawthorne might be spacious, but the house and grounds aren't large enough to avoid each other completely."

"I'm not avoiding you," Austin spoke hastily, his eyes trained on his fingernails.

"It certainly feels like you are. I'll ask you this; if I don't understand what I did wrong, how can I fix my mistake?" I leaned my shoulder against the wooden door post. Austin scuffed his foot along the dark flooring.

"I promise, it isn't you."

"Can you tell me what is wrong, if it isn't me?"

"This place—this time." Austin rolled his eyes and peeked up at the ceiling. "I don't know how to behave, what to say, what to do. This isn't my home." He shrugged, his shoulders deflating. "When will I go home?"

I sympathized. "I'm not certain either. I wish I could tell you what to expect."

Austin nodded, digesting my response. After a few beats, he spoke again. "Rose said I had to wait until that Melinda woman from the bookshop shows up. But what if she's wrong? What if I could find a way back home sooner? I feel silly going through the motions until this extraneous force pulls me out.

I'm essentially waiting to be saved from here. You can call me a damsel in distress."

Hearing Austin refer to my time as something that he needed to be saved from stung. "I see," I said, my voice flattening.

Austin realized what he said and how he said it. "I'm sorry." He frowned. "I didn't mean that. I don't think this time or this place is awful. I am grateful that John and Rose are letting me stay. Everyone has been incredibly nice to me. I just miss my own place."

"I understand," I cut in.

"No, really." He kicked his leg out harder, hitting the floor with an audible thud.

"I should go." I turned around to leave but Austin jumped up.

"Wait," he spoke. I glanced back. "Please?" he added with a hopeful tone. His eyes bright.

I raised my brow but said nothing.

"Let's start over. My circumstances aren't your fault. I shouldn't have taken my frustrations out on you."

"Go on," I said.

"John asked you to keep me company. How about we take a trip today?"

"What did you have in mind?"

"Well," Austin said, looking pensive. "Rose said I should wait and enjoy myself while I'm here. But, I say, screw that! It may not work, but I still want to check out where I originally arrived. Maybe there's a way back. A portal, or a door, or who knows," Austin rambled. "Point is, I have no clue but I'd like to find out. Will you go with me?"

"You could also stop by the place where Rose appeared," I offered.

"Right, she arrived at the pond, didn't she?"

"Yes, John told me he scooped her out after she fell in."

"We could go there first, since the pond is nearby."

I wrung my hands. "I can ask Hugh to ready a carriage while we investigate the pond."

"Thank you," Austin said sincerely. "Can you do that while I finish up here? We can meet back up in the foyer."

"I'll go find Hugh," I agreed.

"It'll be a good thing that you are coming along. If I do find a way back, you can tell John and Rose what happened, so they don't worry," Austin said as I stepped out of the room. I didn't respond. The idea of him leaving didn't sit well with me. It left a strange ache in the pit of my stomach. However, it was what Austin wanted. And clearly Hawthorne was not where he was meant to be. Austin belonged somewhere else, somewhere far away from here, someplace I would never be able to go.

* * *

I found Hugh at the stables, spreading out fresh straw in the stalls.

"Mr. Chambers," he said in his gruff voice. He straightened and leaned on the pitchfork he had been using to move the straw about. "Is there anything I can do for you?" His face was dark and leathery from all the time he spent outdoors tending to the horses and finding random things that needed fixing; Hugh was a real Jack-of-all-trades.

"Mr. Miller and I are in need of a carriage," I said.

"Do you need me to drive you somewhere?" I thought for a moment. We weren't going anywhere far, and it wasn't like we were going to step out the carriage for long. With Austin's plans, it was probably for the best if our party stayed confined to the two of us.

"Not this time, Hugh," I told the man. "However, could you ready the buggy? I shall drive Mr. Miller and myself."

"Right away, sir," Hugh said with a nod, setting aside the pitchfork.

"Thank you. We're just taking a quick walk to the pond and back. We'll return soon to go on our trip."

I left Hugh to ready a horse and buggy. When I entered the foyer, I found Austin waiting for me. He'd dressed for the cold with a thick knitted scarf made from a dark emerald-green thread which highlighted his similarly colored eyes. Austin had even donned a hat, which made me laugh. I'd never seen anyone less suited to wearing a hat. It looked unbelievably out of character, like a child playing dress up.

"What?" he asked. "Do I have something on my face?"

"No," I smirked. "I can't help it, the hat, it looks different on you."

"The hat?" Austin seemed confused. "I thought hats like this were in fashion. I see you and John wear them when you go out. In fact, I borrowed this one from him."

"You are right. It is fashionable. However, somehow it doesn't seem to suit you. I don't think hats are your style."

"Well, I am cold. So, I'm going to wear it," he said haughtily.

"Right you are," I said, smirking.

Austin shot me a peeved look, sighing, he asked, "Did you ask Hugh to get a carriage ready?"

"He's getting a horse ready. Though, we shall take the buggy and I'll drive us."

Austin exited the foyer and held open the front door for me. "You learned how to drive on of those?"

"Any gentleman should be taught how."

"I've never been around horses much. One of my foster parents took me to a petting zoo once. They helped me feed a carrot to a pony; I was scared and cried when its lips grazed my palm. Other than that, I've never been near horses or pony's until now."

"How do you travel around where you are from?" Austin was a grown man. The idea that he'd hardly ever seen horses was unfathomable. Here, they were a necessity— the only means to travel unless you counted walking. And I didn't.

"We use machines that we can sit inside of, kind of like a carriage, but it doesn't need horses to be pulled. Instead, it uses fuel to ignite and propel itself forward."

Then I remembered the conversation we had about the loss of his parents. "A car, right? I remember you mentioning them. That kind of machine sounds miraculous," I said. "I wish I could see one of them."

"Yes, you're right."

"And you have one?"

"Yes."

"You must be a successful man in your own time."

Austin snorted. "I do okay."

I raised my brow. "And why was that funny?"

"It's not what you said. Your comment merely reminded me of my foster family. They don't approve of my job, though I'm good at it. Only my sister supports what I do."

"You must miss your sister," I said. We were walking side-by-side, following the path towards the pond.

"She's staying with me at my apartment. My foster family washed their hands of me as soon as I turned eighteen; she was sixteen at the time. That was six years ago. Alyssa isn't my little sister by blood, but we grew up together. That means more than anything. She lived with our foster parents longer than I did, but she was there for me. She supported me through everything, and when they set an ultimatum, either break off contact with me or move out, she moved out."

"Why would your foster family do that?"

Austin fell quiet. "Some people can't accept a person for who they are."

"I'm sorry." I sensed that I broached a touchy subject, and I didn't want to push him for answers.

"Me too." Austin sighed. "Anyway. We are here. Let's see if I can find a portal that'll take me home." He inspected the water's edge. "Do you remember where Rose fell in?" he said, glancing back at me.

"Why, plan on jumping in? Fancy an ice bath?"

"Very funny," Austin said. "I don't know, I thought that maybe if I stood in the same spot, I'd sense something. I'm not sure what, but I have to try."

Part of me wanted to direct him to the other side of the pond, in case his theory proved to be right. But I didn't wish to lie. "From what Rose told me, she was at the closest point towards Mrs. Ashbrook's estate, so you should move up to that spot over there."

I pointed at the slight curve of the pond from which you could spot the low stone border wall that divided the estates. It was still far in the distance. John had inherited vast lands; a man could walk around for hours without seeing the same spot twice. There was also amazing hunting to be had, though John had never been interested in hosting a hunting party. He'd given his tenants the freedom to hunt for what they'd like, and what amazing stags and deer did roam his fields.

"What are you doing?" I called out to Austin. He'd moved closer to the water and had raised his hands to the sky. With his eyes closed, he replied, "I'm trying to sense if there is something different here." He squished his eyes even tighter.

"Is it working?"

"Of course not." Austin dropped his arms and opened his eyes. "I didn't actually think it would."

"Did you still want to go to where you arrived?"

"I'm not holding my breath, but yeah. I still want to go. Just to make sure."

"I'm sure Hugh will already have a buggy ready for us. Let's head back."

* * *

Hugh had parked the buggy and horse at the driveway near the front of Hawthorne, ready for Austin and I to take for a drive.

"Thank you," I told Hugh, as I took the reins from him. The man nodded and stepped away. I turned to Austin. "You can sit up front with me," I told him. Austin glanced uncertainly at the small buggy.

"Is that thing safe to ride?"

"I promise I know how to drive one," I said confidently. "I've done it many times before. It is fun."

"As long as we don't crash into something," Austin muttered. He acted a bit wary of the old mare. He used the side-step to climb up on the left side of the buggy and took his seat on the driver's bench. I checked the straps and made sure all the buckles were fastened before I pulled myself up and slid in beside him. I peeked at Austin; his skin had turned paler, if that was even possible. He already had a fair complexion to go along with his reddish-brown hair. Today, with the sunlight glinting off it, his hair appeared more ginger.

I held the reins out to Austin. "Would you feel safer if you drove?" He pushed my hand away.

"Very funny. We both know that I don't have a clue how to operate this thing." He playfully bumped my shoulder, though he still appeared tense.

I smirked. "Alright, let's head out." Gathering the extra length of reins beside me, I positioned the whip. Hugh had harnessed one of the older, gentler horses. I sat up straight and waited until its ears flicked towards me— a sign that it was waiting for my command. "Step up," I commanded, and the mare started moving.

"This isn't that bad," Austin said as we drove down the driveway and turned on the road into town. The cold air did make me shiver, so I could only imagine that Austin felt it too. I reached back with my whip hand and snatched one of the folded blankets.

"Here, cover yourself with this while we are driving," I said, pushing the blanket towards him. I returned my hand back into position, the whip hovering to the left. Though I didn't need it, the horse Hugh had chosen was a very good listener. Austin unfolded the beige blanket and spread it out across both our legs. A little warmer for the time being, I led the horse and buggy through every turn and curve until we reached the center of Westbridge.

"Where exactly did John and Rose find you?" I asked. Austin had gotten used to the movements of the buggy; he now even seemed to enjoy the trip.

"It was a smaller road, more like an alley. It led into the street with all the shopping. I believe a dress shop was on the corner."

"Probably by Norah's then," I said, thinking of Westbridge's most fashionable ladies' accouterments store. "I know where that is."

When we reached Norah's, I slowed us down until we came to a stop. Austin climbed out of the buggy first, then I followed and hitched the horse to a post.

"Is this what you remember?"

"I think so." Austin was circling around, taking in the sights. "In truth, I'm not a hundred percent sure." He turned towards me. "I think the whole situation was such a shock that I didn't pay attention to where I was."

"Let's head into the alley first," I said. "That might help your memory." I rested my hand at the small of his back as I led him towards the alley on the left. We passed by Norah's corner entrance with its inviting and colorful displays of fabrics for the fashionable young lady.

"This is where John and Rose were passing through, right?" I asked. We were standing in the alley. It was a shortcut towards the river and the craftsmen setting up shop near it.

"I think so," Austin reached out and touched the red bricked wall, his fingertips skimming the stones. Then he looked back towards the exit to the Main Street. "I believe it was about where I am standing now." Austin tapped his feet on the ground. "I was confused, so I stepped further out into the road." Austin followed his original path. "Then the carriage was heading straight for me. I jumped out of the way and landed on my butt somewhere over there," he said pointing at the ground, closer to where I was standing. "The carriage screeched to a halt a little further up. That's when I got introduced to John and Rose." Austin was walking figure eights, his eyes cast down at the ground.

"Do you see anything?"

"No." Austin glanced up at me. "I don't know what I was thinking. There wasn't anything at the pond, but I kind of told myself that it made sense that there wasn't anything there because that was Rose's spot. I had hoped that it would be different here. But it isn't; this is just an alley. It was never anything else. Trying to find a portal or whatever was stupid."

"It's not stupid," I said, stepping towards Austin. His face hung so defeated, I couldn't help but sympathize. I grabbed both his shoulders and stared him straight in the eyes. "You tried. That's what matters. We'll make the most of the rest." Austin barreled forward and enveloped me in a hug. I wasn't expecting that. His arms squeezed tight around me, and his head rested against my shoulder. The faint scent of lavender floated from his hair; I recognized the smell from the soaps that were generously supplied by Mrs. Avery. Awkwardly, I tightened my arms around him until he finally stepped back, both too soon and not soon enough.

"Thank you for coming with me," he said, his eyes glistening, though he remained stoic.

"Of course. I'm sorry it didn't go the way you hoped."

"Me too." Austin paused and swallowed. "Can we return to Hawthorne? I think I'd like to be alone for a bit."

"We'll go immediately." I led Austin back to the horse and buggy and waited until he was seated to take my place beside him and return to John's estate.

6

Building a School

Today, Austin and I were meeting with John's tenant, Robert McCreary, the man in charge of building Rose's school. Supplies and building materials for Rose's school had been arriving off and on all week. We spent a lot of time together—overseeing the deliveries, walking John's estate when Austin got restless, and I had started to get Austin comfortable around horses. Hopefully, we could go for our first ride soon.

"I brought along the finished drawings of the building for ye, sir," McCreary said to John as he entered John's study. John was sitting in his chair behind his heavy desk. "Did you decide on a location yet? My wee Joan is ever so excited to go to school. Gavin on the other hand says he rather helps me on the farm." The Scot nodded to Austin and I, acknowledging our presence as he stopped in front of John's desk.

John chuckled. "I'm sure the idea of sitting still in a chair for hours doesn't sound too appealing to the little wildling."

"Nay, the lad thinks he doesn't need an education. He told me this all proud with his chest puffed up like some overgrown dandy, then added that he was almost an adult." McCreary shook his head. "The lad's only eleven, and he's been giving me a headache since the day he was born."

I caught John's eye and smirked. He rolled his eyes, probably thinking the same thing I was. McCreary's story about his son reminded me of John and myself as young boys.

John had told his parents the same thing about not needing an education. Though, instead of working a farm, John said he'd join the military. He had been infatuated with the idea for a couple of years, mostly because of my father's military history. I never had another option, but John gradually came to his senses and took charge of his estate.

The deaths of Mr. and Mrs. Easton hastened John's maturity and sense of responsibility. He had to go from a young man with the freedom to do whatever he liked, to the sole caretaker of an entire estate. And he became a parent to his younger sister. The change was jarring to say the least. But he adapted and had grown into a capable and caring man whom I was proud to call my friend.

McCreary untied the ribbon on the leather portfolio he was carrying and laid it flat on John's desk. His eyes shot to Austin and myself.

"Ah yes," John said, pointing at us. "These are my friends, William Chambers and Austin Miller. They'll be staying here for a while and are willing to help with overseeing the construction of the school."

"Good to meet ye," McCreary said with a nod of his head, his gaze calculating. "Do any of ye know how to hold a hammer?" he continued when we both hesitated to answer. "Aye, I'll teach ye. Dinna worry. I'll have both of ye setting up support beams in no time."

"Uh, thanks," Austin said.

John laughed and grabbed the top sketch from his desk. "If they aren't making an effort, McCreary, you can send them to me." He lifted the sketch and held it up to the light. "I think this will do nicely," John murmured before he turned back to his tenant. "My wife wants the school to be near the pond."

"Then the pond is where the school will go," the burly Scot said, deadpan. As they were talking about John's wife, Rose herself entered the room.

"Good afternoon, Mrs. Easton," McCreary said, his tone friendly; he clearly liked Rose. She had that effect on people, even if she didn't always realize it herself.

"Good afternoon, everyone. I just stopped by to sneak a peek at the plans for the school." John handed her the final sketch. Her face lit up as she scanned the drawing. She turned towards the Scottish man. "Mr. McCreary, this looks wonderful. I'm beginning to suspect that you are secretly an artist."

Red fanned across the Scot's fair face. "Nay, Mrs. Easton," he spluttered. "You give me too much credit."

"Well, I can't thank you enough for your help. I can't wait to see the finished result."

John took the drawing from Rose and laid it back down on top of the portfolio. "How long do you think building will take?"

McCreary considered the question. "Depends on the number of men and the weather, I suppose. We'll have to build the support beams and lay the brickwork, thatch the roof, plaster the walls." He thought for a moment. "My Gavin can help with smaller things, but I'll need to hire some men."

John opened a desk drawer and pulled out a few bank-notes. He handed them to his tenant. "Use this to hire as many men as you think you'll need. Do let me know if you require more funds."

"Aye, sir," McCreary said, pocketing the bank notes.

"Well, I will leave you all to it," Rose said. She squeezed John's hand, who looked dotingly upon her. Then she turned towards McCreary. "Before you leave, please stop by the kitchen. Mrs. Avery and I packed a small box with treats for you and your family."

"Thank ye, Mrs. Easton," the Scot said. "My Agnes will be so grateful, and wee Joan and Gavin never shut up about Mrs. Avery's cooking."

"You're welcome," John's wife said with a smile, before leaving the study.

John returned to the task at hand. "So, once you've hired the men, we can start the build?

"Aye, most starting materials already arrived. I can spread the word that we're looking for additional workers and per-haps start in a week's time."

John nodded. "It would be prudent to finish the foun-dation and framework before winter arrives and blankets us with snow."

"Aye," the Scot concurred. "I'll report back to ye, sir, when I gathered the men."

"Thank you, McCreary. When I'm not here, you can share

anything that needs to be done with Mr. Chambers and Mr. Miller; they can make decisions or arrange funds, if and when they are deemed necessary."

The Scot gathered the sketches and Austin helped bind the portfolio closed again. "It was nice to meet you," Austin said, shaking McCreary's hand.

"Likewise, sir," the Scot said, bemused. Then he took his portfolio and left the study to return to his wife, Agnes, with a small detour to pick up the treats from Mrs. Avery.

"When does Rose hope the school will open?" I asked as I stepped forward and leaned against the heavy wood.

"She's hoping to teach in the early spring." John glanced out the window. "It'll depend on the weather; if we can finish most of the structure up before the snow falls, then she might be able to. The plaster work and floors can be done when there is snow outside, as long as there is a roof and there are walls to keep the elements out."

"It doesn't look like it's going to snow anytime soon," Austin offered. "Today is actually pretty warm compared to what I'm used to this time of year."

John rifled through his correspondence. "I hope so. Rose is very excited to start this school, but we'll need to get it finished by March at the latest. I promised Beth we would take up residence in London during the social season." John's face scrunched up as he said it.

"I wish you luck," I spoke.

Just as Austin said, "That sounds like fun. I've never been to London."

I patted my friend on his shoulder. "John here, isn't a fan of the spring in London. Spring means a lot of balls and society ladies. Worst of all, this year Beth is entering society, which means John will have to field a lot of men who will be vying for his sister's hand in marriage."

"More like her dowry," John added darkly. "But she's wanted to join society, and she is getting older." He let out a sigh. "Rose and Beth ganged up on me, to make sure I couldn't say no."

"She is old enough to be responsible. And she is a bit on the old side," I trailed off. John shot me a warning look. "It's true." I shrugged. "Think of Anne Blakeley. She's going on her fourth year."

"Why is this Anne going for four years straight? In romance movies, don't men immediately propose?"

"Movies," John muttered.

I was lost. "What are movies?" I asked Austin.

He seemed to think for a moment, his bright green eyes looking up at the ceiling before returning to me. "Well, I suppose a movie is like a play. Except the people are on pictures that move. I don't really know how else to explain it." His eyes flashed to John for help. My friend nodded.

"Rose told me about movies. William, do you remember the pictures Rose showed us on that strange device of hers?"

"Yes."

"Movies are like those but with movement and sound."

The concept was still strange to me. A twinge of envy coiled through my mind. Austin had come from such a different time and place, somewhere life must have been kind, at least for him.

I was sure that any time and place would have inequalities and poverty. That appeared to be a part of humanity. But someone as gentle and kind as Austin had to have lived a perhaps not sheltered but definitely privileged life. My mind turned back to John's explanation of movies. I might never grasp it, but I nodded. However, I had understood Austin's original question.

"To answer your question about Anne," I said to Austin. "Their family finances are in a bit of a shamble because of her late father and brother's mismanagement. With no dowry to speak of, most men are reluctant to tie themselves to either of Mrs. Blakeley's daughters."

Austin frowned. "Wouldn't the men courting them have money?"

"Not always. It doesn't help that plenty of lords by birth are born so far down the line that they need to marry into wealth in order to secure a decent position for themselves. A third or fourth son generally has to make their own way in life."

"So that's why you are worried about Beth," Austin pointed out. John grimaced at his words. "I guess I would be worried about the motives behind every interaction as well, in that case," Austin added earnestly.

John brushed his hand through his hair and leaned back in his chair. The wood creaking as his weight shifted. "I just want her to be safe and find someone to marry for love," he paused for a moment. "But not for a while, yet," he added. John's expression spoke volumes. "I hope she can enjoy society as a single woman for a few more years."

"I'm sure she'll be more careful about whom she trusts," I said, remembering Danby and his vile schemes. Thankfully, he was still behind bars and wouldn't get out for a long while.

"We shall see," John muttered. "I'm afraid my hair will be

going prematurely gray." He snatched a letter opener from his desk and ripped open a piece of mail.

"Come," I told Austin. I rested my palm on his shoulder. "Let's leave John to his correspondence." Together we left the study.

7

Jerusalem Cherries

"You know what I was thinking," Austin said as we walked through the corridors. "While I'm here, there is something I could do. I would love to draw a picture for John and Rose, as a house-warming present. Or, I guess, a school warming present," he corrected sheepishly.

"You learned how to draw?" I quirked my brow at him. I hadn't pegged him as the artistic type.

Austin picked at his fingernails, something I'd noticed he did when he got flustered or embarrassed. "I love drawing," he said. "It's kind of what I did as a job. You know, back home."

I nodded. "So, you are an artist! I would love to see your work."

He tried to wave away my remark, red blossoming on his cheeks.

"No, I'm not great or anything. We probably should think of something else to give them."

I stopped walking. "I'm sure you are better than you think. In fact, how about you draw something now?"

"I don't have any paper."

"John has plenty in his study." I patted Austin's shoulder. "Wait here a moment," I told him. I retraced my steps and walked back into John's study.

John looked up from his papers. "Was there something else?"

"Can I borrow some paper and pencils?"

"Whatever for?" John scratched his chin.

"Austin would like to draw."

"Well, that is no problem; if I'd known he liked to draw, I could have ordered him some additional supplies. Tell him that if he has any needs, he can tell Rose or myself."

I flashed John a smile. "I'll do that."

John bent forward and pulled open the bottom drawer of his desk. He came back up with a few sheets of blank paper and a box holding a pencil marked Borrowdale. He held the items out for me to take.

"Austin will appreciate this," I told John as I grabbed the papers and box.

"You two seem to get along well," John observed.

"Don't worry. I'm not replacing you as my best friend," I quipped.

John snorted. "I didn't think so." He cracked his knuckles. "No, I'm glad you are becoming friends. He needs someone to look out for him for as long as he's here. And—," John paused.

"And?" I asked.

"Well, you appear happier." I was about to speak, but John hurriedly cut in. "Don't misunderstand me. You've been through a lot. More than you even shared with Rose or myself, I'd reckon." John gave me a pointed stare. "I just want to see you content. But I feel as if you've been more like yourself again lately. It makes me glad to see you more at ease. I can't speak as to if it has anything to do with Austin. My own ego would like to say it's my personal hospitality that's done the trick."

I smirked. "Of course."

John smiled and shook his head. "But, let me ask you this, have you had any of your nightmares?"

"My nightmares?" I froze. I hadn't been paying attention, but now that John mentioned it, it had been days since I had woken up in a sweat, calling out James' name. How hadn't I realized this myself?

"You know we could hear you whenever you stayed with us and had a terrible one," John said gently.

"I know." I held the papers a little tighter. "Thank you for this," I said, clearing my throat. "Austin will appreciate it."

"Will," John trailed as I headed towards the door. "You know I'm always here to listen."

"I know," I said. Then I left John behind again to work in his study.

Heading back down the same corridors, I found Austin leaning against the wall as he waited for me. He pushed himself to standing once he saw me approach. I shook off the sense of gloom John's conversation had left. I pushed James out of my mind, even if it felt like a betrayal.

"I've got all an artist needs," I said, lifting my hand to show Austin the blank papers.

"Is there anything you'd like me to draw?"

"I'll have to think about that," I said, handing Austin the box that held the pencil. "However, I do have a location in mind."

"And that is?" Austin asked as he opened the box and marveled at the pencil. He slowly took it out and observed it from all angles.

"I figured we could go to John's hot house."

"Okay, we can do that." Austin lowered the pencil back into the box and closed it. "I'm sure I can find a good subject to draw there."

"John mentioned he'd recently repotted his Jerusalem Cherries and transferred them indoors."

"What are those? I don't really know much about plants." Austin shrugged apologetically.

"You'll see when we get there," I said. "I like them."

Together, we exited John's home through the servants' entrance in the back and winded our way to the hot house. The bleak winter sun glinted sharply off the glass panes, blinding me. I raised my hand to my forehead to protect my eyes from the glare. Next to me, Austin pulled up his collar. His breath came out in visible puffs every time he exhaled. It was cold outside, though the temperature hadn't dropped enough for the pond to be frozen over or the whole world to be blanketed in snow.

Once we reached the door to the hot house, I opened the door for Austin, and let him enter first. I followed and quickly closed the door behind me.

Austin let out a whistle. "It's nice in here." He strode towards a bench and small cast iron side table, which was set up in the middle of the room for flower watching. He dropped the papers and the box containing the pencil on the side table, then he rubbed his hands against each other. "I think my fingers need a moment to warm up before I can draw," he said, turning towards me. "So, which ones are those Jerusalem somethings?"

"Jerusalem Cherries," I corrected.

"Yeah, those."

I looked around the room and spotted the signature red berries lined in pots on top of a work bench in the corner of the hot house. "It's these," I said, motioning Austin towards the plants. He walked up to the bench and touched one of the vivid red berries.

"I'd wager these aren't edible." He let go of the plant and stuck his hands in his pockets, bouncing a little on the balls of his feet.

I scratched the back of my neck. "I'd wager you're right."

"So, what would you like me to draw?" Austin said, his eyes resting on me. The intensity of his gaze pierced my defenses. I didn't know how to answer. Austin must have sensed my wariness because he continued. "I could draw you..." he suggested, letting the question trail.

I glanced to the side. "I'm not sure. I don't think I'm a very interesting subject. Perhaps you can try a still life?"

Austin shook his head. "No, I think I'd like to draw you. Don't worry, I won't bite."

I smiled and nodded. "Alright. What do I do?"

"Just a moment," Austin told me. He snatched a chair from a different corner and set it up across from the bench. Once he finished, he asked, "How about you sit on the bench?" His tone of voice, direct and deep, made it sound more like an order. I bit my lip and sat down on the wooden surface.

"What would you like me to do now?" I asked. I folded my arms and crossed my legs. Then I immediately shifted again, re-folding and re-crossing my limbs. I'd never been more acutely aware of every single muscle in my body and more unsure of how to use them.

"You can relax," Austin said, a smile playing at the corner of his lips. He could probably tell I was less than comfortable.

"I'll try." I sighed and stretched my back, feeling my muscles roll between my shoulder blades. Then I rested my left arm on the armrest and let go of the tension lingering in my body.

Austin had found a tray, which he'd turned upside down in his lap to use it as a flat surface to draw on. He pulled up his legs until he sat cross-legged, pencil at the ready.

"Did you want me to look in a specific direction?"

"You can look at me," he said, his eyes scanning my features. The pencil moved across the paper in steady lines, his hands nimble and clearly used to sketching. Austin kept moving his gaze between the paper and myself. I felt his eyes stop at the scar curving from my eyebrow along my cheekbone. Without thinking, my hand reached for my face and gingerly rested against the permanent reminder of war etched on my face.

Austin lowered the pencil. "Do you mind me asking what happened?" He nodded his head to indicate he meant the scar on my face.

"I fought in the war against Napoleon. I got injured during my final battle."

Austin's eyes grew wider for a moment before he spoke again. "What happened? I mean, you don't have to tell me if you don't want to. I'd understand if it's too difficult."

I hesitated. "My battalion was overrun by Napoleon's army. We'd set up camp outside of Ligny, but we hadn't expected the French forces. Our own leaders were away, visiting a nearby house for a party, when the French troops arrived. It meant we didn't have anyone to lead us. Napoleon's soldiers completely took us by surprise. We had no idea what was coming." I glanced at Austin who was listening intensely. "My men and I decided to join the Prussian army in the hope that we could have a chance of pushing back the French forces. However, they were too many to hold off." I shook my head while memories flooded my mind, as if I could flick them away if I just tried hard enough. Not that that had ever worked before. My fingers tensed as I remembered the screams so clearly, I could have sworn I was back at the battlefield. Back at the base of that windmill that should have been the best outlook post, the air heavy with the scent of gunpowder and pennies.

James' face flashed through my mind, clearer than it had been in a long while. It was strange how as time passed, I started to forget the exact shape of his face. The way his mouth curved, luscious and primed for a smile. What the exact shade of brown his eyes were.

Now, I remembered them perfectly, their color vibrant like a rich cognac. We'd prayed together. I told him we'd make it through, that we'd get back home. And then we were thrust into chaos, the smoke so dense we couldn't distinguish our enemies from our allies. The smell of rotten eggs choking us while volleys were being shot from both sides. Muskets firing overhead, their explosive sounds overwhelming any sense left.

I'd primed and shot my weapon a few times, aiming at an enemy I couldn't even see, before I noticed that James had stopped next to me. Lowering my weapon, I called out his name. No response. I'd reached out for him, my palm coming away sticky with his blood.

I swallowed deeply as I returned to the present. My hand trembled; I wiped it on my pant leg, even though it was clean. Some part of me was trying to wipe away James' life blood though it had long since been shed. Austin was still patiently waiting for me to continue my story. His expression made it clear that he was concerned about my reaction. I stopped wiping my hand and forced it to lay still on my thigh. Then I picked up where I'd left off.

"We couldn't see them coming. They... They charged us out of nowhere. A French soldier stabbed his bayonet at me, flaying open the side of my face. He must've thought he killed me, judging by the amount of blood I was covered in and how still I lay. I was lucky that he merely sliced my skin, and that he continued on without checking to make sure he finished the job."

I didn't mention to Austin that at that time I didn't feel lucky at all. James' death had left me feeling so unequivocally and irrevocably numb that I'd wished that soldier had killed me. To plunge me into darkness the same way one of his fellows had done to my love. For, at that time, I thought, how could I go on living if James didn't?

As I recovered at the medical camp, I despaired and

thrashed, and cried. I remembered yelling at the nurses to leave me be, to let the fever set in and take me. Thankfully, they didn't pay attention to an injured and delirious military man shouting at them. At night, my own worst thoughts haunted me, telling me I should have died on that battlefield.

Eventually, I realized that wasn't true, but it took a while. I realized James would have wanted me to live and be happy. It's what I would have wanted for him if he were in my stead. But it didn't stop the guilt and the nightmares from tormenting me. I would have to repeat to myself what James would have wanted for me; sometimes I actually believed it. More often than not, I didn't.

Austin softened his voice. "I'm so sorry that you had to go through that. I can't imagine what that must have been like for you." He lowered the tray to the floor and stood. He held on to the paper as he sat down next to me. Austin held the drawing out towards me. I glanced at his sketch. It was still rough but, in a few lines, he'd managed to capture my likeness, scar and all.

"You really are an artist," I noted. He shot me a faint glimmer of a smile.

"It helps when I have a good subject to draw."

"My scar isn't too off-putting?"

Austin shook his head. "On the contrary. No one is perfect. I think your scar is a part of you; it tells a story about who you are and what you've survived."

"That's a nice way of phrasing it."

Austin grinned. "I mean it. We all bear our scars; some are just more visible than others. And if I'm being honest, I think it gives your face some character."

"Well, I appreciate your honesty," I said amused. I moved to stand but Austin stopped me.

"William," he said, his eyes boring into mine. "I am here, you know, if you need someone to talk to. I know I'm a stranger still—and who knows how long I'll be here— but even so, I'd like to be your friend. That is, if you'll let me."

"I'm not sure why everyone feels the need to point that out. John said a similar thing earlier." I said it jokingly, but the comments had hit home. I'd been trying to act like nothing was wrong. Frankly, I thought I had been doing a rather good job of it. Apparently, I couldn't have been more wrong.

Austin's bright eyes softened. "Great minds think alike," he said. The corners of his mouth gently lifting into a smile. Then he straightened, a small crease appearing between his brow. "I mean it though. And if it isn't me then—that is, if you feel up to it—you should talk to John. But I am here if you want to talk."

"I'd like nothing more," I confessed. I'd never met anyone so direct, so wholly themselves. I envied his strength, which was evident not in displays of power but in being kind and by being true to himself no matter what.

8

The Brocklehursts

Mrs. Avery appeared this morning, while we were all gathered for breakfast, with two letters on a silver platter. She held my letter out to me, so I could take the piece of dreaded correspondence. Then she held out the other towards Austin. The wax crest with the large, embossed B immediately told me who the letter was from, Mrs. Brocklehurst. She'd finally decided to call in the invitation she'd given us when she visited. Austin ripped open his letter.

Beth laid down the piece of bread she was chewing. "Go on, read it to us," she told Austin eagerly. Austin started reading the letter.

Dear Mr. Miller,

My daughters and I would like to invite you over for supper at Filton Grove. We shall await your appearance.

Cordially yours, Mrs. Brocklehurst

"We knew that was coming," I said.

John laughed. "Am I glad that I am through with that." Austin dropped the letter next to his plate and continued eating.

"So, that's why you married me," Rose winked.

"Of course, I had to find a way to get out of those blasted dinner parties. Now that I'm a married man, I'm not nearly as interesting."

"And you were before?" Rose quipped with a teasing smile.

"You can answer that question better than I can. You married me, after all." John raised his brow at Rose.

Austin turned to me. "Our visit is only a few hours, right?" he said in between bites of egg.

I nodded. "Just remember to stay civil and to keep your distance. You don't want Mrs. Brocklehurst to press you into marriage with Arabella, Fanny, or—what's the youngest name?" I directed at Beth.

"Letitia," she said.

"Or Letitia," I emphasized.

"So, no touching, no talking, no eye contact," Austin ticked off on his fingers.

"Certainly, no time spent alone with one of the girls," John teased.

"Oh, stop it you two," Rose ordered. "Stop scaring Austin." She turned to him. "Don't worry. Just enjoy the food and the experience, and don't let John or William discourage you." She shot me a stern look.

I held up my hands. "Fine, I won't tease any longer. But I stand by my point that it is dangerous business. Many a wealthy gentleman have left for a dinner party and returned engaged."

Rose shook her head. "Think of it this way. You find yourself in a situation that most people would never even dream of. Just enjoy the strangeness of it all. Make plenty of memories to take back home." Rose winked at Austin.

* * *

The memory in the making had started off reasonably well. Hugh had driven us to Mrs. Brocklehurst's home in the middle of the woods. Filton Grove lay halfway between Westbridge and Bowerfield—a smaller community in Kingswood County. Austin had once again borrowed John's hat, which Mr. and Mrs. Brocklehurst's butler dutifully accepted upon entrance to their home.

"Mr. Miller, Mr. Chambers, how wonderful that you are dining with us this evening," Mr. Brocklehurst bristled from beneath his rather enormous mustache. The protruding facial hair vaguely reminded me of a boot brush. He waved his hand. "Come in, come in." Austin and I followed him into the drawing room where Mrs. Brocklehurst and her three daughters were occupying themselves with making sure that they appeared as if they weren't expecting us that moment, while also looking their best.

"How wonderful to see you again," Mrs. Brocklehurst said

politely from her seat, her hands demurely folded in her lap. A woman, whom I presumed to be her eldest daughter, sat next to her in a similar fashion, her neck strained from sitting as straight as possible.

"You've already met my wife," Mr. Brocklehurst said. "Let me introduce my daughters. This here is my eldest, Arabella."

"How do you do, Miss Brocklehurst," I said with a small bow to Arabella. She smiled shyly. Austin mirrored my movements.

"Then we've got Fanny and my youngest, Letitia." Mr. Brocklehurst pointed at the two girls standing behind their mother and sister.

"Nice to meet you Miss Fanny and Miss Letitia," I said. The youngest girl giggled, covering her mouth with her hand. She couldn't be more than fifteen.

"Do you like music, Mr. Chambers?" Mrs. Brocklehurst asked as her husband ushered me into a chair. Austin took his seat in a chair beside me.

"I don't think I know anyone who isn't fond of music."

Mrs. Brocklehurst looked pleased. "Everyone always remarks how talented my Arabella is. Perhaps she can play a few tunes while we wait for dinner to be served."

Arabella stood and went to the piano forte in the corner.

"I'd be delighted to hear Arabella play," I said pleasantly. The oldest daughter spread out her dress as she perched herself at the bench and started playing a lighthearted tune.

"So, Mr. Chambers," Mr. Brocklehurst began. "At last year's Bragg recital, we heard from acquaintances that you have taken up apartments in Albany."

"You know them," Mrs. Brocklehurst shot in. "Lord and Lady Westham." She was eager to drop their name so it made their connections in society seem of higher quality.

"I have indeed. I've encountered Lord and Lady Westham a few times out on the promenade and during other social engagements in London."

"And are you planning to stay in Albany as a gentleman or will you rejoin the military service somewhere else?" Mr. Brocklehurst held out a glass for his footman, who filled it with brandy.

"Would you like some brandy, sir?" The footman asked as he moved towards me.

I nodded. "Please." He supported the bottle with a white napkin to ensure no drop was accidentally spilled, and gently poured me a glass. I savored a small sip as I thought about my answer to Mr. Brocklehurst. Meanwhile, the footman poured Austin a glass as well.

Mr. Brocklehurst continued. "I heard some rumors about a local militia that's being formed."

"I've finished my duties. Now I've returned to society. After all, I do want my father to keep an heir." I said it lightly, but everyone connected in polite society was aware of my father and our falling out. It was quite a scandal at the time, being left with John's parents. I'm sure Mr. and Mrs. Brocklehurst were aware of it. But I remained the only heir and if anyone is certain of anything, it is that society mothers will push their daughters on anyone with good prospects. And those I had in spades.

"And what about you, sir. What do you do?" Fanny, the middle daughter, asked Austin. All three daughters greatly resembled their mother. Though the youngest was the plainest of the bunch, perhaps she would still grow into her looks.

"I own a house in America and run a business," Austin said. I shot him an encouraging smile when he glanced at me. We'd practiced his cover story on the way over.

"And why did you come to England?"

Austin crossed his legs and took a swig of brandy. "Well, Mrs. Easton and I were childhood friends and when I received the good news about her marriage, I decided I should pay a visit. It had been such a long time since I'd seen her. Mr. Easton has been a most gracious host."

"How marvelous," Fanny exclaimed. In the background, Arabella switched to another tune, this one more dramatic.

"Arabella dear, how about you play something a bit more joyful?" her mother said. Arabella stopped playing and picked through her sheet music.

"Can you play that Mozart piece, sister?" the youngest girl asked.

Arabella smiled indulgently at her sibling. "Of course, I can." She pulled out a handwritten sheet of music from the stack and laid it on top.

"Will you play after your sister is done?" Austin asked Letitia.

"Oh, no. I do not play the piano," she said, blushing up at Austin. "I'm afraid my fingers aren't fast enough for the music."

Mrs. Brocklehurst fanned out her dress. "Only my eldest daughter inherited my talent for playing music," she said loftily. Arabella had started on a popular arrangement by Mozart. Mrs. Brocklehurst pointed at the elegant musical instrument.

"That piano forte was given to me by my father. Now, it is my daughter's instrument to play."

"Would you honor us with an example of your musical prowess?" I said to the proud mistress of Filton Grove.

"Oh, I couldn't possibly. I'm far too old to play now," she said, waving her hand. "No, it is Arabella's time to shine now."

"Spoken like a doting mother," Mr. Brocklehurst grumbled from underneath his giant mustache. His wife shot him an appreciative smile.

"Have you heard," Fanny spoke. "Lord and lady Westham got a barouche."

"I can't say I have. Thank you for the interesting news," I said politely.

Austin leaned towards me. "What's a barouche?"

"A barouche is a more luxurious carriage," I whispered back.

Mrs. Brocklehurst perked up. "I must know what you two were whispering about," she said. "Have you learned of any gossip?"

"None of the sort," I replied. "Austin was simply telling me how wonderfully Arabella is playing."

Mrs. Brocklehurst nodded, a grin on her face like a cat with cream. "Yes, all my daughters are very accomplished. You must sit next to Arabella during dinner, Mr. Chambers. I'm sure she'll keep you entertained."

"I'd be delighted to sit next to Miss Brocklehurst." Arabella was staring at me from behind the piano forte.

"And Mr. Miller can sit next to my Fanny. I'm sure they'll find something in common."

Austin turned towards the middle daughter. "What do you like to do, Miss Fanny?"

"My Fanny makes silhouettes," Mrs. Brocklehurst cut in before Fanny herself could answer. The girl blushed and chewed the corner of her lip while her mother continued on. "Why, that piece on the wall over there is one of hers." Austin and I followed the direction of Mrs. Brocklehurst's pointing finger. In between the two exterior windows was a collection of art displayed as a collage on top of garish purple wall covering. One of the pieces was a silhouette of a woman on a white background with a walnut frame."

"It's lovely," I said. "You have such talented daughters."

"Who is it a silhouette of?" Austin asked Fanny.

"Oh, it's..."

"She modeled it after me," Mrs. Brocklehurst jumped in again. "Can't you see the resemblance?" Fanny frowned behind her mother's back while Mrs. Brocklehurst tipped her head to the side, to let us admire her in profile."

"Now that you mention it, Mrs. Brocklehurst, the resemblance is striking." I winked at Fanny, who immediately averted her eyes and chose some other spot in the room to focus on.

"My dear Hyacinth and I are very proud of our daughters," Mr. Brocklehurst said. He reached for his glass of brandy and took a deep swig. Then, he plopped back into the chair, the wood groaning beneath the strain of his weight. His mustache almost seemed to dance on his face as his small, pink tongue flitted out and licked his lips. "Do you have any recommendations on where to stay in London?" the man asked me.

"Are you renting Chelton House this year, if I might ask?"

"I dare say it is likely. My wife and daughters have enjoyed our stay there each year. I was merely inquiring a man as yourself who has made London their home."

"Well," I said, pausing for a bit. "I've chosen my apartment in Albany because of my status as a bachelor. However, I doubt there are any places finer than Chelton House."

"See, didn't I tell you, Papa," Arabella said. "I like my rooms there."

"Yes, dear. You might've mentioned it a few times."

"Our Fanny will be entering her first season this year," Mrs. Brocklehurst said. "My dear husband wanted to make sure we would be staying in the most fashionable part of town still."

"I assure you, it is."

"Will you be staying in London during the season?" Arabella asked from beneath her eyelashes.

"I haven't decided yet."

"My daughter shall save a spot on her dance card if you do," Mrs. Brocklehurst said. I smiled and nodded.

"And what about Mr. Miller?" Fanny added. "Will you stay in England for a while?" she asked Austin directly.

"I'm afraid I don't know yet. It depends," Austin said.

"On what?" Fanny asked.

Austin froze for a beat before he answered, "On the company, of course."

"Then I suspect we shall all find ourselves in London," I said.

Fanny hid her smile behind her hand.

Mr. Brocklehurst's valet entered the drawing room. "Dinner is ready, sir," he announced to his employer.

"Thank you, Bronson," Mr. Brocklehurst said while waving his valet away. With a groan, our host stood from his chair. Then he addressed the room. "Let us all retreat to the dining room." He held out his hand towards his wife, who gladly took it. Arabella played one more run on the piano, finishing the piece she was playing, and closed the lid on the ivories.

Fortunately, Austin and I managed to get through dinner unscathed. We sampled some delicious hunter's stew, made from venison shot on Mr. Brocklehurst estate. We finished the evening with a sweet treat of apples in brandy. Austin's cheeks were quite red when Mr. and Mrs. Brocklehurst and their daughters were waving us out from the front steps. My own face felt flushed as well, the heat from the alcohol rushing up to my head.

"How wonderful it was to have you for dinner," Mrs. Brocklehurst said.

"Thank you for your hospitality." I gave her a nod and put on my hat.

"We should all go hunting together sometime," Mr. Brocklehurst said. "Some of the finest hunting grounds in the whole county can be found on my estate."

"I don't doubt it, Mr. Brocklehurst. I should be delighted to hunt with you."

"Then that is settled," he said, nodding gravely. "I shall extend an invitation to you and Mr. Miller when next I'll host a hunting party."

9

Small Hand Pies

I pulled on my boots, so I could head to the spot where the school was going to be built. The weather was incredibly drab. I hoped one of the maids would be able to salvage my boots after, as they invariably would be covered in muck. However, it was still early. Perhaps the day would brighten still. Austin and I were getting ready to meet McCreary and a few other tenants and workers from the village near the pond.

Austin and I were walking down the back path when we ran into Mrs. Avery, Hugh, and a mousy girl in a worn dress. They were walking towards the servant entrance.

"Good morning, Mrs. Avery. Good morning, Hugh. What are you doing out here so early? And who is this?" I asked, glancing at the girl. First, I thought she was shy, however, she lifted her chin and pointedly stared back at me.

"This is my niece, Clara," Mrs. Avery said. When she noticed that Clara didn't move, Mrs. Avery gave her a small tap on the shoulder. "Curtsy and introduce yourself," Mrs. Avery hissed. The girl narrowed her eyes and curtsied as minutely as possible.

"No need to curtsy on our account," I said, wondering what the girl's hostility was about. Mrs. Avery wasn't about to let it slide though.

"Go on then," Mrs. Avery told the girl. She gave Clara another small tap and a scowl. The girl finally spoke.

She glanced at her feet when she mumbled, "Nice to meet you, sirs."

"Nice to meet you too," Austin said.

"I apologize for Clara's behavior," Mrs. Avery said. "Coming here was a bit of a shock, but she's to learn how to be a maid."

"Good luck, Clara," I told the girl. I turned to Austin. "Come on. We need to hurry, or we'll be late for our meeting with McCreary." I smiled at Mrs. Avery. "I wish you luck with getting your niece settled."

"Thank you, sir," she said, more formally than usual. But that was probably for Clara's sake. Mrs. Avery was part of John's family, all things considered. She'd been here even before he was born. But the casual way we all interacted with the staff at Hawthorne was not the norm for most houses.

I'd been in plenty of homes where the mere notion of a gentleman speaking to the help was considered unseemly, let alone the cook addressing them by their Christian name. I'm sure Mrs. Avery wanted to set the right example for her niece. I couldn't fault her for that; Clara seemed to have some fire in her.

Austin and I continued on our way to the pond while

Mrs. Avery, Hugh, and Clara slipped in through the back door. When we reached the meeting spot, McCreary was busy tapping stakes into the ground with ropes tied taut between them. Another man, who I hadn't met yet, was helping him steady the wooden spikes, a wheelbarrow with a few spades and other supplies parked behind them.

"Ah, Mr. Chambers and Mr. Miller. How wonderful to see ye," McCreary said as he stood and brushed dirt off his wide hands. He clapped his hand around the other man's shoulder. "This here is Bledsoe; he'll be helping me set up the foundations."

"How do you do," the man said with a tip of his hat.

"Are you a tenant here?" I asked. The name sounded familiar.

"No, sir. I run a shop in the village."

"Bledsoe!" I exclaimed, as the answer came to me. "You must be the shoemaker."

"Indeed, I am," Bledsoe said. "How kind of you to re-member."

"If you make shoes, why are you helping McCreary with building the schoolhouse?" Austin asked.

"My father was in construction, sir." More quietly, he added, "And I could use the extra money."

McCreary spoke up. "Bledsoe is looking to retire and hand over his shop to his eldest son."

"Is that right?" I said.

"It is, sir. This is the perfect test to see how Arthur does without me."

I smiled at the shoemaker. "If you taught him all you know, I'm sure he'll do fine."

"Thank you, sir."

I glanced at the markers outlining the shape of the building to come. "This will be the spot?" I asked McCreary.

"Aye, sir." He tamped his foot on the ground. "The ground is firm enough to support the structure and Mrs. Easton wanted it near the lake. For the view, I suppose."

I grinned. "Certainly, for the view." Austin lifted his leg and stepped over one of the ropes. He walked the inside of the outline, casting cursory glances side-to-side.

"Mapped out like this, it seems small," Austin remarked to McCreary and Bledsoe.

"It'll be grand enough when it is built, I assure ye." Mc-Creary nodded gravely. He'd stiffened up a bit after Austin's comment.

"I have no doubt. Since Austin and I have no knowledge of such things, we shall defer to you, McCreary."

"I am honored, sir" he said, loosening up again.

"What's next?"

"I've taken the liberty of ordering a few men to bring up the supplies from the main house. But first we need to uncover the first layer of ground. Bledsoe and I will begin digging as soon as you and Mr. Miller leave."

"Don't wait on our account," I said. I walked towards the wheelbarrow and snatched up one of the spades. "I can help. Just tell me what to do."

Bledsoe appeared mortified. "But, sir. This isn't a job for a gentleman."

"Perhaps not. But I'd like to get my hands dirty."

"Then ye shall do just that," McCreary said. Bledsoe

glanced at McCreary with utter shock. Austin followed suit and grabbed one of the other spades.

"Where do we start?" he asked.

Bledsoe hurried towards the wheelbarrow and picked up a spade, wielding it almost as a weapon.

"We only need to remove the topsoil, sir," McCreary said. "Piling the dirt to one side."

"Since we'll be working beside each other, let's resolve to drop the honorifics."

"If you insist, sir," McCreary said, then he stammered. "Mr. Chambers."

I shook my head and laughed. "William will do." I thrust the spade into the ground. Using my foot, I pressed the metal deeper into the dirt and removed the first layer of soil.

The four of us worked side-by-side for hours. Despite the chill in the air, my brow was covered in sweat and my arms were covered in a fine layer of dirt. We managed to strip most of the grass. Evidence of our labor was a burgeoning mound near what would be the entrance to the school. The men McCreary hired had been coming on and off with wagons, dropping materials beside the wheelbarrow.

"William! Austin!" a voice called. I lowered the spade and glanced behind me. Beth was heading towards us carrying a basket.

"Beth, what are you doing here?" I said when she walked up to us.

"I knew you were busy working today so, with Mrs. Avery's help, I decided to bring you all something to eat." Beth looked Austin up and down. "It appears I was right. You all look like you could use it." She decidedly strode towards a soft patch of grass and set down the basket. Rummaging around, she pulled out a blanket. "Can you give me a hand?" she asked Austin.

"Of course," he said, stepping away from the construction site. He swiped his hands against his shirt before helping Beth. He grabbed one corner of the blanket and helped her spread it out.

Beth peered up at me. "Well. Come on. Let's have a seat." My hands were dark from the dirt, but I did the best I could by brushing my palms against my trousers. I spread out on Beth's right while Austin sat down on her left.

McCreary and Bledsoe watched awkwardly, spades still tight in their hands.

"Mr. McCreary, I brought enough for all of us," Beth said.

"Oh no, Miss. We can't take yer hospitality," he started.

"I insist." Beth pointed her arm towards the open spots on the blanket. "Please have a seat and let me say thank you for your hard work."

McCreary and Bledsoe laid down their spades and joined us. Now that I sat down, fatigue settled in my muscles. My spine strained from the repetitive movements and a blister had developed beneath the tender skin at the bottom of my pointer finger.

Beth opened one side of the basket and pulled out honeyed buns, which she handed to each of us. The sticky sweetness didn't help my hands feel any cleaner, but it tasted like heaven after shoveling dirt. At least John couldn't accuse me of not being helpful, not that he would.

Beth pulled out drink ware and poured us lemonade from a glass bottle. "What needs to happen next?" she asked while we sipped our tart drinks.

"A few lads from town are coming in tomorrow and wheeling away the dirt," McCreary said, licking his lips. "Then we're gonny lay down the foundation and start the brickwork."

"How exciting." Beth clapped her hands. She turned to me. "Will you help with that as well?"

"Oh, I don't think so. I'm afraid that I don't have a clue how to build a wall. Austin and I will merely check-in regularly to track how the work commences."

Beth frowned. "Then why help today?"

Austin laughed and glanced at me. "I think I can answer that one."

"Do go on. I'd like to hear the answer," Beth said as she pulled small hand pies from the basket.

"I think shoveling dirt is the only thing we can do without having any prior knowledge. At least once the building is finished, we can say we helped, even if it was just to prep the topsoil."

"I'll have to tell John that," Beth laughed. She pushed savory pie into my hands. The four of us finished eating while Beth entertained us with conversation. Once our bellies were full, we stood, helped her pack up, and said goodbye.

"Let's get back to it," Bledsoe said, after he waved Beth out. He pushed his sleeves back and bent to pick up his shovel. McCreary, Austin, and I joined him and continued digging up the last patches of grass until everything within the boundaries of the stakes was a smooth layer of dirt. We tamped the ground down with the blunt sides of our spades for good measure.

"I appreciate you working beside us today, Mr. Chambers and Mr. Miller," McCreary said once we were done.

"It felt good to be useful," I replied.

"I agree," Austin said with a smile. He wiped his brow with the back of his hand and left a dark mark across his forehead.

"When will you both come by again?" McCreary asked. He took Bledsoe's spade and his own and returned them to the wheelbarrow.

I took the spade from Austin's hands and walked towards the wheelbarrow. "Probably later this week to check the progress. However, if something changes or you need us to come sooner, you can send someone to fetch us," I said, while dropping the spades.

McCreary held out his hand. He gave a firm shake once I grasped it. "See ye soon, sir."

"See you soon," I said before turning to the shoemaker. "Nice to meet you, Bledsoe."

"Nice to meet you, sir."

I bumped against Austin and together we headed back to Hawthorne.

"I'm ready to lay down and sleep," he said, exuding a deep sigh.

"I feel the same. Although, a bath may be warranted first," I said. I glanced at the dark streak on Austin's forehead. "You've got a bit of dirt there," I added, pointing at my own forehead.

"Here?" Austin said, swiping his fingertips along the skin, making it worse.

A laugh bubbled up. "I don't think that helped."

Austin lifted his right brow. "You can laugh all you want, but you don't look like a clean gentleman either." He smirked at me.

"You are right; we both need to wash up or in the morning, we'd find our bed sheets covered in the dirt we spent all day shoveling." I stopped and pulled a kerchief from my inner breast pocket. "Here, let me at least fix your forehead. That way our faces are presentable when we return, even if our clothes aren't." Austin stopped walking. I grabbed the white fabric, folding the clean side out and lifted my hand. Stepping closer, I gently brushed the kerchief against his skin, wiping away most of the dirt. My hand lingered at his temple. Austin raised his hand and enveloped my fingers. His lips parted slightly as if he wanted to say something. Just for a moment, we stood in complete stillness. Our breaths in sync. Then he lowered my hand with his.

"Thank you," he said, his voice deep, green eyes bored into mine. I swallowed thickly and averted my gaze, uncomfortable by his stare and what it could mean. Or perhaps, by what I dared hope it could mean.

Neither of us spoke. But the way he parted his lips and gazed at me. It felt like an invitation. A summons. To reach for him and taste him, if only I dared. But I couldn't take advantage of his friendship.

And what if I was wrong? What if I dreamed it all up in my head? The curious glances, comments, and touches since he arrived could all just be written up to him being from the future and not used to the way we interacted. Did I even want to risk anything if he was interested? Could I ever truly be with someone after James?

I stepped back, returning the kerchief to my pocket.

Austin seemed disappointed when I said, "Let's get a move

on," and continued walking. Austin joined up, and we both returned to Hawthorne without speaking.

When we entered the foyer, Austin turned to me and broke the silence. "Will you still give me another riding lesson tomorrow?"

"I promised," I said wistfully as we parted ways.

10

Horseback Riding

The next day, I woke up and found Austin already in the stables. He was petting Maggie, a gentle older mare, and feeding her winter carrots.

"You are up early," I said.

Austin turned his face to me and nodded. "I didn't sleep very well."

"Bad dreams?"

"No, I was going to ask you the same thing. I think I heard you last night?" Austin's eyes bored into mine, a pensive look upon his face.

"I wasn't sure if you could..." Perhaps I needed to ask John for a change in rooms. I didn't want to disturb Austin with my nightmares. I walked to the pen and picked up a brush.

"It's okay, you didn't bother me. I had a lot to think about. My brain wouldn't shut up."

"Anything you'd like to talk about?"

Austin smiled his crooked smile. "Oh you know, same old, same old. Man ends up back in time."

I handed him the brush. "Worried about your sister?" he grasped the brush and started combing out Maggie's mane. The mare bristled and nuzzled against his hip, searching for more carrots.

Austin sighed. "Yes. It doesn't matter that Rose told me time essentially is frozen. I keep thinking, what if. What if time did continue and Alyssa is worried sick about me? We're sharing an apartment; if I'm not there to pay the bills, she'd be turned out."

"And you miss her."

Austin nodded. "It's tough. I miss my life; I miss Alyssa. And I get where Rose is coming from. This is a once in a lifetime opportunity; I should enjoy the experience, take in as much as I can. But I suppose I'm a bit of an overthinker. I can't stop worrying."

"I don't know how to fix that. But don't keep it bottled up." Austin's brow lifted. I grinned bashfully. "I know, I know. I'm not one to talk. It may be challenging for me to share my private thoughts with others, but that doesn't mean I don't understand how it can be helpful."

Maggie sniffed my hand while Austin considered.

"I'll keep that in mind. I did make you the same offer."

I picked up another carrot from the bin outside Maggie's stall. "Besides, Rose had just as much of a rough time adjusting when she first arrived. However, I think she's forgetting those details now that she and John are in love." The mare chomped down on it with delight.

"Rose looks so happy," Austin said.

"She and John both. I never imagined such a wonderful love match for my friend." I patted Maggie's head and turned to Austin. "Do you think you're ready to try saddling up?"

"I guess." Austin smiled ruefully. "What goes on first?"

I led Austin to the racks and nails that held all the horse tack and saddles. Thrusting a blanket into his hands, I said, "First, you lay this over Maggie's withers. After that, we'll add a saddle."

"Which one?" Austin asked, pointing at the different saddles hanging over the racks.

I pointed to the first one. "This one is a side-saddle; it's only used by the women."

Austin stared at the two pommels. "How does that work?"

"A lady can use it to sit sideways. Those extensions are called pommels; the rider would hook her right leg around the second one."

"That doesn't seem comfortable."

I grinned. "I wouldn't know. You could ask Beth for her opinion, though she prefers to ride astride when alone." I picked up the next saddle. "This is the one we'll be using."

Austin returned to Maggie and planted the blanket across her back. I handed him the saddle and helped put it on.

"Now what?"

"See those straps?" Austin nodded. "You'll have to tighten it and adjust it to Maggie's girth." I waited for Austin to finish buckling the straps before checking if they were secure.

"The last things we need are the bit and reins. If you can grab them from the hook over there," I said, pointing at the hook beside the mare's stall. Austin snatched the reins, and I showed him how to put them on Maggie.

"Was that it?"

"Yes, now you can saddle up and take Maggie for a ride."

"Oh," Austin stammered. "Well, I don't know. How do I even...?" The faces he was making were sending me into hysterics.

I tried to smother my laughter. "Don't worry. I'll help you mount. I will hold on to Maggie the entire time."

Austin flashed me an annoyed glance. "Fine. I'll try it. But don't you dare make fun of me if I fall off."

"I swear," I smirked.

"Okay, before I can change my mind. Let's go."

Holding Maggie's reins, Austin and I left the stables. I figured we'd stay close. All I would be doing was leading Austin around in circles.

"Are you ready?" I asked. Austin bit his lip and stared Maggie up and down.

"Do I step in those?" Austin was looking at the stirrups.

"Yes. I'll hold Maggie steady. Then use your left foot to step into the stirrup and kick off with your right. It takes a bit of practice to learn how to swing your leg over." I grasped the reins a little tighter and positioned myself near her head. "Go ahead," I told Austin.

Austin grasped the pommel and stepped into the stirrup. He was off to a decent start, but then he hopped awkwardly. He was trying to lift his leg but not swinging it high enough. I schooled my face.

"I don't think this is working," he remarked.

"Just a moment," I said. "Be a good girl," I told the mare. I dropped the reins and joined Austin. "Here, I'll help you. Step back into the stirrup." Austin followed my commands.

"Alright. Now. When you kick your right leg away from the ground, I'll help you lift. Alright?"

"Okay," Austin sank into his knees a bit more and jumped. I snatched his waist and used his momentum to push him up and over. Softly, he landed into the saddle. I immediately grabbed a hold of the reins, before Maggie could make a run for it. She was a good choice for a beginner rider, though, calm and well-behaved. But mounting tended to set off any horse. I'd seen plenty of gentlemen trying to mount, only to topple off the other side when their horse trotted forward. Always accompanied by much amusement from the crowd.

"How does it feel?" I asked Austin. He was moving his back, trying to position himself.

"Uncomfortable," Austin grinned. "I feel like I'm sitting incredibly straight."

"Try to get a sense for her. Pay attention to her movements while I lead you around."

I led horse and rider in a large circle. Maggie had her ears turned up, clearly enjoying the outing, while Austin remained as stiff as a board.

"Loosen a little," I shot out. I laughed. "By the looks of it, you are riding to your doom."

"I am trying. This is my first time."

"Hopefully, a few more lessons will help you get accustomed to Maggie. I would love to go for a ride out in the countryside."

Austin lifted his brows. "I'll do my best. But I'm not sure if I'll learn fast enough." I continued stepping backwards, leading them around. An idea formed in my head. One I probably shouldn't have, but I couldn't help myself. Austin looked so handsome mounted on top of Maggie, I wanted him to experience a real horseback ride. And a small part of me didn't mind that in order for my idea to work, I'd have to be right behind Austin as well.

"Would you like to go for a ride?"

"How?" Austin's face was apprehensive.

"I'll sit behind you and steer."

"There isn't enough space." Austin peered behind him.

"Trust me," I said, handing him the reins. "Take your feet out of the stirrups and stay steady. I'll mount behind you."

Austin glanced around worriedly and removed his feet. I stepped up and swung my leg over, landing behind him. I was seated on Maggie's bare back, my legs pressed against Austin's thighs.

"How can you ride like that?" he asked.

"It's a bit unorthodox, and I will certainly be covered in horse hair and sweat once we return, but other than that, it's much the same."

Maggie bristled. Austin was clutching the reins a little too tightly. I took them from him, slackening the tension.

"We shouldn't burden Maggie with both our weights for too long, but where would you like to go?"

Austin glanced down the driveway. "We could try that direction." I nodded and applied pressure to Maggie's left side, turning her towards the driveway.

Austin remained stiff as we trotted down the path. "You don't have to sit so straight; you can lean into me," I told him. He nodded, relaxing against my chest, moving with me.

After a while, he remarked, "This is less uncomfortable."

I smirked. "Oh?"

"I don't need to work my muscles as much." It was because I was taking the brunt of the exercise. But I didn't breathe a word. I liked the feel of him against me. "I can see how riding a horse could be fun once you know what to do."

"I like the solitude. When you are riding you don't have to focus on anything but the well-being of your horse. Everything else falls to the wayside. You can just be."

"Peace and quiet," Austin muttered.

"Yes." We trailed all the way down to the end of the driveway, then I turned Maggie around to make her way back to the stables. "When you can ride by yourself, we should venture out past the pond. There are some well-kept riding trails leading up to Mrs. Ashbrook's estate.

"I promise I'll try," Austin said. "But one step at a time."

Back at the stables, I dismounted. I held out my hand and helped Austin to the ground. "Let's clean Maggie off," I said. I led her back to her pen. Together, we took off the saddle, bit, reins, and blanket. Then we used rags to wipe away the slight sheen of sweat. There wasn't much since we hadn't gone far. I handed the mare another carrot and thanked her. She nipped at my coat. I closed the stall, and together, Austin and I returned indoors.

11

A Hunting Party

"What a marvelous day for shooting," Mr. Brocklehurst exclaimed. Austin and I stood together with the owner of Filton Grove, admiring the large clearing which was perfect for shooting birds. Small half-walls were lined up across the field, providing cover for the shooter. We'd received the invitation for the hunting party a few days before.

An array of footmen gathered, holding fowling pieces as they waited for the additional hunters to arrive.

Mr. Brocklehurst clapped his meaty hand on my back. "Let us compare at the end who is the better shot." He let out a hearty laugh. "Or should I worry about Mr. Miller taking home the prize?"

"I don't know about that. Shooting isn't really my thing, but I'll try my best."

"I'm sure you'll do fine. Just be sure to aim forward. We

don't need to hunt our own." Mr. Brocklehurst's thick mustache bristled as the man laughed.

"I hope there are plenty of pheasants," a man walking up said. I froze. I recognized that voice.

"Captain Tremblay, welcome," Mr. Brocklehurst said as he turned to the newcomer. "We are still waiting for the other guests to arrive. Let me introduce you to Mr. Miller and—"

"Officer Chambers," Captain Tremblay answered.

"You are acquainted with each other?"

"Yes," I said, squeezing my hands. "Though I'm no longer in service. It's just Mr. Chambers now." My knuckles turned white; with a painful pop the half-healed blister on my right hand reopened.

Captain Tremblay gauged my response for a moment then answered Mr. Brocklehurst. "Mr. Chambers and I fought together against the French."

"How delightful. You must catch-up and tell us all about your shared experiences." Mr. Brocklehurst looked pleased, as if he couldn't have planned it better himself.

I didn't expect to see Captain Tremblay again. Not after he visited me at the field hospital after the victory at Waterloo. He spoke to me when I was being readied to travel to the boat that would take me from The Netherlands back to good old England. I didn't want to return to our British shores at the time. My mind was too preoccupied with losing James.

I stared at Tremblay's outfit, the brass buttons and glaring red fabric of his military coat took me by surprise. I couldn't help it, but my heart was pounding in my chest. Shivers ran along my spine. I forced my feelings down, pretending I was fine.

"Are you okay," Austin whispered, concern furrowing his brow.

I nodded my head slightly and tried to unclench my fingers. I turned away from the men, pretending to observe the hunting grounds. Counting my breaths, I inhaled and exhaled until I felt my heart rate slow.

The other guests arrived and circled around Mr. Brocklehurst, excited about the prospect of shooting. Austin slipped next to me.

"We can leave, if you'd rather," he said in a lowered voice right when Mr. Brocklehurst started his announcement.

"It seems everyone has arrived so let us go to our spots and may the best man win."

I forced a smile before answering Austin. "I'll be fine."

"Will you tell me what's wrong? Is it that Captain Tremblay?"

"Later," I told him.

"As long as there is a later." He gave my wrist a soft squeeze.

One of the footmen followed me to an unoccupied low wall. He handed me a fowling piece— a smooth double-barreled shotgun— which I cocked and readied. Mr. Brocklehurst acted as the overseer of the hunt since it was his estate. He had taken up a spot in the middle.

Now, all we had to do was wait until the beaters drove the prey towards us. Then, Mr. Brocklehurst would shout the command.

I rested the butt of the shotgun against my shoulder and aimed, waiting to release my shot. I glanced to my left where Austin was trying to do the same. His footman was animatedly explaining how to hold the weapon. My gaze returned to the field in front of me, which consisted of thickets and underbrush. Servants on the other side of the field shouted and stomped through the field to flush the fowl out of hiding. The first sounds of rustling headed our way, and before long, a flurry of pheasants headed skyward in front of us.

"Aim and shoot," Mr. Brocklehurst shouted as he aimed at the birds.

Left and right of me, men shot and reloaded. But not me. My finger stilled on the trigger. Smoke filled my nostrils. Heat scored my cheek.

"Aim and shoot!" Another round of shots sped past me.

My breath hitched. My hand trembled, and I dropped the shotgun. I squeezed my eyes shut, but I still saw the flames. I could hear the high-pitched screams of men as they lay dying in the field, burning alive because they were too wounded to move. And James—my James— cradled in my arms, my uniform stained dark red from both his blood and my own.

Someone moved past me as my legs buckled, and I sank to the ground. James' body was heavy in my arms. I held him until the shooting stopped and the smoke cleared. But it hadn't stopped. They were shooting now. Someone grabbed my shoulders.

"William, Will. Can you hear me?" I shook my head. No, I was with James. James was dead. I was... was I?

"Come on. I need you to get up," the voice pleaded. He pulled at my arm.

"No," I shouted. "I can't leave him. I can't. It's not safe. I promised to protect him."

"He's not here," the person pulling at me said.

"No," I choked out. I tried to look at James' face, but he

was no longer cradled in my lap. "Where did he go?" I cried, tears streaking down my face.

The other person knelt in front of me and grabbed my face.

"William. You are stuck in the past. What you are seeing has already happened." He pulled me in to a hug. "Come back to me," he whispered in my ear. I recognized the man's voice.

"Austin," I muttered, burying my face in his neck, fat tears soaking his shirt.

"It's alright," he murmured, caressing my back. "You are alright. You are here with me, and you are safe." I gripped him tightly as I returned to the here and now, my breath heavy and labored. Shame and embarrassment coursed through me as I became aware of my surroundings. Here I was crying in another man's arms, making a scene at Mr. Brocklehurst's shooting party.

"I can't," I said, pushing myself back. Scrambling to my feet, I felt the stares of all the men present. "I need to leave," I urged Austin. He stood and gripped my arm to steady me. A hush fell across the group.

Mr. Brocklehurst stepped forward, his scatter gun forgotten by his side. "Do I need to call for a doctor?"

Austin shot a quick glance at me. "I don't think it's necessary. Hugh can take us back to Hawthorne." My limbs trembled as if they could no longer support the weight of my body. I felt tired. So tired. Emotionally and physically drained.

"Just take me home. Please," I told Austin.

"We are going now," he said kindly. He shifted his weight and slung his arm around me.

"Are you certain?" Mr. Brocklehurst said, his gaze pityingly scouring my frame.

"I am," Austin remarked firmly. "I apologize for the inconvenience to your shooting party. Please don't stop on our account. I'll take Mr. Chambers to Hawthorne where he can be seen to by Mr. Easton."

"Send us word on his recovery."

"Will do," Austin said. He gripped me tighter. Together, we walked the mile or so to the main house. Hugh jumped out of the carriage when he saw us limping towards him.

"Anything wrong, sir?" he asked me.

Austin spoke up. "Nothing is wrong. However, we would like to return to Hawthorne as soon as possible. Mr. Chambers is a bit tired."

"Right away, Mr. Miller," Hugh said. He gripped the carriage door and opened it for us. Austin helped me inside to one of the benches. Once he made sure I was comfortable, he sat down across from me.

"How are you feeling?" he asked once the door closed and Hugh had taken his seat at the front.

"Exhausted," was the only word that came to mind. Anything else felt either too small, too enormous, or not appropriate. Austin leaned forward and took my hand in his. He faced me, staring straight into my eyes. His thumb skimmed across the soft skin on the back of my hand.

"Was it seeing Captain Tremblay?" he asked. I frowned and averted my eyes.

"Perhaps a little," I confessed.

"Does this happen often?"

Did it happen often? I bit my lip. "No. Not like that."

"Like what then?" Austin prodded gently. The carriage jerked forward as the mares started their trot homeward.

I returned my gaze, catching his vivid green eyes, and bared my soul. "I told you about my nightmares. Those horrible nightmares." Austin nodded.

"Usually, they happen only when I'm sleeping."

"About James," Austin stated.

My hand tightened in his. "Where did you hear that name?"

"I heard you shout it just now."

"Oh," I sighed. "Did everyone?"

"I'm not sure. You rambled on a bit and most of the men were distracted with the birds."

My lips tightened. "Nothing I can do about it now."

"No, I suppose not," Austin added matter-of-factly.

"What you must think of me," I said, sorrow permeating every word. I pulled my hand back, but Austin snatched it again.

"No. You listen to me, William. And you hear me." He squeezed my hand and laid his other hand on my knee. "I was worried about you. Heck, I *am* worried about you. But none of this is your fault." I jerked my head, but he moved his hand to cradle my cheek. "I mean it. Whatever happened back then and whatever happened just now, none of it is your fault. You are a good man."

"You hardly know me."

"I have seen enough to know that you do your best for others. You are there for John and Beth no matter what they need. And you've been here for me, a stranger thrust upon you from out of nowhere."

"I don't mind," I started.

"That's my point exactly." Austin's voice had slowly gotten louder, but now he softened it again.

"Do you want to tell me about James? About what you were seeing when you fell to the ground?"

I paused. I couldn't, not now, not everything. Not to Austin.

"Will you let me guess?" Austin asked. I leaned back against the thin padded backing of the seat and nodded.

Austin waited, as if to gather the right words. "Let me know if I am wrong," he said. Slowly he added, "I think you loved James." His eyes assessed my expression. "And he loved you." The wet heat of a tear rolled down the side of my face. "You lost him in the war?"

"Yes," I said glumly. Austin's expression told me he'd registered my admission. I was waiting for him to pull away and look disgusted. To my surprise, he never did.

"I am so sorry."

"Me too."

"He must have been a wonderful person if you loved him so strongly," Austin said. I glanced up, surprised at his comment.

"He was." Those two simple words felt too small to describe everything James had meant to me, but it was a start. "James was the only one I could be myself with," I told Austin. "He was such an integral part of my plans for the future."

"I can understand that."

"In an instant, he was gone. Years fighting side-by-side with only minor wounds. And to add insult to injury, Napoleon's forces were defeated the very next day. My dreams and our plans out the door. James in a shallow grave and me with a scar that reminds me of what happened every time I look in a mirror or catch my reflection in a window."

"I don't know how to help with the grief, but if it hurts, doesn't that mean it was real. That you really loved each other? I envy that. However short-lived it may have been."

I pondered Austin's statement. "I am grateful for his love. Even if I had known what was coming, I wouldn't have changed a thing." I shot Austin a wry smile. "My grief has gotten better. My nightmares have been less frequent. It was today, seeing Tremblay and the shooting. It transported me straight back to Ligny. I'm sorry you had to see me like that."

"Don't apologize for something you couldn't help. I am just glad I was there to support you."

"It would have been a lot more awkward if one of the other men had to get me away," I added flippantly.

Austin smirked. "What if it had been Mr. Brocklehurst that hugged you?"

I fake shuddered. "His great mustache tickling my neck." I sighed, my face turning serious. "I'm glad it was you." My eyes were still on the verge of welling up. I rubbed them with my knuckles. "Today took a lot out of me." I pulled a timepiece out of my pocket. "Good lord," I exclaimed. "It's only nine a.m. But I feel like I've been out an entire day. When we return, I think I need to sleep."

Austin's intelligent eyes appraised me. "I think that's for the best. However, I'd be more comfortable if I could keep you company for a while. At least until you are sound asleep, in case you have more nightmares immediately after going to bed."

"You don't have to," I hurried to say, but I liked the idea of having Austin near as I drifted off to sleep.

"I insist."

12

Nightmares

I appreciated Austin taking charge. When we returned to Hawthorne, he fielded questions from Beth and John. They were both wondering why we were back so early since usually hunting took some time, not to mention the gathering after. He held them off with simple excuses and followed me upstairs to the room I was staying in.

The windows were open, bathing the entire room in bright light, but Austin bounded towards them and with a swift jerk, closed the baby blue drapes. I sank down on the edge of the bed and, in one fluid motion, pulled off my shirt and threw it over a decorative stand. With my elbows resting on my knees, I cradled my face in my hands.

"Hey, you're okay," Austin said softly. He sank down next to me and caressed my back. "Let's put you into bed." Austin reached behind me and pulled the coverlet back more. I crawled in and rolled to my side. Austin grabbed the blanket and covered me with it. He patted the blanket. His weight shifted off the mattress. I grabbed his wrist.

"Will you stay with me? Just for a little while?" I dropped my hand to let him decide. I had no right to ask him to stay but I hoped he would. Somehow, this man I barely knew made me feel safe, and I sure needed that.

"Don't worry, I said I'd stay. I'm not going anywhere." Austin moved in behind me, pressing flush against my back, slinging his arm around me. I grabbed his hand and held it tightly against my chest. Against the back of my neck, his breath rhythmically heated my skin with every breath he took. I had expected it to be awkward, but it wasn't awkward at all; it felt comforting to be this close to another human being again. I hadn't been this cared for and safe in a long time. I enjoyed being held in someone's arms while I drifted off to sleep.

* * *

Waking up to see Austin next to me sprawled out across the bed was exhilarating somehow. His arms were stretched out crookedly above his hair, which was adorably disheveled, and his mouth opened slightly in an adorable pout. The sight of him in my bed was so disarmingly innocent and yet enticing; I could observe him like this for hours. His shirt had ridden up while he'd moved around and now, as I glanced at his abdomen, I noticed the start of a symbol.

"Good morning," Austin muttered. He was sleepily looking

at me. "Or is it good afternoon?" He yawned and stretched his arms a little more.

"It's still light out, so I doubt we missed dinner," I said.

"Did you sleep well? How are you?" Austin asked as he remembered the reason we were in my room.

"I think the nap helped. Thank you for staying with me."

"It looks like I needed some sleep too." Austin snorted.

"Can I ask what the mark on your stomach is," I said pointing at the dark symbol starting right below the edge of his shirt.

Austin quirked a brow. "Were you watching me sleep?"

"No," I stammered. My skin flushed.

"It's alright," he said with a grin. Pushing off the bed, he pulled his shirt up and over his head, revealing an intricate design covering his left shoulder and chest, ending at his lower rib cage.

"I never noticed before."

"Well, usually my tattoo is covered with clothes."

"How did you get this done?" I reached out to touch him but stopped short. I glanced up at Austin. "Can I touch you?" Austin nodded, so I traced my finger along the dark lines that were etched in his skin.

"One of my friends did this," he said, his voice soft as I continued tracing the tattoo with minimal pressure. His skin was smooth and silky beneath my fingertips.

"I like it."

Austin genuinely looked happy about my statement. "I am glad," he said. "This. Or, well, tattoos like this are what I do for a living. In my own time, I work as a tattoo artist."

"And that's why you draw so well."

"Yes."

"Do you think you could do something like this to me?" I loved the sight of his tattoo— exotic and different. The idea of having something that Austin created permanently painted on my body sounded like a wonderful memento. A unique memory I could carry with me always, even when he invariably returned to his own time.

"If I had the right equipment. I'm not sure where to get that here," he said, frowning at whatever he was thinking. I was still unconsciously tracing my finger along his skin.

"I'm sorry. I should leave you alone," I said, pulling back my hand.

Austin looked at me wistfully. "I don't mind."

"Still. I've kept you here all day. We should get up and see what time it is."

"Find some food," Austin added. His eyes scoured my face. "You really feel better? Because you can tell me if you don't. I'm willing to listen."

"I'll keep that in mind," I said, keeping the tone of my voice light. I sat up and sidled off the bed. John and Beth were probably still wondering what we'd been doing up here all day, so it would be best to get dressed. I retrieved my shirt, which I'd haphazardly thrown over the ornate stand, then, using water from the washing basin, I straightened out my hair. Behind me, Austin also got ready.

With us both getting dressed again, a distance grew between us that hadn't been there when we were dozing and chatting in the bed. Austin's carefree conversation stilled. Perhaps it was only in my mind. Being around Austin was easy, too easy. I was afraid that if I grew too close to him, I'd be devastated when he left, and leave he would.

I had no business getting attached to him when he was only here temporarily. I wasn't sure of his feelings, let alone my own. For all I knew, he would do this for any friend. But then again.... the future couldn't be so different—even if they had mechanical vehicles— that a person would get so close to another human being without at least reciprocating some tender feelings.

My heart fluttered whenever I saw Austin. I wondered if he experienced the same. Not that I had any right to pursue such a feeling. No, I was too broken for that. Austin deserved someone whole and unspoiled. I felt guilty about even thinking about Austin. How could I like anyone after James?

I turned to Austin. "How about we find something to eat first. We can go to the kitchen?"

"Sounds like a plan," Austin replied. He gave my palm a gentle squeeze before dropping his arms, as we left my bedroom.

Out in the corridor, the new maid was busy dusting the wooden frames that adorned the walls, artwork depicting centuries of families living at Hawthorn— the latest being John and Beth as children with the late Mr. and Mrs. Easton.

The new maid—Clara, I remembered— curtsied as we passed by her. Then she immediately returned to dusting another frame, this one a stern family portrait of John's great-grand parents. John's great-grandmother looked especially old-fashioned in an expansive baroque dress covered in ornamental frills, the opposite of the sleek silhouette that was en vogue today.

Walking down the main staircase, I had the sudden urge to look behind me. The maid's eyes were trained on our backs, the duster forgotten at her side. I shot her a quick smile and continued walking as she hurriedly resumed cleaning. Her stare struck me as a bit odd, but I decided it was more than likely because she was still getting used to Hawthorne.

Downstairs in the kitchen, Mrs. Avery was bustling around getting dinner ready.

"Mr. Chambers and Mr. Miller, I reckon you're in here for supper," she said, while moving roasted chicken legs from the pan to a serving platter. Once the meat dropped on the plate, she let go of the pan and patted her sweaty forehead with a cloth she kept at her waist. Mrs. Avery frowned and glanced around the kitchen. "Did you see Clara anywhere?"

"She was busy dusting upstairs in the guest wing," Austin replied.

"Och, that girl is giving me a headache," Mrs. Avery said bluntly. She snatched a wooden spoon from a rest and stirred a cream-colored sauce bubbling away on the stove. The smell was making my stomach growl.

"Would you like me to fetch her?" I offered.

Mrs. Avery's eyes crinkled, and she smiled affectionately. "No need." She sighed as she turned her head back to the stove. "I've sorted it all myself now anyway."

"Can I help?" Austin said.

"You are Mr. Easton's guest; I wouldn't let you help." Mrs. Avery ladled a clear broth into a soup bowl. "Mr. Chambers and yourself can go to the drawing room and announce that dinner will be served shortly, if you don't mind."

"We don't mind at all," I answered in tune to my rumbling stomach.

Mrs. Avery continued plating food. She hardly glanced up as Austin and I left the kitchen. Perhaps Mrs. Avery's niece would come in handy once she was properly trained up. Mrs. Avery seemed a tad overwhelmed with dinner service this evening.

Usually, I commended John for his unorthodox way of running his estate, especially the lack of servants and formality. Besides Estelle, who was Beth's lady's maid, Mrs. Avery who acted as cook and head housekeeper, one scullery maid whose name I couldn't remember, Hugh who essentially was a Jack-of-all-trades, and George the valet, there wasn't any staff. If there was a special party or dinner, John would hire footmen and a butler from town. But Mrs. Avery was getting on in years, and it was a rather sizable estate. I hoped Clara would help lighten Mrs. Avery's workload.

I stopped Austin in the hallway, my hand on his shoulder. "Austin, I don't—" I started.

Austin cut in. "It's okay. I won't say anything. This has nothing to do with me, so it's up to you to decide whether you want to tell any of them."

"It's not that I don't want to," I tried to explain.

"I'm not judging." And as he said it, I realized he genuinely meant it.

"Thank you." My deepening voice conveying my gratitude.

Unfortunately, just because Austin wouldn't betray me and tell everyone what happened at Filton Grove, didn't mean that John wasn't perceptive enough to realize something was wrong.

He pulled me aside after Austin and I announced that dinner would start soon. Beth, Rose, and Austin left for the dining room, which meant John and I had the drawing room to ourselves. Which was a good thing because I didn't want to say anything in front of Beth and Rose. Beth still thought of me as an uncomplicated honorary brother, and I intended to keep it that way.

John pursed his lips and looked at me. "Can you tell me what happened? You were supposed to go shooting with Mr. Brocklehurst, then you return early, pale as death, supported by Austin. I waited all day to find out what happened while Austin spent his time with you in your room."

"You aren't worried about Austin's virtue, surely?" I remarked jokingly, deflecting his pointed remark.

"Should I?" John said. His tone made it clear he wasn't amused.

I sighed. "No, you don't need to worry about Austin. He was merely with me as a friend."

"You know that's not what I meant." John glanced at the doorway. "I'd be glad for you, if..."

"I know," I hurried to say. "But we aren't. He's just a friend." The words sounded more despondent than I meant them to be.

John frowned. "Then what was going on?"

I moved to close the door. With my back turned towards John, I started talking. "You know about my nightmares?"

"Yes," he confirmed, though we'd already had a conversation about them.

"Sometimes they happen even when I'm awake."

"And that is what happened today?"

I nodded and turned around. "I'm sure I'll be the exciting topic of many conversations to come."

"Perhaps we can speak with Mr. Brocklehurst," John said, but I waved him away.

"It's too late now."

"Why didn't you ever tell me?"

"I didn't know how. I've been wrestling with it myself. The nurses at the field hospital called it 'soldier's heart' or 'the blue devil', though that doesn't sound nearly as horrible as it feels."

Embarrassment crawled up my spine and made me shudder. John was sympathetic but his sympathy didn't feel deserved. I hesitated. Then, all at once, the words tumbled out of me.

"When the shooting started, I thought I was back at the battle of Ligny. It felt so real, James dying, holding his lifeless body in my arms. It wasn't until Austin spoke to me that I realized what I was seeing had already happened. That I was safe. I don't deserve his friendship."

"That's not true," John cut in. He gripped my arm. "You are my best friend, Will. Always have been."

"And you are mine," I laughed awkwardly as I swallowed away the lump in my throat.

"Since I wasn't there, I'm glad Austin could help you. I like him." John's eyes twinkled as he said the last part.

"I do too." The words weighed heavy on my heart. I had no business liking Austin. It felt like a betrayal to James. And what if he left? What if I let myself hope, and I was left behind again, alone? I didn't think I could bear it.

"Just promise me that you'll do what makes you happy,"

John said, unaware of my thoughts. "You don't need to pretend with me."

Nodding, I answered him. "I'll try. That's all I can do for now." I would have to do what was best for me. I didn't know why John sent for me in the first place, why he needed my help with Austin. Perhaps he wanted to keep an eye on me, or perhaps I was reading too much into it, and he simply wanted to spend more time with me.

Regardless, I was worried about my future. I couldn't let myself grow closer to Austin; my heart couldn't take much more. I was afraid it would shatter if I had to say goodbye to one more person.

I wanted to stay close, but it was best if I returned to London. I could visit John again once Austin had left, a clean break. A twinge of regret burst in my chest, but I ignored it. I would pack up and make plans to leave in the morning. The only issue was saying farewell. Perhaps I could leave a note. John would be angry if I left without a word, but time apart would soften him.

13

Albany

When I returned to my apartments in Albany, I wondered if I had done the right thing. My chest ached the entire carriage ride back to London. John would probably have read my note by now. I could only imagine his reaction. What did Austin think? No, I couldn't go there. We were both better off like this.

"Welcome back, sir," my butler said. "I hope you enjoyed your stay with Mr. and Mrs. Easton."

"I did, Parsons. But I am glad to be home." I handed him my coat.

"I'm afraid we weren't expecting you, sir. If you'd wait in the drawing room, I'll fetch a chambermaid to air out your rooms and light a fire."

"It's my own fault. I left in rather a hurry. Take your time; I'll be fine in the drawing room."

The butler inclined his head and hung my coat in the

closet. "In the meantime, I'll have some tea sent up, or would you prefer something stronger?" he asked once he turned back to me.

A whiskey sounded appealing, but I decided against it. "Just tea, please. Oh, and perhaps some light refreshments." It had, after all, been a long carriage ride.

"Right away, sir."

Parsons picked up the suitcase I had dropped off near the entrance and headed to the servants' area. I retreated to the drawing room and put myself up in a comfortable leather chair.

It was quiet. Normally, I would've enjoyed a moment of silence. But not now. I had gotten used to being around people again. At Hawthorne, there was always some kind of noise. Beth giggling or arguing. John and Rose chatting animatedly about whatever topic was important at that time. Even the hustling and bustling of Hugh and Clara, or the kind words of Mrs. Avery. And I'd gotten used to having Austin around.

I sighed, leaning back into the chair. Parsons returned soon, followed on his heels by a girl carrying a tray of tea, biscuits, and cold cuts. She set it down on the table in front of me.

"Thank you," I told her. She bobbed her head and poured my first cup.

"Cream or sugar, sir?"

"A splash of cream, please."

Once she finished, she curtsied and left the room.

"Is there anything else I can do for you in the meantime?" Parsons asked. "Annette is readying your room as we speak. I could order some water to be heated for a bath."

I shook my head. "No, thank you, Parsons. Fresh water next to my washing basin will be sufficient tonight. Although, if you could alert one of the footmen. I haven't decided yet, but I may head into town this evening."

"Certainly, sir."

Then, my butler left as well, and I was alone again. I ate a biscuit and some cold cuts. The tea was hot and fragrant, but it all ended up at the bottom of my stomach where it clumped together and made me sick.

I kept wondering. Had I done the right thing? The pit in my stomach was growling, no.

* * *

That evening, I decided that I *was* going to head out. I'd spent hours wandering through the rooms of my apartment, lost in thought. I needed some human interaction or at the very least, some liveliness around me. A dark cloud was following my every move and I needed to divert my mind.

One of the footmen drove me to Covent Garden. From there, I walked the familiar streets until I reached The Waddling Duck. There weren't many people out on the streets, but once I entered the establishment, I was welcomed with warm lights and cheerful noises. The place was filled with a heady mixture of cologne and liquor, and traces of tobacco.

"'Aven't seen you for a while," Mary Duck said from the bar.

I tipped my head and took off my hat. "Always a pleasure. I was away visiting a friend."

"Such a charmer," she said, in her broad accent. She waved

one of her boys over with a tray of drinks. I accepted a glass of whiskey.

A few couples were dancing near the piano while one of the guests was playing an upbeat tune. By the time I'd found a chair, the music had turned into a waltz. One of the couples, two men, swayed together in time to the song. They were whispering in each other's ear. I averted my eyes, envious. Another couple trailed away from the dance floor, kissing.

I sipped my drink. Strangely, my night here felt like an echo of my previous visit to The Waddling Duck. I'd sought this place out to not feel so alone but seeing everyone around me enjoy themselves merely made me feel lonelier.

I didn't even know if Austin liked me as more than a friend. And now I would never know. But it would have been wonderful to dance together like the couple dancing the waltz, whispering sweet nothings in each other's ear.

Sighing, I took another swallow of whiskey. Did I actually like Austin, or did I miss the connection I had with James? Was I looking for the same connection with another?

Guilt shot through me whenever I thought of finding someone else. Because it would mean he was well and truly gone from my life. But, no, I couldn't compare Austin to James. They were incredibly different. I think James would have liked Austin, but he was carefree and outspoken, where Austin was thoughtful and caring.

Perhaps it was only friendship on Austin's side, but I liked him for who he was. And I couldn't help the attraction I felt.

I needed to move on with my life. James was gone and Austin would soon leave as well. Perhaps it would be easier to find a woman who was easy to be around. I'd considered

Rose, once upon a time. But the thought of sharing a life with someone I could never be attracted to, that I could never love, left a bad taste in my mouth. I wanted a full life with someone I adored.

I returned my gaze to the dancers, watching them as they glided across the floor in each other's embrace. That's what I wanted. Austin, my mind conjured up. But it could never be him.

Crossing my legs, I drained my glass. It was quickly replaced by another. I tipped Mary's servant well. I leaned my head against the back of the chair and closed my eyes, listening to the sounds of laughter at Mary's establishment.

I was about to take another drink from my glass when one of Mary's runners, a small girl, burst through the door.

"Raid," she screamed. "The constables are on their way."

Mary Duck's face blanched. "Go, warn the guests," she ordered her servers. The men sped off into different directions. One headed up the stairs, probably knocking on the doors of the private rooms. The others ran to the gathering rooms downstairs.

"'Ow long do we have?" Mary asked her runner.

"Couple 'o minutes. No more," the girl answered before she ran off.

The piano music had stopped, and the dancing couples were now standing frozen in the center of the room.

Mary Duck stepped forward. "Everyone. We can head out the back. You can follow August over here." She waved over one of the servers. He nodded.

I stood as did the rest. We didn't have long. August hurried through the corridors, leading the guests and myself to the back of the house. There, he opened the door for us. Men and women were racing down the stairs and exiting the other rooms, pushing past one another to get out the door.

Heavy knocks sounded against the front door. Mary had stayed back.

"What's this, constable?" she asked. "There's no one here."

"We'll be the judge of that," a man spoke. "We have a reason to believe this house is being used for illegal activities." Then, I could hear the constables file into The Waddling Duck, spreading out in every direction.

I tried to exit the door, but the small corridor functioned as a bottleneck, and I was shoved harshly into the wall by frantic people fleeing.

"Here," one of the constables shouted as he turned into our hallway. The rest followed, grabbing hold of and arresting any person that got within their reach. I grunted, lifting my hand to the back of my head. One of the constables slammed a woman in menswear against the wall. I had to keep my face hidden. Another constable reached for me. I jerked my arm away and pushed against the crowd blocking the door until I managed to burst through.

I ran, heart beating in my throat. My head and shoulder hurt from the shove into the wall. I heard the constables shout stop, but I ignored anything around me and kept moving, turning and twisting past the back streets until I was alone. I nearly collapsed. My lungs burned as I tried to catch my breath. A stitch in my side prevented me from standing upright.

Had I gotten away? I couldn't risk standing around. I needed to keep moving. No longer running as fast as I was able, I walked, heading further away from The Waddling Duck.

That was just my luck. First night back and the place got raided. I hoped Mary would land on her feet. My heart went out to the poor bastards that got caught. I winced when I touched the back of my head, a bump already developing. Only a little further and I could hail a carriage.

I wound my way back to Covent Garden. Once I reached the well-lit street, I let out a breath and slicked back my hair. Then, as if nothing had happened, I approached a driver parked on the side.

"Can you take me to Albany?"

14

The Parthenon Marbles

It could have gone so wrong. I'd tossed and turned the entire night, my mind playing over the events at The Waddling Duck, mixing in with memories of James and my military service.

Now, I was splashing my face with cold water from the washing basin. The back of my head and my shoulder smarted. I didn't think anyone recognized me, but yesterday startled me. I'd broken my promise to John; I didn't keep out of trouble. I was lucky to get away. The poor souls behind me had probably spent the night in jail and were now awaiting sentencing. I could have been one of them.

And for what? I hadn't enjoyed myself. I spent the entire time I was there thinking about James and Austin, wondering if I'd made the right decision. Perhaps I was being a fool. Perhaps I should pack my bags and return to Hawthorne. Perhaps. Perhaps. Perhaps. I sighed.

I threw on some clothing and dragged myself down the stairs. Parsons had arranged for breakfast, so I ate in silence at the dining table. What was wrong with me? I swallowed a bite of streaky bacon. John was worried about me, and I repaid him by running away and only leaving a note. Was it really easier to leave and not say goodbye? What if Austin left and I never got to see him again? The food turned to ash in my mouth. I tried to rinse my mouth with a big gulp of tea.

Parsons returned to the dining room. "Sir, Mr. Easton is here to see you." John? He traveled here for me? Before I had a chance to process or answer my butler, John strode into the dining room.

"Who leaves without so much as a word?" he said angrily, frowning.

Parsons turned to me and muttered, "I'll see myself out, sir." I nodded, stunned. The butler backed out of the room as John continued.

"Why did you go? And why did I have to find out with a note?"

I stood from my chair. "I apologize. Frankly, I was already reconsidering my decision. I was about to pack my bags and return."

John softened his frown. "After the hunting party, you must've realized we were worried." I noted the 'we'— wondering if that meant Rose and himself or Austin as well.

"You didn't have to travel all this way," I said.

"Well, what did you expect me to do?" He shrugged. "Besides, I was the one who said we should wait a day. Austin wanted to leave as soon as I read the note you left out loud."

"He did?"

"Yes, you fool. Everyone was worried. You didn't seem the most stable. I thought you promised you would talk to me?"

"I should've, I...I just thought leaving was for the best."

"It wasn't. And now we're all here." John gripped the back of a chair.

Wondering if I heard that right, I said, "We?"

"Yes, we. Beth wouldn't miss the chance to go to London."

"Of course," I laughed.

"And Austin wanted to come, and Rose did as well."

Heat flushed my cheeks. "I can't believe you all traveled here for me. Where are they?"

"Rose wisely suggested I head in first. I was a bit angry that you left. She figured you'd appreciate a bit of a notice." John's gaze was direct. "Will you return with us?"

I bristled a bit. I knew I should have spoken to him, but he was my peer. He couldn't order me what to do. "I am my own man, if you didn't know."

John sighed. "Will, I didn't mean it that way. I just hope you'd return with us and stay a while longer. But you can do as you wish and return whenever."

I shook my head. "No, I'm sorry. Yesterday... I." I sank back down on my chair and pointed at the seat John was gripping. He sat as well. "I had a bit of a night."

"What happened?"

"I needed some diversion, so I visited The Waddling Duck." Understanding flashed in John's eyes. "But the place got raided."

His eyes trained on me. "Will," he said.

"I know. It was stupid. I could've gotten caught. But I didn't."

"I'm glad you are fine."

"Yes, well." I glanced to the side. "We should probably give the others the good news that I am returning with them. Though, since you traveled all this way, I'll have Parsons ready the guest rooms." I flashed John a grin. "We owe it to Beth to visit Bond Street and perhaps we can take a detour and stop by the British Museum."

* * *

Beth was ecstatic to learn we'd be going shopping. The five of us ambled along the cobble-stoned streets peeking in and out of different store fronts.

"I'll be only a moment," Beth said, as she darted into a haberdashery shop.

"More like an hour," John muttered. He shook his head and laughed. "I don't know where she gets her love of fashion from."

"Your mother was quite fashionable," I pointed out. "But I have an idea. How about, while we wait for Beth, we try the cream puffs?"

Rose nodded eagerly. "Those were delicious the last time I had them. You do have to watch out for the powdered sugar."

"I'll get them while you wait here," I said.

Austin followed. "I'll come with." When we were a bit further away, he asked, "Was it something I did, or did you need space to recover?"

"I think I felt a bit overwhelmed," I told him. "But, as I

told John, I wanted to return almost as soon as I arrived in London."

"Okay. It's just... I don't know when I'll go back home and I wouldn't want to leave without saying goodbye."

I turned to Austin, a warm smile plastered on my face. "You won't need to. I'm returning to Hawthorne, and I promise that I'll stay this time.

Austin let out a breath. "Okay. Well, then. Let's get those puffs."

We returned to Rose and John with a bag of treats. We ate the cream puffs, careful to keep the powdered sugar off our coats.

"These are delicious," Austin told Rose.

"Yeah," she said, wiping her face with the back of her hand. "They are very good. I remember Beth and I were covered in the sugar last time." She shot me a pointed stare. "And John and Will were making fun of us.

Beth returned from the haberdashery, holding a new reticule. Her eyes flew to the cream puff I was finishing off. "Ooh, did you save one for me?"

"Of course. We would never forget you." I handed her the bag with the last treat.

She moaned as she bit into the fluffy exterior. "We ought to visit London more often."

"You'll be staying for a long time, come Spring." I grinned.

"Yes, I can't wait." John rolled his eyes behind her.

"Come on, let's find a driver and visit the British Museum. I've been wanting to see the Parthenon marbles. They are part of an exhibit."

"That name sounds familiar," Austin said. "I don't know why." He smiled. "But yes, I'd like to see more of London."

We strolled down the rest of Bond Street, browsing other stores. I ordered a few Christmas gifts for Austin at a menswear shop. One would get delivered later. The other, I sneaked into my pocket.

John hailed a carriage at the end of the street which took us past Kensington gardens and dropped us off in front of The British Museum.

Beth raced past the tall, wrought iron gates, excited to enter. John and Rose ambled behind me, arm in arm. We walked across the gravel driveway, flanked by decorative trees and the occasional Roman statue.

Once we reached the top of the steps, a porter ushered our party in through the large doors.

"Where would you like to go first?" I asked Beth. Her eyes spied the sign near the entrance detailing the different exhibits.

"Can we go to the upper floor first?" We followed her up the wide staircase until we reached the next floor. Beth inspected the various shells and fossils displayed in the first room with a sense of awe. Other rooms held stuffed birds and preserved lizards in jars.

I turned to Austin. "Would you like to skip ahead and explore the gallery?"

He smiled. "Yeah, we can go."

"John," I said, before he could turn into another corridor. "Austin and I are going to the Greek exhibit. We can meet up later, near the entrance?"

"Go ahead. We'll most likely be there soon."

Austin and I trailed down the staircase and wound our way through Montagu house until we reached the gallery. I'd been interested in seeing the Parthenon marbles since I read about them in the paper.

Part of a Greek frieze was displayed against a long wall; other worn but impressive statues stood throughout the space.

"To think that Elgin shipped all these from Greece," I muttered.

Austin let out a laugh. "I imagined something completely different when you mentioned marbles."

"What did you imagine?" I asked.

"Those little balls kids used to play with."

"Oh, yes. I can understand the confusion." I grinned. "No, I was interested in seeing these. There's been a bit of a fuss about them."

"About what?" Austin examined one of the statues.

"Mostly the legality of them being here. Lord Elgin, who sold the marbles to the British Museum, took them from The Parthenon in Greece. Not everyone agrees on whether that was allowed. Many people spoke out against it; Lord Byron wrote verses about the plundering."

Austin nodded. "That's why the name was familiar. The same questions are still being asked in my time. Greece wants the artwork returned to them."

"It is a shame," I said. "Imagine how magnificent this must have been intact." Austin agreed.

We took our time taking in the different pieces. I pondered Austin's words. To think, over two hundred years from now, there will still be people arguing about the marbles. Austin's own time was too far in the future to even comprehend.

"Did you enjoy London?" I asked Austin when we returned to the entrance.

"I had fun," he said. "It's interesting to see what the city looks like in this time period. I just know it from TV. The moving pictures," he corrected himself. "London is very different in my time. I mean, some buildings are the same. But others, not so much."

John, Rose, and Beth were waiting for us by the porter. We returned to my apartments, where Parsons had prepared the guest rooms. In the morning, we'd return to Hawthorne.

15

A Military Man

I'd settled back into life at Hawthorne after my flight to London. I was enjoying a cup of tea and reading the paper in an uncharacteristically quiet manner. John had taken Beth, Rose, and Austin out for a morning walk, while I opted to stay back. They'd be back soon, and Hawthorne would once again be filled with chatter. This past week had left my nerves a bit frayed and now that I was alone, I needed time to think.

"Sir, there's someone here to see you," Hugh said upon entering the drawing room.

I closed the paper and uncrossed my legs. "You sure they are here to see me? Did they say who they were?" I asked Hugh.

"No, sir. It is a military man, sir."

My mind immediately conjured up Captain Tremblay, though I wouldn't know why he'd come here after our brief conversation at Filton Grove. "Can you show him to the drawing room?"

Hugh nodded and shuffled away. My instincts were right. Moments later, Hugh returned with Captain Tremblay in tow.

I stood as a sign of respect.

"No need to stand," Captain Tremblay said. "By the looks of it, you are feeling better?"

"I am," I acknowledged, sitting back down. "Please, have a seat, Captain Tremblay. I'm afraid that John—Mr. Easton— is out for the moment. He'll be back soon, though."

"Please, call me Tom," Captain Tremblay said. "And I don't mind. In fact, I'm here to speak with you."

I glanced at Hugh, still waiting near the doorway. "Hugh, could you warn Mrs. Avery that we have a guest and get her to bring some refreshments?"

"Right away, sir," Hugh bobbed.

I turned my attentions back to Captain Tremblay—Tom. "What is this about?"

"After you left in such a hurry during the hunting party, I wanted to make sure you were alright."

"Well, I am."

Captain Tremblay continued, undisturbed. "We military men need to stick together, after all."

I stayed silent, waiting for him to make his point.

"I've got the assurances of all the men who were present at Filton Grove that they will keep what happened to themselves. We don't need word to come out about your little outburst." My mouth flopped open. I didn't know what to say. Captain Tremblay fiddled with the ring on his left hand before continuing. "I believe they mean to honor their promises."

"I'm not sure what to say."

"A thank you might be in order," Captain Tremblay suggested, his voice still as cocky as it was when he ordered me to return to England.

"Thank you. But, why?"

"Why what?"

"Why help me?"

Captain Tremblay shrugged. "You aren't the only soldier who has returned with certain afflictions." He glanced at the jagged scar marring my cheek and let go of his ring. "Not physical scars and wounds but afflictions of the nervous kind." Weirdly enough, the idea that others were having similar issues felt comforting in a way, just not the way he said it. "Our military is the corner stone of our kingdom. The last thing we need is for civilians to detect weakness in our officers."

For a moment there, I thought he was being kind, but I knew better. Captain Tremblay didn't do a single thing if it didn't further his own career. Weakness indeed. His comment left a bad taste in my mouth.

Clara ambled into the room carrying a platter with a pot of tea and cups, and some of Mrs. Avery's apple tarts. John's cook must have had some leftover from the night before. She slid it on a stand and curtsied. She giggled as she handed Captain Tremblay a steaming cup of Darjeeling. The captain didn't seem to mind the maid's girlish attentions, though, some tea sloshed over the porcelain and landed on his jacket.

"Sorry, sir," Clara said, her cheeks flushing. She pulled a

kitchen towel out of her apron and started patting the wet fabric.

Flustered with the girl's attentions, Captain Tremblay snatched the towel from her hands and began dabbing his jacket dry himself.

"I'll be fine," he said, handing the towel back. "And, it's Captain. Captain Tremblay."

Clara bobbed. "Captain Tremblay," she said, pronouncing his last name slowly, savoring the syllables. She stepped back and poured my tea. I caught her shooting repeated glances at the captain. Once she was done pouring the tea, she spoke again, her words directed at Tremblay. "If you need anything at all, I'm down in the kitchen."

"That will be all, Clara." I shot out, making her pout. She hurried back to the kitchen, leaving the tray behind.

"I apologize," I told Captain Tremblay. "The girl is new at Hawthorne. I'm not sure if she's the right fit to be a maid, but she's the niece of Mr. Easton's cook."

Captain Tremblay took a sip of tea. "It's kind of Mr. Easton to take in one of the more unfortunate."

"I wouldn't necessarily put it that way. Only that Clara still has some ways to go to learn her duties."

Captain Tremblay nodded. "Now, there was one more matter I'd like to discuss; since you've been staying in the countryside, you probably haven't heard that I've been forming a militia group of my own. The justice of the peace appointed me to oversee local militia and keep the peace on our home ground."

"You are right. I haven't received any word on that." I scratched the back of my neck, wondering where Captain

Tremblay was going with this. I did remember a comment about a local militia from Mr. Brocklehurst.

He stirred his tea lazily. "Since I heard the news that you'd rented apartments in London, I've been meaning to come call on you."

"What for?"

"I'd like you to consider returning to service and joining my militia. After your display a few days ago, I am certain it would be for your best. Structure and easy to follow commands will be what you need to—"

"Now, wait a minute." My voice raised as I shot up out of my chair. "I am no longer in military service. You don't outrank me here, Captain Tremblay. And I don't appreciate being spoke to in this manner in my friend's home."

Anger flared in Captain Tremblay's eyes; however, he managed to keep a lid on his emotions.

"You may think what you will," he said, biting his tongue. "I'd still like you to reconsider."

"I doubt I will," I said plainly.

"Then you won't," he shrugged. "Either way. I'll have offered."

I huffed and returned to my chair. Now, I just had to get through his visit. I wasn't sure if I truly disliked him or if it was because he reminded me of some of the worst days of my life. I decided to remain friendly and distant. "Try one of the tarts. Mrs. Avery is one of the best cooks in Westbridge."

Captain Tremblay grabbed one from the tray and bit into the golden pastry with gusto. After he wiped crumbs off his face he said, "You didn't oversell your cook. That was delicious. I might have to steal her from Mr. Easton."

From the doorway John's voice said, "I'm glad you like my cook's food, but I'm afraid I won't let her go, and I doubt that she'd want to go."

Captain Tremblay turned his head and stood. "Mr. Easton, how wonderful to meet you."

John extended his hand. "The pleasure is all mine. Hugh, our valet, told me you were here to visit William?" Captain Tremblay shook John's hand.

"I am. Though I should probably leave now. I'm heading back to London tomorrow."

"Where are you staying?"

"At an inn called The Black Stallion."

John nodded. "The inn is a popular place, but," he continued, quickly glancing at me, "surely we can't let a friend of William's stay at an inn when there is plenty of room at Hawthorne."

"I wouldn't want to impose."

"Not at all. I'm sure my wife and my sister would like the diversion."

Captain Tremblay paused, thinking. "Fine, you've twisted my arm," he smirked. "We can't disappoint the ladies. I'll accept your hospitality."

"That's settled then. How about we move this to the dining room and introduce you to them. We just returned from a long walk, so we were going to sit down for a bite to eat."

John motioned for Captain Tremblay to walk ahead of him.

"I wish you hadn't done that," I whispered in John's ear as I passed him by. My friend just shot me a puzzled look.

"Why?" he mouthed.

I shook my head. "Later."

Beth had her mouth stuffed with bread when we entered the dining room. She chewed and swallowed as fast as she could before smiling at Captain Tremblay. "How nice to meet one of Mr. Chambers' friends," she said, her face red from the cold and her hair wind-beaten. Beth remembered the state of her hair and quickly smoothed her hands across her scalp to tame the wild blonde snarls. Since Rose had the foresight to tightly braid her curly hair, she looked the most presentable, though she sported equally red cheeks.

"It is my honor to meet you both," Captain Tremblay said.

John pointed at Beth. "This is my sister, Ms. Easton. And across from her sits my lovely wife, Mrs. Easton."

"Welcome to our home," Rose said, as if she'd been doing it all her life. I was proud of how my friend had adapted to life at Hawthorne.

"And you've met our other guest, Mr. Miller."

"I have indeed," Captain Tremblay said, nodding his head at Austin. "Good to see you again."

"Likewise," Austin added.

"Please, have a seat," John told Captain Tremblay. "I'll just ring for Clara." He pulled a cord in the corner of the room. I sat down next to Austin, while Captain Tremblay joined Beth on the other side of the table. John took the head of the table, wedging himself between his wife and his sister. Clara bounded into the room, straightening as her eyes skimmed the room and settled on Captain Tremblay.

"Clara, Captain Tremblay is staying the night. Could you ready one of the guest rooms and inform Mrs. Avery that she'll have one more mouth to feed for dinner?"

"Yes, sir. I'm sure that'll be fine, sir," the maid said, bobbing her head. "She's making a big pot of soup already."

"Thank you. That will be all, Clara. Once you are finished preparing the room, you can return to the kitchen and help your aunt."

I caught the maid sneaking another peak at Captain Tremblay before she left. It was the military jacket, I was sure. For some reason, women enjoyed seeing a man in uniform. Perhaps it was the promise of adventure or even danger that lay beneath the bright red fabric, something most highborn ladies knew little of. I begrudged them their innocence sometimes.

Aware of Captain Tremblay, Beth now took small dainty bites, followed by even smaller sips of tea. The sight made me grin when she usually had the appetite of a bear.

"So, Captain Tremblay, what did you need William for?" Rose asked.

He hesitated. "I'm afraid that is a private matter. I couldn't speak of it until William gives me an answer."

"Oh, but William, we'd love to know," Beth said.

"Captain Tremblay offered me a position in his new militia."

"How exciting," Beth gushed.

Right when I added, "which I declined."

"Oh," Beth uttered.

"I've given Mr. Chambers time to change his mind," Captain Tremblay added magnanimously.

John grabbed an apple from a bowl. "I'm sure Will knows what he wants."

I smiled at John for backing me up.

From the stiffening of his limbs, I could tell that Captain Tremblay was offended. "It is a great opportunity," he boasted. "Anyone would be proud to be a part of a militia that has been appointed by the justice of the peace."

"I won't reconsider."

Austin's fingers trailed up my leg and gave my knee a little squeeze. I dropped my arm under the table and gripped his hand. It felt good to know that Austin and John were here supporting my decisions. Especially, the warmth of Austin's hand in mine, showing his support. I'd only known him for such a short period. But now, I couldn't imagine not meeting him.

16

A Midnight Snack

My dreams were plaguing me. It was another restless night tossing and turning, getting tangled up in my own sheets, seeing the faces of the men who died at the battlefield whenever I closed my eyes. I'd be glad when Captain Tremblay left in the morning. He could proposition me again, but I would never accept his offer; I was finished with wearing a uniform.

His personality had been grating on me all day. Flirting with Beth, regaling everyone with heroic war stories which weren't remotely true, pretending we were friends. I was grinding my teeth through dinner when he started talking about my stay at the field hospital.

"Captain Tremblay," I said as a warning.

He opened his arms and in a smarmy tone, announced, "We are amongst friends here."

John tried to cut in. "Perhaps we should talk about something else. Will, doesn't—"

"Nonsense." Captain Tremblay waved his hand to show how ridiculous he found John's comment. "I'm sure Mr. Chambers has told you all about Ligny and the nurses at the field hospital who took such good care of him." I clenched my jaw when he pointed at me. "Look how well his cheek healed. I dare say, it is a talking point for the ladies now." He shot me an exaggerated wink. "You'll have to join me at an outing in London." He lifted a glass of wine to his lips.

Austin tried to change the subject, directing his attention to Beth, in hopes that her bubbly and talkative nature would take over the room. "Have you decided what you and Ms. Blakeley will go as for Mrs. Ashbrook's masquerade?"

"Well, Anne and I have been discussing it," Beth said. "But we haven't decided. I would like to keep it a surprise." She turned to Captain Tremblay. "Do you like masquerades?"

He gazed at Beth in a way I didn't like. "Yes, masquerades are quite fun. You never know who lurks where," he said, lowering his voice for dramatic effect. Beth gave her best efforts, but eventually, Captain Tremblay managed to turn the conversation back to me.

"Is that why you don't want to take my offer?" he said to me.

"Why?" John asked him nonplussed by the vague question.

Captain Tremblay turned his face into a charade of pity. "Because Mr. Chambers was in quite a state when I found him at the field hospital, calling out, crying and begging to be relieved from life itself."

Rose jumped up. "I've heard enough. We've offered you our hospitality since you appeared to be a friend of William. Now

I know that isn't true. Who would dare speak about his friend like this?" Rose said angrily. "Calling you an acquaintance would be too good."

Captain Tremblay grabbed a napkin and patted his lips. Then, lowering it slowly, he said," I can tell when I am not wanted. It is too late to leave, so I shall retire to my room."

"I think that is for the best," John said. Captain Tremblay stood with great airs and huffed as he walked away.

"Screw him," Austin told me.

I caught Austin's meaning. "He sure is a bounder," I agreed.

"Bounder?" Austin giggled. "I'm sorry. I can't help it. Almost everything sounds so different in your British accent, but I can't make head nor tails of that one."

I flashed a smile. "Your speech is incomprehensible sometimes as well. Half the time, I have to piece it together by context."

"I didn't realize."

"It's fine. I like hearing you speak," I said. "And, if you must know, a bounder is someone with no regard for anyone but themselves."

"That sounds about right," Austin said.

After that, I'd left my friends behind. The whole dinner with Captain Tremblay had worn me down, not to mention that I was still exhausted from the day before.

Now, it was in the middle of the night. Or no... I peered at the dark sky paling by the minute. It was already close to dawn, judging by the light. Feeling restless, I untangled myself from the sheets. Mrs. Avery would be getting up soon to start baking, but she wouldn't mind if I went to the kitchen and prepared myself something to drink. I remembered the last time I went to the kitchens in the middle of the night. Then, Rose had been with me, keeping me company.

I wouldn't stay away long, so I didn't bother changing out of my nightshirt. However, I did grab a robe from the door hook and swung it around me. The stone floors of Hawthorne got cold in the winter.

Soft footed, I walked across the hallway and down the stairs. John's home was so quiet at nighttime, it felt peaceful to be surrounded by nothing but the gentle settling of the walls—a soft creak here and low groan there as the old house breathed in and out. I navigated my way to the kitchen using only the scraps of light the moon provided through the windows. I hadn't brought a lantern.

Tying the robe a little tighter around me, I hoped the thick material would warm me a bit more before I could get some tea in me. The kitchen had a fire burning day and night. I used some of it to light the stove, so I could heat the kettle.

There was only a short wait until the kettle whistled, signaling the water had boiled. I gathered a cup, strainer, and some loose-leaf tea. Then I picked up the kettle, pouring the hot water over the leaves. Tea at last. I sat down at the kitchen block, holding the cup in the palm of my hands.

I blew across the surface and took a sip. Light slowly filtered through the windows, turning the dark shadows into a lighter gray. Putting down the cup, I turned my ear towards the kitchen entrance. Footsteps thumped down the hall, much too heavy to be Mrs. Avery. Perhaps Hugh had awoken. I didn't want to be a nuisance once the staff arrived.

Depositing the teacup by the washing tin, I turned to

leave the kitchen. That's when I spotted his foppish hair and the red coat slung across his arm. Captain Tremblay, busy straightening his shirt from whatever he had been doing.

I stopped. "What are you doing here?"

Captain Tremblay glanced up, a cocky smirk appearing on his face once he saw it was me. "William. I could ask the same of you. Didn't think I'd find you in the servant quarters. No.....Not with the servants." I caught a glimpse of his teeth.

"You should return to your room." I brushed past him to leave. But behind me, Captain Tremblay continued.

"Does your friend understand *who* you cried for? Would he still defend you, if he knew?"

I turned on my heel, surprising him with my speed. "You have no idea what you are talking about," I spat.

"Don't I?" he said, taking a step back. "Come now, William. We don't need to tell lies." He paused a moment, staring me down. His mouth formed the words "James", exaggerating it. Mocking it.

I gritted my teeth. "You. Will. Leave." Anger seethed beneath my skin. I could feel my hands tremble.

Captain Tremblay strutted around, trailing his finger along a decorative vase. "I don't think so," he declared, smirking at me. "I still need you to join my militia."

My mouth practically fell open. "Why would I ever do that? What in the world would make you think I'd join after your display if hostility?"

"I quite disagree." He picked up the vase, judging its weight. "I've thought it through, you see. You'll join, then, with the help of your name...and fortune, might I add, I'll be able to align myself with the upper echelons."

"This is about my money?" I glared at him, his hands still twirling the porcelain. "Put that damned thing down," I snapped.

"Fine," he said placing the vase back on its stand. "It's about your money and your name."

"You're a captain. What do you need me for."

"I'm not highborn, which some people won't let me forget, despite my military accolades."

"And how is this my fault?"

"How is it that you. You! Knowing full well what you are. How can you return to society and be treated like a hero, when I'm only being invited places because of the justice of the peace? No mother wants me to marry their daughter while they throw themselves at you, and you don't even want them."

"Perhaps it's not me you should worry about, Captain Tremblay. We've all heard whispers about your trips to the Birds of Paradise. You must need me because you've all but gambled, drank, and fucked your life earnings away." Captain Tremblay's face turned an ugly purple, which only spurred me on. "I suppose the money lenders are after you now? Settled on a spot at a debtor's prison yet? I heard the Marshalsea is nice this time of year. At least the stench from the Thames isn't as strong during winter."

"Say all you want about me," Captain Tremblay snarled. He poked his fat finger at my chest. "But what will everyone say when I tell them about you. Will Mr. Easton keep you as his guest, hmmm? I can report you to the authorities, have you tried in court. Society won't want you then."

I glared at the horrid man. "You've got no proof." No one

had ever seen me in a compromising position. It would just be his word against mine, and I'd win that battle.

"No?" Captain Tremblay glanced behind him, down the hall that led to the servants' sleeping quarters. "I had a lovely evening with your new maid." He smiled lewdly, brushing his hand along his shirt. "And she told me the most remarkable story about you and the other guest, Mr. Miller, I believe? She said that the two of you were awfully close to each other. Too close, in fact. She told me in confidence that she'd seen the both of you leave your bedroom together. And that Mr. Miller had been there all day."

My face blanched.

"You can imagine my surprise to hear such a damning story. Now, if I get what I need, then that's what it will be. A story. However, if you don't comply, I can report you and I doubt the judge will dismiss *two* witnesses."

My hands clenched. I wasn't about to let this spineless ingrate tell me what to do.

Captain Tremblay tapped his foot. "I don't have all day. Or... should I speak with Mr. Easton now. Surely, he has a right to be informed about the person staying under his roof." He laughed. "James, don't leave me....," he mocked. "What a display. All of us made fun about you, even the nurses."

He'd hit a nerve. I pulled my arm back and hit him square in the face. The cartilage crackled beneath my knuckles. "You bastard," I said as he doubled forward and clutched his nose. His eyes welled up and blood spurted from between his fingers.

"You broke my nose," he exclaimed in shock, his words muffled by his swelling sniffer. "I will tell everyone."

"Go ahead," I shouted. "See what I care." I threw a napkin at him which he snatched and pressed against his nostrils. He bounded towards the foyer. His struts fast and angry, I followed him as he climbed the stairs and headed straight towards the main bedroom. He rapped twice, loudly, and entered the room without waiting for a response.

"What is the meaning of this?" John bellowed. Rose shot up and clutched the blanket to her chest.

"William?" she questioned me. She frowned at the sight of Captain Tremblay clutching his bleeding nose.

"He," Captain Tremblay said, stumbling further into John's room. "Assaulted me."

John leaped up from the bed. "Good."

"What..."

Rose asked again. "William, what is going on here?"

Captain Tremblay got over his moment of stunned silence. "I'm here to tell you about William." His speech was slurred from the swelling.

I stood silently in the doorway. Austin sneaked up behind me. "I heard the commotion. What's going on?"

Captain Tremblay shouted for all to hear. "You need to turn him out. That. That. Molly."

John's eyes darkened. "You are to leave my house at once and will never speak of this again. If you breathe even a word of this, I will make certain the law hears about your slander, with a full account of your despicable nature. Jealousy of a fellow brother in arms is such a damning quality, is it not?"

"You know what he is, and you don't mind?" Captain Tremblay gasped.

"You heard my husband. Get out!" Rose said firmly from the bed.

"If I were you, I'd listen to my wife." John stepped towards Captain Tremblay who, now that the tides were turning, backed away from the room. He pushed past me and Austin.

John looked at me. "Don't worry. That sorry excuse for a man doesn't have a leg to stand on."

I nodded. "We should speak to Clara though. She's been telling him stories."

John thought for a moment. "I'll consult Mrs. Avery on what to do with the girl."

"Should someone check if he's actually leaving?" Rose said. "I'd like to be sure he's gone and not lurking in a cupboard somewhere. I was having such a good dream before he burst in."

John turned towards her. "About me, I hope?"

Rose quirked her brow. "You wish." I shook my head. John and Rose always managed to flirt, no matter the situation.

"I'll go," Austin offered. He turned and left the room.

"Wait. I'll come with." I followed Austin down the stairs.

In the hallway, Captain Tremblay was barking orders at Hugh, who had sleepily emerged from the servants' quarters. "Fetch me my horse, immediately." Tremblay's voice was still thick, but his nose had stopped bleeding. Rust-colored stains marred his shirt. "I won't stay here a moment longer."

Hugh looked up at me, his face questioning. "Go ahead, Hugh. See that Captain Tremblay leaves," I said.

"Sir," he said with a nod.

Captain Tremblay's eyes narrowed. "This won't be the last

you hear of me. I promise," he said, pointing his finger at me, as if he was scolding a child.

"I think it is," I said. "Good day."

"Don't let the door hit you on the way out," Austin added. I snorted. Captain Tremblay looked entirely disillusioned as Hugh practically herded him out the front door. I turned to Austin, laughing. When I did, my smile turned into a frown. I caught a glimpse of Clara; she had sneaked up to the foyer and watched the exchange from behind a door post. Her eyes grew wide when she saw me stare. She quickly turned on her heel.

"Wait," I commanded. The girl froze and glanced back, her light brown hair messy and loose around her face. She bit her lip. "Clara. We know that you spoke with Captain Tremblay." Her face paled.

"I," she started, her mouth opening and closing like a bullfrog. "I didn't..."

"Never mind that. If I were you, I'd return to your room. Mr. Easton is going to have a talk with your aunt. I'd wager you'll be wanted for an explanation soon."

"Sir. Please don't tell my aunt—"

"That Captain Tremblay visited you this evening?" I finished her sentence. Clara nodded.

I paused. The girl looked worried. "I'll discuss it with John, but I don't think it'll be necessary."

Her eyes shot to Austin. He nodded as well. Relief washed across Clara's face. "Thank you," she said.

"I'd return to your room now," I told her. She hurried off to the back of the house.

17

A Road Trip

"What did Mrs. Avery say?" I asked John, while he strutted around his office.

"She wasn't pleased to hear that Clara had been telling tales to Captain Tremblay."

"You didn't..."

"No, I did as you asked. Though I don't know why you are being so kind to the girl. She hardly deserves it."

I shrugged. "It's not all her fault; Captain Tremblay can be very persuasive. I'm sure he helped her think the worst of me."

John frowned. "That's no excuse."

"No, it isn't. But she is young, and I hope with time, she'll learn to do better. Besides, she's Mrs. Avery's niece."

John sighed and walked to his desk. He decanted a bottle of whiskey and poured himself a glass. He held up another empty glass.

"A bit early, no?"

"Not after the morning we've had. I think it is all we deserve."

"A little then."

John poured the whiskey and handed me a glass. "I told Mrs. Avery that Captain Tremblay had persuaded her to tell secrets when she was serving us at dinner. She wasn't pleased to hear that Clara would run her mouth about our household." John scoffed. "I practically had to beg Mrs. Avery to keep Clara on."

I shook my head. "That sounds like her."

"Yes. She was particularly outspoken on the subject. I think her niece is going to get an earful." John threw back his whiskey and set down the glass. "William, are you sure about this?"

"I am."

"Well. I've told Mrs. Avery that Clara might need some more supervision. Rose came up with it by the way," he added. His face lit up with pride. "Clara will take lessons with Rose to learn how to read and write and perhaps if she does well with the other classes, she'll be able to help with the school."

"That sounds like an interesting plan."

"Only something Rose would come up with," John said fondly. "Speaking of my wife," he said, changing the subject. "Rose is still upstairs; I think I shall surprise her with breakfast in bed."

"Have fun," I said, patting John on the shoulder.

As John left the study, I drained the glass of whiskey I'd been nursing. It was still early and despite my interrupted night, a kind of restless energy buzzed through my body. I decided that I'd make good on my promise to John and check on the building site. It would be interesting to see how far the men had gotten.

* * *

Austin joined me at the building site. The men McCreary hired from town were making swift progress. Last time we were here, we'd dug up the topsoil with McCreary and Bledsoe. Now, instead of a bunch of turned up dirt, there stood the beginnings of a house. Four walls, an opening for the door, and holes for the windows.

"Rose will be happy to see the progress," Austin said. "It looks like I need to hurry up with my drawing."

"How is that coming along?"

"What can I say," he shrugged. "An artist is his own worst critic."

"Which means it's probably perfect already." I watched as the men were preparing the top beams for the slate roof that would top the building.

Austin pondered. "The drawing is almost finished; I just need to add the final touches. I think we should find a frame for it."

"If you know the measurements, we can have one made in town."

Austin tapped his right pointer finger against his lips, his mind clearly occupied. I wondered what he was thinking. "You can take the measurements whenever you like. Then, sometime this week, we can venture into town. Besides, we have more errands to run. I doubt you've ordered your mask for Mrs. Avery's party yet. Christmas and New Year's Eve are getting nearer, and we don't want to wait too long."

"True," Austin said, dropping his hand. "But I have a proposition."

I opened my mouth to ask what kind of proposition he was thinking of, but Austin rapidly continued. "Hear me out first. I don't need an answer right away. I'd like you to think about it." He paused for my confirmation.

"I'll agree to hearing you out, but I must confess that your seriousness is making me nervous."

Austin's lips twitched, showcasing his dimples. "I promise it's nothing to be nervous about," he said, his palms out towards me. He glanced at the men hard at work on the school building. McCreary stood near the entrance, minding the building plans, occasionally shouting orders. None of the men, including McCreary, were paying us any mind. "You know what. How about we go somewhere else to talk? Somewhere we can sit down?"

I smiled kindly. Austin beamed back at me in return. "Yes. We can. If you'd like it to be somewhere private, we can talk in John's hot house? I just have to speak to McCreary before we leave."

"Sounds good to me." Austin pressed his hands into his pockets and stayed put while I walked over to McCreary.

"What'll ye say about that," the Scot said when I stopped by his makeshift desk. He'd rolled the building plans out and secured the edges of the paper with some random rocks.

"I'd say it's progressing nicely."

He clapped his meaty hand on my shoulder. "Aye, sir. I reckon the building'll stand before Christmas."

"Impressive," I stated.

The man's chin was turned skyward, pride beaming on his face. "Aye, the lads from town have worked verra hard."

"You yourself have as well, I reckon."

"Might have," McCreary agreed.

"I'm sure Mrs. Easton will be delighted to hear how the building is going."

"Gi' her my best when ye leave, sir."

"I shall return to the house shortly, though Mrs. Easton has bid me to tell you that there's a basket of scones and other pastries waiting for you and your family up at the kitchens, should you like it."

"My wife would like it verra much." McCreary's eyes twinkled. "My wee ones too."

I said goodbye to the friendly Scot and joined Austin. We walked the path leading back to the main house. Ducks quacked and spluttered as they swam their rounds, disturbing the smooth surface of the pond. Austin tucked his chin into the thick scarf wound around his neck, his hands still planted in his pockets.

"Whatever you wanted to tell me..." I trailed, watching him. "You could say it while we're walking. There isn't anyone around."

"Maybe you're right." Austin breathed and slowed his pace. "I was just thinking—you know, about Captain Tremblay— and everything else you've told me."

"What about Captain Tremblay?" Worry squeezed my heart, making it hard to think over my labored heartbeat. Austin had been present when Captain Tremblay was making his accusations in front of John. John knew and supported who I was, however, not everyone was like him. I'd already shared a lot with Austin, but I didn't want him to reconsider his friendship.

"It made me think about your James. I think you've never had a chance to properly grieve him."

"I-I don't know."

"Was there a funeral? Some place to say your goodbyes?" Austin caught my gaze, his eyes bright in the morning light.

I shook my head. "No, I went from the battlefield, to the field hospital, then straight to London. The war with France had ended, and I was expected to be grateful and joyous for the outcome. The fallen soldiers who died on foreign soil and us, the ones returning home a bit worse for wear but alive, being lauded as heroes."

"I know it isn't the same," Austin said. We slowly headed towards the hothouse, an impressive structure of glass and welded iron protruding against the back of Hawthorne. "My parents died when I was young, too young to understand what the loss meant or know how to grieve the absence of them. Then, growing up, moving from foster family to foster family, I really started to feel the absence of my own parents. The sadness and sense of loss, my wishes and what-ifs about what could have been, grew and grew, until it felt all encompassing. It drained me and clouded every happy moment I had. Finally, my foster sister snapped me out of it." Austin smiled wistfully. "I think you'd like her. She's fierce and outspoken, funny and smart. She's my best friend."

"How did she help you through your grief?" I glanced up, curious for his answer. Austin tilted his head to the sky.

"She said we were going on a road trip and wouldn't take no for an answer."

"And a road trip is your plan for me?"

A laugh bubbled up from Austin. "Not exactly. The road trip wasn't the point. No, Alyssa ordered me to put on clean clothes and dragged me out of my room. Then she drove without telling me where she was going. I didn't know what her goal was until we arrived at a place I recognized. I'd looked it up all the time. She parked in front of a small house, one of many Victorian homes on a long street. Blue paint peeling off the porch. A different family lived there then. I could see an abandoned tricycle laying on its side in the middle of the lawn, and children's boots kicked off in front of the door. It felt strange seeing my childhood home lived in by other people, even if it had been a lifetime since I'd lived there. Heck, I hardly even remembered my life before the accident. But Alyssa took me there for a reason. She brought flowers, a cheap gas station bouquet." Austin paused. I opened the door to the hot house.

"Did it help?" I asked as I followed Austin to a bench.

"Yeah. Alyssa has decent ideas sometimes," Austin snorted. "It gave my feelings a place to put them. I never had a chance to let out what I was thinking and feeling. I never got to say goodbye. Our little memorial helped me do that. It must have been weird for anyone walking by to see two teens kneeling on the sidewalk, but it helped me. We left the flowers."

"It was very thoughtful of your sister to do that for you."

Austin nodded. "I got lucky with her." He leaned into the corner of the bench and pulled off his scarf. "But, to get to the point I was making. We could do something like that for you. What do you think?"

"I'm not sure," I stammered. "It's not like I can return to Ligny." I thought back to the green valley overlooked by a picturesque windmill. At least, that was what it looked like before the attack. After the gun smoke cleared, there was hardly any green left; fires had swept away any living thing, until the soil was barren."

"Have you been to James' home?"

"Never."

"Did he mention where he was from?"

James mentioned his home all the time. I couldn't help but smile. "His father lives near Blackpool."

"You don't have to, but I would like you to consider going there. I could come with, or you could go by yourself, if you'd like that better. Regardless, I think it would do you good to see his home, maybe meet his dad. Say goodbye to him at a place you know he loves."

I sat in silence, mulling over Austin's words. He must've understood that I needed to think because he stayed next to me—quiet but constant. His presence, ever since I'd met him, seemed to comfort me. I turned towards him. He looked up, patiently waiting for whatever I decided to say.

"I think you are right, and I'd like you to join me. It would take us a couple of days to get to Blackpool. Perhaps a mid-week to get there and back when all is said and done."

Austin beamed at me. "That's fine."

"It is a long journey."

"I guess I'll get to see more of the country," he added

cheerfully. "You don't have to give me an out. This was my idea, so if you want me to come along, I will."

"Then it is settled." I quirked my lip.

"When do you want to leave?"

"The sooner, the better, I'd say. Though, we'll have to make a stop in town to get the masks for the masquerade designed, and I'd wager you'd like to place an order for a frame."

"Ah, yes. I hope we can get it before Christmas."

"How about we stop in town tomorrow to run our errands and take the coach from there?"

"I'll follow your lead. I have no idea how to travel in this time." Austin shrugged bashfully.

"I guess we'll have to pack." Despite the reason for going on the trip, the anticipation made me giddy. I'd never seen James' home. Now that I was going, the idea that I would stand where he grew up and see everything he used to talk about made me excited. It would be a glimpse into his life that I had never had before.

18

The Confectionery Shop

Hugh dropped us off at the main street. I noticed a sign tacked up in the window of the milliner as we strode along the boulevard. It advertised that during winter, they'd also design masks and other accessories needed for a ball.

A small bell tinkled as the door opened. Inside, displayed on stands, were rows upon rows of hats. Bonnets with long and fluffy feathers, bonnets with a colorful display of artificial flowers or fruits, top hats, caps made from lace or straw, and lots and lots of ribbons in all manner of sizes, shapes, and colors.

"Can I help you, sirs?" a man asked. He stepped out from behind the counter, greeting us both.

"We read your advertisement in the window—"

The milliner nodded gravely. "You must be here for Mrs. Ashbrook's masquerade. I've had quite a few orders already; in fact, I helped another gentleman just this morning." His eyes sized us up. "Do you have any particular designs in mind?"

Austin nudged me.

"What is it?" I asked.

"We should order separately. Keep our outfits a surprise from each other."

"That is a fine idea, sir," the milliner said to Austin. "I can help you first?"

Austin looked at me for confirmation. I nodded.

"Yes," he replied.

The Milliner turned and headed towards a back room. "Please, follow me, so we can discuss your order in private."

While Austin was ordering his mask, I decided to take a look at the hats. My eyes were drawn to one in particular— a luxurious stovepipe hat made from beaver wool. The black felt had such a beautiful sheen to it, I couldn't help but reach out. Its texture was smooth, almost silky, beneath my fingertips. The price tag was a bit more than I usually spent on a hat, but I envisioned myself wearing it around town. I would order a mask and I would also purchase the hat, then I could wear it on our trip to Lancashire.

I wondered what kind of mask Austin was ordering, though I doubted I'd have any difficulty recognizing him; I'd spot his eyes from miles away. Ordering didn't take them long. Soon, Austin returned, and the milliner waved me towards him.

"What are you looking for," the milliner asked. "Perhaps a jester's cap, or a spook?"

"Can you make a mask like a wolf?"

"Certainly," the hat maker said. "That won't be a problem. Will this all be charged to Mr. Easton at Hawthorne?"

"Yes," I nodded. "And I'd also like to add the black hat on the display rack."

"A fine choice, sir." The man bowed and followed me to the display, where he gently lifted the hat off the shelving. Would you like a box?"

"No need. I intend to wear it straight away."

"By all means," the man said, handing me the hat with a flourish. "Thank you for your business."

I found Austin leaning against the front of the building, our luggage resting by his feet.

He quirked his brow, a crooked smile playing on his lips. "You found a hat?" His eyes darted to the headwear I had tucked into the crook of my arm.

"I liked it." Then I passed him by. "Come," I ordered him. "We have a bit of time before the coach leaves. The stop is right up there." I pointed at a signpost near the modiste's shop. "Before we leave, we should get some treats from the confectionery." I lifted the hat and plopped it on my head.

"Dashing," Austin remarked, in an attempt to mimic my accent.

"Is that what you think I sound like?"

Austin acted affronted. "I thought it was a rather good impression."

Snorting, I told him, "It wouldn't have fooled anyone."

Austin lifted the bags and handed me my suitcase. Together, we walked down the street, passing by Norah's as we reached the confectionery shop. Another small bell tinkled when I opened the door; I let Austin enter first.

"Welcome," a woman said from behind the counter. We

were early, so she was still busy setting out the treats. "Please, have a seat. I'll be right with you. Would you like some tea?"

I checked the clock on the wall; we had plenty of time. I nodded.

Austin and I sat down at a small, white cloth-covered table. The woman brought at a steaming teapot and two cups. "Any treats?" she asked.

Austin glanced around the shop. "What's good around here?"

The woman looked surprised when Austin opened his mouth. "Oh my, you aren't from around here."

"No, I am visiting."

"Well, I shall bring out a selection then," she said, perking up. She poured the fragrant tea into our cups and headed back behind the counter. I saw her bending and picking an array of treats.

"This is too much," I said when she returned.

"Nonsense, whatever you don't eat, I can box up for you to take with you." She smiled wide and dropped the tray of treats on the table. "Enjoy."

Austin nibbled at a soft, mini, layered cake, while I dunked a sugar biscuit into my tea.

He closed his eyes and sighed. "This is delicious."

"Don't tell Beth we went here; she loves this place."

Austin bit into another treat. "I promise I'll keep it a secret."

The whole shop smelled like the inside of a pie— sugary, sweet and irresistible. I poured a splash of milk into my tea and stirred it with a spoon. Austin preferred his tea black.

The woman returned to our table. "And?" she asked Austin. "What do you think?"

"They're wonderful," he said, finishing the pastry he was holding. She beamed at him.

"We would like a box, though, since we have to catch the coach," I interjected.

"I'll be right back." She whirled away to return moments later with a small pastry box.

Once Austin and I finished our tea, we boxed up the left-over pastries and headed to the counter. I paid her for our food, and we went on our way.

A few people had gathered at the coach sign; an elderly woman with a young girl, and two men perhaps a decade older than Austin and me.

It was a tight fit when the coach arrived. I shared a bench with the two men while Austin sat beside the elderly woman and the child. The girl was eyeballing the box from the confectionery.

"Would you like some?" he asked her.

"Mary, what do you say?" the elderly woman said, her hair obscured by a lace head dress favored by the older generation. I assumed she was the girl's grandmother.

"Yes, please," the girl added in a slight lisp. Austin held out the box to her so she could choose which one she wanted.

"Would you all like one?" I asked the other passengers. We had plenty to go around. The two men and the little girl gladly accepted.

The little girl and her grandmother exited the next town over but the two men— bankers— stayed with us until Birmingham. They had been in Westbridge to oversee the funeral of a member of their bank and to make sure the will was enacted, the younger told us.

We waved them off when they got out at their stop. Then it was just the two of us; we could both stretch out on a bench. Blackpool was a long way. We'd have to make a stop and spend the night at an inn before journeying on to Lynton Hall. I was equal parts nervous and excited. I think Austin could sense my fidgeting.

"Try to relax," he told me.

"I'm not sure if I can."

"Either way, I'm here to help if you need it. And if at any time you decide you don't want to do this, we'll turn back. No questions asked."

"Promise?"

He smiled, resting his head against the window curtain. "I promise."

19

Lynton Hall

Now that we were here, I started to regret my decision to come. The coach dropped us off at the nearest stop on the main road, which meant Austin and I would still have to walk about two miles to get to Lynton Hall.

Lancashire was beautiful, all rolling hills and reflective lakes. Then there were the woods. Aspen and oak, poplar and sycamores, standing tall beneath the sun, waiting for spring to return. And everywhere, hedges of buck thorn, with their bright orange berries that remained even in winter. The landscape was resplendent enough that Wordsworth could compose a poem about it.

As we got closer to the stop, my stomach seemed to knot in on itself more and more, until I was certain it would never be able to untwist itself.

The driver left us at the sign post. Now all Austin and I had to do was follow down the road and turn right into the long driveway that would lead to the large house. I plopped my new hat back on my head and gripped my suitcase.

"Should I have sent a letter ahead of us?" I asked Austin. Uncertainty made me furrow my brow. He swung his satchel across his shoulder.

"We left pretty quickly. I doubt a letter would have arrived before we did. Or if a letter did make it before our arrival, it would've been barely."

"You are right. Of course. I-It's just... Now that I'm here, I'm not certain this is the best way. What if his father turns me away at the door?" I pursed my lips as the scenario played out in my head.

"Why would he? He doesn't know you."

"No, I suppose not." I closed my eyes, steeling myself. I nodded to Austin. "Alright, let's go."

"Okay."

We turned right and followed the long lane towards Lynton Hall. The gravel lined path crunching beneath our feet with every step. We'd walked perhaps a mile and a half when the line of trees opened up to reveal manicured lawns with full bushes. At the center stood Lynton Hall. The country house was a fine example of Stuart architecture; rows upon rows of sash windows that could be opened, columns and baroque stonework, hipped roofs adorned with dormer windows.

I rapped on the door with the decorative brass knocker. Moments later, the door opened to reveal a broad faced footman.

"Can I help you, sirs?" the footman asked. He glanced at the pair of us. "Do you have an invitation?"

Gathering myself, I needed to remind myself that I was

William Raphe Chambers, a gentleman and a veteran. I had every right to be here. Standing a little taller, I continued, "I am Mr. Chambers and this here is my companion, Mr. Miller. We are here to call on Mr. Tyndall."

The footman nudged his head. "If you can wait right here, sirs. I shall notify Mr. Tyndall of your arrival."

"Thank you... What is your name?

"Baldwin, sir."

"Thank you, Baldwin."

The footman promptly turned and strode down the hall, leaving us behind to wait on the stoop. Moments later, Baldwin returned with an older gentleman, dressed smartly in coattails and an intricately knotted kerchief. There was no mistaking the family resemblance. Mr. Tyndall stood tall with a firm jaw and the same brown eyes as James. The only significant difference was the graying hairline and deepened creases in his face.

James' father stepped forward, clasping my hands, and giving them a firm shake.

"Mr. Chambers, or can I call you William? How wonderful to finally meet you." Mr. Tyndall moved on from me and proceeded to shake Austin's hand. Of all the things to expect, this certainly wasn't it. James' father already knew my first name and was clearly glad to meet me.

"I'm afraid that I'm a little confused," I confessed when Mr. Tyndall turned back to me. "I wasn't aware you knew about me."

"Did James never tell you? He wrote to me all the time, telling me all about his comrade William. "

I smiled fondly. "I did notice him write a lot; I just never asked."

"I missed my son dearly while he was away, but his recounting of everything you both experienced while in service provided plenty of diversions." Mr. Tyndall went silent for a moment, lost in thought. His smile faltered, only a second, then he picked it up again. "Why, whenever a new letter would arrive, even the staff asked to be present for the reading. However, not all parts were always suitable for those of the female persuasion. Mr. Tyndall beckoned us. "Please, come on in. Follow me." He glanced toward the footman. "Baldwin, can you tell Mary to bring us some tea and refreshments." He paused for a moment, thinking. "She can bring it to the parlor."

We followed Mr. Tyndall to the parlor, a heavily carpeted room with a velour chaise lounge in one corner, flanked by a small side table. A settee and deep leather chair were in the other. The furniture was clearly of good quality, though a bit worn.

"Please, sit down," he said, motioning towards the different seats. "Now, William, you must tell me the story about that one man from your squadron." Mr. Tyndall scrunched up his face. "Argh. I can't remember the name. It's somewhere in James' letters. The one who got really drunk."

"Oh, I think I know who you mean." I laughed and shook my head. "Bilberry."

"That's it." Mr. Tyndall slapped his knee.

"What was the story?" Austin asked.

"You tell your friend," Mr. Tyndall guffawed. "I wasn't there; I don't think I could do the story justice."

I went over the events and thought of the best place to start. "James and I— well, and our entire squadron— we had been holding camp, observing the siege lines. Slowly but surely, our food supply dwindled until all we had left to eat was stale biscuits. The siege had affected our supply chain, so it would take a few more days before we'd be restocked. One evening, when we all had been down in our cups, Bilberry strolled off into the darkness to take a piss. A lot of time passed. We all wondered where he had gone off to, worried he'd went ahead and gotten himself captured by the French. We were just about to go look for him when, all of a sudden, Bilberry returns, wrangling a squealing pig. It was screaming its head off. We were baffled, not one of us spoke, while this pig was trying its best to get away from Bilberry. However, waste not want not. And we were famished. Together, we butchered the pig and roasted it over our fire. The men asked him where he got the pig, but he never told us. At the time, the appearance of the pig felt like a miracle, as if God himself had smiled down upon us and blessed us with this hearty gift. Full bellies make for happy men."

Intrigued, Austin stared up at me. "Did you find out?"

I smiled and shook my head. "Not until the next day when one of the officers angrily complained about the thieving French scum who stole the pig. The pig that was kept to be roasted for their supper."

Austin grinned and said, "And the officers never found out?" Mr. Tyndall slapped his knee and heartily laughed.

"No." I smirked. "We ate all the evidence." I glanced at Austin. "And to this day, it was the best bacon I ever ate." Mr. Tyndall let out a hearty laugh while Austin shook his head.

I turned to Mr. Tyndall. "Bilberry is now the viscount of Pembrington."

"You don't say?"

"I ran into him once after the war, in London. Nowadays, though, he prefers to stay at his country estate. His cousin died at Waterloo which meant the title transferred to him."

"War," Mr. Tyndall exclaimed. "We lost too many good men fighting those bloody French. And to believe that Little Boney was allowed to live in exile in Saint Helene when my....my son." Mr. Tyndall's voice cracked. He swallowed deeply, turning his face away. "I hope I never endure another war again."

"Yes," I agreed. A slight wisp of a girl entered the parlor and supplied us with tea and biscuits.

"Now, what was the purpose of your visit?" Mr. Tyndall asked.

I decided to stick as close to the truth as I could. "I miss James; he always spoke so fondly of his father and of his home. By my reckoning, I ought to visit and say goodbye."

"Were you there?" Mr. Tyndall's voice had grown quiet, the meaning of his question very clear.

I nodded gravely. "I was right by his side."

"Is that where..." he pointed at my face.

"Yes. I was lucky, but if it hadn't been for your son, I'm not sure if I would have made it either. James was the bravest man and soldier I ever met."

Mixed emotions warred on Mr. Tyndall's face— pride at his son's accomplishments, sadness about his loss. "I'm glad to for the knowledge that his friend was by his side when my son passed."

"He didn't suffer. James died quickly and painlessly."

The older man nodded, a slight sheen in the brown eyes that were so like James. "Thank you."

My grief didn't necessarily feel smaller, but sharing it with James' father helped lighten the load. To have this shared kinship with another person. I never thought about it this way before, but I had been lucky to meet James. To have had his light shine on me, however short it may have been. For a while, we had found each other and both our lives had been the better for it. Despite the heartache, I was glad for loving him, for it showed me that I could.

Austin nibbled on one of the biscuits, a crumbly short bread pastry.

"Mr. Tyndall, Austin and I will have to leave soon to catch our coach. However, would you mind if I walked down to the lake? James used to tell me about the days he spent fishing out there. I would love to see it."

Mr. Tyndall scratched his chin. "The scenery isn't as nice this time of year. You ought to come back in spring when everything is in bloom. But, of course you can." He picked up his cup and swallowed some tea. "However, isn't it a bit late for the coach? You both are welcome to stay the night."

My eyes shot towards Austin. He simply shrugged, leaving the decision up to me. "I thank you for the offer, though I'd prefer to get back on the road since we have other engagements. The next coach should drive by around four p.m."

"You must let my driver drop you off at the sign post. No need to make you and your friend walk my entire driveway."

"I'll gladly accept that." I smiled warmly at James' father. "Would you like to join us?" I offered.

"No. No," he waved. "My old bones are too weary to walk in this cold." Mr. Tyndall didn't seem weary to me. Perhaps he simply sensed that I could use the privacy to mourn my friend.

I lowered my head. "Thank you, sir. I'm glad I got to meet James' father."

"Likewise, my boy. It brings my heart such joy to know he had a friend by his side." Mr. Tyndall returned to the warmth of his comfortable home while Austin and I set out for the lake.

The view was as beautiful as James had described to me. Though in his description, the trees were full and green and the air perfumed by red roses. There was a small pier with a wooden boat tied to a post. The boat had seen better days. Mr. Tyndall clearly no longer used it. I could imagine James out here fishing, joking and laughing his big hearty laughs.

Austin and I stood side-by-side watching the soft winter sun reflecting off the water.

"Take your time," Austin said gently. But it was time. And Austin was right. This was the perfect place to say goodbye to James. To wish his memory farewell in a place that he loved. I stepped onto the pier. "Do you want me to..." Austin started.

"No." I shook my head. "This is something I have to do myself." I walked down to the edge of the pier. Fishing around in my jacket pocket, the pocket closest to my heart, my fingers pulled out a ring. Two cranes and two roses made up the symbol on the ring, the Tyndall family crest. James had gifted it to me as a sign of the promise we made to each other. To live our lives together. I gently placed my lips against the metal, kissing it, before laying the ring down at the end of the pier.

"Goodbye, James. Goodbye, my love," I whispered to the wind, hoping it would sweep my words up to the heavens. There wasn't more to say. I was certain James knew how much I'd loved him. With the back of my hand, I swiped away the wetness coating my cheeks.

I found Austin solemn and still, watching me as I returned to him. He brushed my cheek when I reached him and grabbed my hand. Then, in solemn silence, we returned to Lynton Hall.

* * *

Mr. Tyndall's driver was already prepared and waiting when we reached the front entrance. Austin had just sat down on a seat. I was about to enter the carriage, when Mr. Tyndall ran from the house.

"Wait. Just a moment," he shouted. I turned my head and stepped back to the gravel. He hurried towards me with a bundle of papers in his hand. "I want you to have these," he said as he thrust them into my arms.

"What are they?"

"They're James' letters. He wrote so much about you. I think he would have wanted you to have them."

"I-I don't know what to say. Are you certain?" I held them out towards him.

"Quite, my boy." He pressed my hands into my chest. "You keep them and read them every once in a while. That way, I know there will be someone thinking of my son even after I die. Can you promise me that?"

"I promise."

"Good, now, go on the both of you, before you miss the coach."

"Goodbye, Mr. Tyndall," Austin said from the carriage window.

"Goodbye," I echoed, and joined Austin in the carriage.

20

Hart & Fox

We'd stopped at a roadside inn with a whitewashed exterior with wooden sidings, and dark green finishes, including a metal sign with the name Hart & Fox. It was the same one we had stayed at going to Lancashire. Once we entered, I headed straight for the inn keep, a gangly fellow with a long face that reminded me of a horse. I dropped my luggage on the floor and took a seat at the bar

"Two rooms, please," I said, laying down money on the counter. "And two beers."

"I'm afraid I've only the one room left," the innkeeper said while polishing a glass. Austin took his seat beside me.

"We'll take the room," Austin said. The inn keep nodded and set down the glass. Behind him, he picked a key off a hanger. He handed it to Austin.

"Juz' a moment on the beer," the inn keep said. He pocketed the money I laid down on the counter, leaving behind the fare for the second room, and poured some drinks for other guests sitting at the bar. Then, he returned to us with two pints of beer, a thick layer of foam on each of them.

Austin licked his lips and took a swig.

"Do you have anything on special?" I asked the inn keep.

"Mutton pies, sir. My wife made 'em juz' today."

"We'll take two."

The inn keep nodded his long horse like face and called towards a plump woman serving two gentlemen sitting in the back. "Two pies, Mary. For here." He pointed at us.

"Coming right up," the woman shouted back.

I paid the inn keep for the food, and he returned to his other customers. He dropped the mutton pies in front of us not much later. The pastry was lukewarm at best; however, I was starving. Switching between bites of pie and swallows of beer, I wolfed the food down, barely tasting either, which was perhaps a good thing. I certainly had better food at other inns and guest houses. Austin had also finished most of his mutton pie. Now, he was picking at the last piece of crust. He yawned loudly.

"Oops. I should've covered my mouth," he said jokingly. "That wasn't very gentlemanly." I snorted. He lifted his eyebrow. "What, you disagree?"

"Not at all," I teased. "I definitely don't see a gentleman."

Austin bumped his shoulder against me in mock affront. I flashed him a smile and finished my beer.

"Do you mind if I retire to our room?" I asked. "Today has been a long day."

"I'll come with. I'm ready to stretch out as well." He dropped the last bit of crust on a napkin and stood, the stool scraping against the wood. We both picked up our luggage and took the stairs to the upper floor. Using the key, I opened our room. I should have known it was the same layout as the room I had stayed in before.

"Oh," Austin said as he entered the room and realized we would have to share a single bed. He was a decent sport about it though; Austin set his satchel down in an empty corner and said," I claim the wall side."

"I could lay on the floor," I hedged.

Austin quirked his brow. "I think you forgot we've already slept in one bed together. So, we can do that again." I hadn't forgotten. In fact, I thought about that night quite often. Heat crept up my neck. "Though, I must admit, this will be a tight fit," Austin continued. He sized me up. "Yes, your bed at Hawthorne is much more spacious."

"Alright, I guess I'll prepare for bed," I said, hesitating. I took James' letters from my jacket pocket and laid them on the desk. Then, I started peeling off my clothes. Austin's eyes flitted to the bundle of papers tied together with string.

"Are you going to read them?" He nudged his head towards the desk.

I hung my jacket from the chair. "Not now. I don't think I'm ready just yet," I said, glancing at Austin. "But eventually I will. I did promise."

"I think it was kind of Mr. Tyndall to give you his son's letters."

"Yes." I paused, not knowing what else to say.

Austin sat down at the edge of the bed. "Did visiting Lynton Hall help? To say goodbye?" he asked as he took off his shoes.

I untucked the kerchief around my neck. "I think it did," I admitted. "I wasn't certain at first. But there at the lake, it felt right, like James was there with me and approved." I shrugged, pulling off the kerchief. Next, I unbuttoned my trousers. "I know it sounds silly."

"It doesn't sound silly," Austin said. His American accent got stronger the more he tired. I liked hearing the way he spoke, the foreign way he formed his vowels.

"Thank you for suggesting this," I said. "I would've never gone on my own."

Austin chuckled. "I think you give me too much credit."

I disagreed. "Never enough." Austin pulled off his shirt and threw it across the room, where it landed somewhere near his satchel. Moments later, his trousers followed. He climbed in under the covers and scooted up against the wall as much as he could. I moved in behind him, dressed solely in my shirt.

The bed was a tight fit and I had to lay flush against Austin or else I would tumble over the edge. I tried my best to give him space, but he snatched my arm and pulled it around him.

"There's no room," he said. "I don't mind." Taking his word for it, I snuggled up closer. My face pressed against the back of his neck, his scent intoxicating as I practically buried my nose in his hair.

It was difficult to put into words to the way he smelled. Austin simply smelled like Austin. My thoughts and feelings were conflicted. It felt right to hold him in my arms, but I couldn't know if he felt the same. And there was the matter of him leaving. Even if he did have the same regard for me, he would still leave and return to his own time. I couldn't ask him to stay. I felt selfish for even considering.

I pushed the intrusive thoughts away. For tonight, I just enjoyed the feel of his supple body against my own, the gentle rise of his chest as he breathed, and his scent beneath my nose. I would stay here forever, if I had a choice, bundled up together in a cramped bed.

* * *

Come morning, I found myself flat on my back with Austin draped over my chest, sleeping soundly. I stifled a laugh. He snored in gentle rhythmic bursts. I remained still as to not wake him. His face relaxed and pressed against my shirt; I brushed back a lock of hair that had fallen across his forehead. He stirred.

"Morning," he mumbled, rubbing his eyes.

"Morning," I repeated. Austin shot me a crooked smile as he gazed up at me through heavy lidded eyes. "Did you sleep well?" I asked.

Austin shrugged. "I've slept on worse. Though," he said pulling his arm back and rolling off me and onto his side against the wall, "It seems I've commandeered all your space as well. I'm sorry. I hope you weren't too uncomfortable."

I smirked. "I've slept worse as well. Besides, you are entertaining when you sleep."

"Ooh," Austin said, wiggling his brow. "You were watching me while I slept?" His tone taunting. "I'm not sure if I should be flattered or disturbed."

Snorting at his taunt, I said, "Certainly disturbed."

"I'll take it under advisement," he answered, raking his fingers through his hair.

I sat up at the side of the bed. Bending over, I snatched my trousers from the floor. Glancing back at Austin, I asked, "Are you hungry?"

Austin propped himself up on one arm. "I'm starving. That meat pie didn't do anything for me."

"Good. Let's get a fry up before the coach arrives." I stood and buttoned my trousers. Then, at the small dresser, I splashed some cold water on my face. Behind me, Austin also got out of bed to get dressed. I pulled a comb from my luggage and dipped it in the water to style my hair. Austin's was short on the sides and didn't need much maintenance. He stepped next to me and dipped his fingers into the basin as well, using the clean water to wipe the sleep from his eyes.

It felt strange but also natural how we were interacting with each other. Despite our close quarters, I didn't feel stifled or overwhelmed by his presence. Instead, his nearness brought me comfort and companionship.

Though the things I felt whenever I saw him or thought about him had nothing to do with a simple companion. In fact, I was afraid that I might have to confess my feelings. It wasn't fair on either of us to continue like this. I wanted to know where I stood with him and Austin needed to know, so he could make an informed decision about any time we spent together.

If Austin only saw me as a friend, then that was that. I would have to live with that. It would be his choice and I'd respect it. But spending the night in the same room without knowing how I felt, wasn't right.

I finished getting dressed and packed, then opened the door for Austin. Together, we left the room and followed the stairs down to the first floor. We snagged a table near the fireplace.

"We've got the best spot," Austin said as he sat down. "Perks of being early, I suppose."

The inn keeper's wife swung by our table. "What can I get you?" she asked in her heavy Lancashire accent.

"Two fry ups, please."

Not much later, she returned, her arms weighed down with two full plates of eggs, bacon, bread, and black pudding. My mouth watered at the savory smell of breakfast. I could use a filling meal that would stick to your ribs, after yesterday. Austin must have thought the same because he practically inhaled his plate of food. Halfway through the eggs, he slowed down a bit and poked at the black pudding.

"What's that?" he asked, the tines of his fork pushing against the sausage.

"Just try it. It's scrumptious." Demonstrating, I took a big bite.

He regarded me for a moment, questioningly. "I'm not sure."

"It's black pudding, a kind of blood sausage, a staple of a full English Breakfast. I promise that it tastes delicious."

Austin pinned a piece of sausage down and lifted it up to his face. He sniffed the meat and carefully bit a small piece off. His eyes scrunched up in the same way they would when he was thinking or considering something. Austin chewed a bit more, before saying, "The texture is a bit different, chewy actually, but it's not bad."

"Are you going to eat more?"

"I think I will." He ate the rest of the sausage on his fork. I finished my plate and wiped the juices down with the last pieces of bread. Using a napkin, I wiped my face and placed it on the plate. I patted down the front of my jacket to make sure any crumbs were gone. My hand glided over my inner pocket that was now empty, the ring that I had kept there for so long left behind at Lynton Hall.

I felt lighter somehow, hopeful. I looked forward to the future, whatever that might be, which was something I hadn't done in a long while. Not since James died. Part of it was Austin, his assistance and support. But the other part was coming to terms with what happened, not denying it or shying away from it. Realizing that James' death wasn't my fault.

Saying goodbye to him at his home had been the right thing for me to do. However, that didn't mean I wouldn't still miss him, and it didn't mean that what we went through on the battlefield wouldn't haunt me. It just meant that I was healing and growing, finally seeing a future with real possibilities.

Whether Austin would be a part of that, I couldn't know. I hoped he would be. However, regardless of Austin, I knew I deserved a place in this world. I deserved happiness. My lips quirked into a small smile at my realization. Tension I had been unconsciously holding in my body slid away, loosening my shoulders.

"What are you thinking about?" Austin asked. "It looks like you're a million miles away."

"I was just thinking how glad I am that we went to Lynton Hall. For the first time in a long while, I'm enjoying myself without sadness permeating everything that I do. I feel calmer." I gazed at Austin. He looked at me, his eyes shadowed in the dimly lit inn, early morning light barely breaking through the windows.

"That's good. You are my friend, William. I'd like to see you happy."

I nodded and scraped my throat. "Well, we should probably get ready for the coach."

"Yes. We don't want to miss it." Austin stood and slung his satchel across his shoulder. I followed him to the front where I paid the inn keeper for breakfast.

Austin's words cycled through my brain. I needed to restrain my feelings. He was from a different time, and I was reading too much into his behavior. Austin made it abundantly clear with his words that I was merely a friend, though, my friends called me Will.

I hadn't corrected Austin, simply because I liked the way he said William. From his lips, my name sounded intimate, like a promise of things to come. Not that they would. I was fully capable of keeping a friendly distance. My relationship with Austin could remain purely platonic, the same as my friendship with John. And if I ever doubted our friendship, I merely needed to remind myself that he would soon depart.

21

James' Letters

I was glad to be back. Hawthorne might be John's family home, but I practically grew up alongside him. I would always think fondly of the place and all its nooks and crannies, the hiding spaces in the parlor and the music room, the expansive gardens we used to roam as boys. A part of me always felt like I was coming home whenever I crossed the threshold.

Today, John was clearly apprehensive about my mental state as Austin and I returned from Lynton Hall. I was lifting my luggage into the hall, ready to climb the stairs and retire to my room when John sauntered in behind me and stopped Austin in his tracks. I could hear every word he said even though he was trying to whisper. John had never been very subtle.

"How is Will?" John asked Austin. I glanced over my shoulder, catching John's concerned face.

"I can hear you, you know." At least John had the smart sense to look apologetic.

He continued, louder this time. "I was only asking Austin how you were."

I dropped my luggage and walked towards them. I smiled warmly and clasped John's upper arm, giving it a gentle squeeze. "No need to walk on eggshells around me. I know I've been... well, not myself." I sighed. "What I mean to say is that I am genuinely starting to feel better." I glanced at Austin, taking in his calm face. "Our excursion to Lancashire helped. So, feel free to treat me like normal." I gave John a pointed shove, throwing him off balance.

His brow quirked as he regained his equilibrium. "Back to teasing and such then."

"What is this I hear about teasing?" Rose's voice floated in from the doorway leading to the back end of the house. "Welcome back," she greeted Austin and I. She stepped up to John and slung an arm about his waist. "How was the trip?"

"William made me eat black pudding," Austin said.

"Oh, I still won't touch that," Rose said, shaking her head. "I can't get over the idea of eating blood, though, John has been convincing me I should."

"It is delicious," John and I replied in tandem.

Rose laughed. "That may be, but I will never know. That stuff is all yours."

"The black pudding really wasn't that bad," Austin offered.

"Where is Beth?" I asked John. Normally, his sister would be right here bursting with questions.

John leaned against the banister. "She's spending the night at the Blakeley's. Anne invited her for an evening of music."

Rose returned her gaze to me. "How was Lynton Hall? How was James' father?"

"Taking over Beth's role?" I joked.

"Maybe," she grinned. "Someone has to."

"His father was a kind and hospitable man," I answered truthfully. "Lynton Hall is a beautiful place. You'd love the lake," I told Rose. "It was...helpful. To share memories with someone who knew and loved him." My thoughts flared to the letters tucked away in my luggage. "Mr. Tyndall gave me some of James' personal letters. I planned on reading them tonight, when I was back in my own room."

John frowned. "Are you sure—"

"John, it's up to Will whether he wants to read them or not." Rose gave her husband a pointed glance.

"I'm just looking out for you," he said to me.

"I understand. However, I meant what I said; I am starting to feel better." Sterner than I meant it to be, I added, "I don't need to be coddled."

John grinned at that. "That's the Will I grew up with!" he exclaimed. His voice softened. "All I've wanted was my friend back. I missed you."

A lump formed in my throat. I swallowed deeply before answering. "I've been here."

"Not fully. Not since the war. Not for a long time," John said, his eyes a bit brighter, a bit shinier than usual. "I'd catch glimpses now and then but mostly you kept everything to yourself. Kept yourself locked away from me, from us." John pointed to Rose and himself.

Hanging my head, I said, "I know. I'm sorry. I didn't understand what to do with my emotions. Sometimes, it felt like

I would burst with the sheer magnitude of them, and other times, I felt like I was lost, searching for help when there was none to be found." It saddened me to think that while I was so lost in the grief and pain of losing James, I never noticed that John was worried about me.

John placed his hands on my shoulders, our foreheads nearly touching. "I'm merely glad I've got my friend back." Then, he enveloped me in a hug, his arms tightening around me. From the corner of my eye, I saw Austin smiling at us.

"Alright, alright," I told John, a bit embarrassed. I wasn't exactly used to wearing my heart on my sleeve. He moved back from the embrace. "I am ready to retire for the evening." I eyed my luggage which held the bundle of letters. Then I nodded to John and Rose. "I will see you at breakfast."

"Good evening," John replied.

* * *

Dressed in my night shirt, I nestled into the plush covers. On the stand next to the bed, a candle flickered gently, emitting a faint smoky scent.

In my hands were the letters I received from James' father. I untied the string holding them together and rifled through them, my eyes skimming the different dates scrawled on the paper.

Picking out a letter from 1811, I unfolded the paper. My heart skipped a beat as I recognized the messily written letters. I used to make fun of him for the way he jotted down his words. I held the letter closer to the flame.

From the deep creases in the paper, I could tell that Mr. Tyndall had read and refolded James' correspondence over and over again. It must have been a great sacrifice on his part to give them to me. However, the kind man had seemed unburdened once he had given them to me. I read the opening line.

Dear father,

Being away from home these past few weeks has reminded me how much I love Lynton Hall. Had I been there, I would have spent countless hours on the lake, fishing. Then, at supper, we'd eat what I caught. Mrs. Grantley always appreciated when I supplemented the larder.

Do you remember that enormous carp I caught a few years back? Our cook thought I was telling a Canterbury tale until I dragged the deuced thing into the kitchen. She was nearly in vapors. Do send me word on the goings-on at home. I shall be glad to read about every meal and social visit while our rations are tight as we march to Cadiz.

Though the food is lacking, our spirits are high as we are proceeding bravely towards the Corsican monster. One of the ensigns is skilled with a pencil and draws caricatures of Napoleon whenever we have a break. Perhaps I'll request one to send to you in a future letter.

Your loving son, James

My lip curled at the mention of the caricatures. I remembered one drawing that the men passed around at the campfire— Napoleon struggling to put on a hat as tall as himself. We all had a good chuckle about that one. I wondered if James ever added a caricature to one of his letters.

I rifled through the stack and pulled out another one. The date jumped out at me, only a week before our final battle. I checked the other letters to make sure but couldn't find a more recent date. The letter I now held in my hands was James' final correspondence. Slowly, I unfolded the paper, thumbing the edges. My eyes drifted to James' chicken scrawls. The tone of the letter was jarringly light. Though, I only felt that way because I knew what was to come.

Dear Father,

We have left Spain behind. Our troops are driving the French forces ever North. My regiment is being led by Duke Wellington, though I haven't had a chance to meet him in person. Hopefully, I'll be able to before the war is over. I admire his assertiveness and command of the military.

Before I forget, William has urged me to wish you well and to thank you for extending your invitation to visit Lynton Hall when we are once again free to do so. I doubt it will be long before I get to take the boat out on to the water. We'll have to show him what Lancashire is like.

William wants me to visit his friend's estate in Westbridge. From what he's told me, it's a small town; however, it would be enjoyable to travel around once again for leisure and not war. After visiting you and his friend, we plan to take up lodgings in London. I hope you'll support me in my future endeavors.

Your loving son, James.

Carefully, I refolded the paper, stacked the letters, and tied them back together. It was strange to read about that day, to think about our light banter and excitement for the future.

Reading his last letter, the precursor to our shattered dreams, saddened me, but it also drove home how lucky we had been to find each other. James had loved me wholly and undoubtedly, just as I had loved him. His happiness at that moment in time almost burst from the page.

We didn't get to have a future together, but just because it was short, didn't mean it wasn't important. And, it didn't mean I couldn't find happiness again. It was a strange sensation to think of James and not feel like I couldn't breathe, my chest squeezing with every thought of him. My happy memories were no longer clouded by his death. Once again, I could think of a funny memory and smile.

I breathed a sigh of relief and tucked the letters away into a drawer on the stand next to the bed and dampened the candle.

* * *

The next morning, Austin ushered me into the hot house, away from prying eyes. He checked to make sure no one else was around before closing the door.

"It's finished," he whispered excitedly.

"The drawing?" Austin nodded, leading me to a workbench against one side of the glass paneling. Displayed on it was the drawing, a beautiful rendering of John and Rose. Austin had captured them perfectly, right down to the proud lift of John's chin and the mischievous twinkle in Rose's eyes.

I whistled at the piece of art in front of me. "This is beautiful. John and Rose will love it." I turned to Austin and flashed him a smile.

"I hope so," he said. His face was so earnest, I contemplated teasing him. I decided against it because the way he cared about other people was one of the qualities I liked most about him. I never wanted him to lose that.

"Oh, before I forget," Austin said, spinning around. "Maybe you can give me a hand with this." He conjured up a thick box from behind a large potted plant next to the work bench. He laid it flat on the wood and lifted the top. "The frame arrived yesterday. Hugh handed it to me, and I stashed it away in here." He lifted the frame out of the box.

Austin had chosen a simple but elegant design that I knew Rose would like. She didn't prefer ornate or elaborate decorations; for her, simplicity was best. The plain design of the frame would instead put focus on Austin's skilled drawing.

He opened the backing to the frame. "Can you help me place the drawing?" he asked, his face turned up towards me, waiting.

I carefully lifted his drawing and settled it into place in the frame. Austin returned the backing and turned the frame over, admiring the end result. He set it down, leaning against the glass panel, and took a step back.

"I like it," he said, bobbing his head.

"You will have the best Christmas gift of us all," I said. Austin smirked. "Well, I did my best."

"Show-off," I retorted. Austin shrugged and laughed.

22

Christmas at Hawthorne

Christmas arrived at Hawthorne, and with it came the first flurries of snow. Everyone living at the estate assembled in the hall, ready to head to the Christmas service at the local parish church which was led by Mr. Willoughby. Mrs. Avery and Clara were dressed in their finest clothes, scarfs pulled tight around their necks. Hugh was already waiting out front by the carriage. The drive didn't take long.

At the church, the pews already started filling up. There were many familiar faces from around town. Mrs. Blakeley and her two daughters, Anne and Mary, were sitting primly at the front. I glanced around for Randolph and found him in the back, speaking with Mr. Rigsby, the silk merchant, and his wife Jane.

Most of John's tenants were here as well. John and Rose were held up by McCreary; he handed John a small gift. It was a custom for tenants to give a token of appreciation to a generous landowner. And John had always been generous with anyone living on his lands, something he'd learned from his parents. John graciously shook the Scot's beefy hand and pocketed the gift before heading towards our pew. I moved to the corner while Austin slid in next to me.

"How does this work?" he whispered.

"You've never been to a Christmas service?" I asked.

He shook his head and continued whispering. "My foster family is Christian, but I personally don't have a religion."

"The service shouldn't take very long. It's mostly sitting through the sermon, then we can return home to celebrate the festivities at Hawthorne. Although, Mr. Willoughby does like to posture and hear himself speak."

"Who's that?"

I pointed at the thin man with slicked back hair standing alone near the front of the chapel. The vicar was thumbing through his notes, clearly running some last-minute lines. "Did you know that when Rose first arrived, he proposed to her at a dance?"

"Nooo!" Austin exclaimed a little too loud. He snorted with laughter. Glancing around in embarrassment, he lowered his voice again. "What did she do?"

"From what she told me, John swooped in and saved her from having to dance the waltz with the vicar."

"Small mercies," Austin snickered. "Did the vicar find a wife?"

"No takers yet, as far as I've heard."

"Can't blame them," Austin said, glancing back at Mr. Willoughby, who plastered back his greasy hair even more.

I lifted my brow and laughed. "Indeed."

John and Rose joined us in our pew while Mr. Willoughby stepped up to the dais. We sat through a few hours of sermonizing and singing hymns. Austin actually knew a few of the carols; he said they were still popular in his time. Finally, we were able to return home. We wished the other churchgoers a joyful Christmas. Beth hugged Anne. The sky outside had turned slate gray, the flurries of snow getting thicker and heavier as they stuck to the ground.

* * *

Back at Hawthorne, Clara hurried to stoke up the fires that warmed the house and Mrs. Avery headed to the kitchen.

"What's for dinner," I asked her as she pulled off her bonnet and gloves.

The middle-aged woman smiled kindly. "Christmas goose," she said.

"And the rest you'll have to wait for to find out." She wagged a finger at me. "No sneaking into the kitchen."

"Cross my heart," I grinned, drawing an x on my chest. "There'll be fruit pudding though?"

Mrs. Avery looked suspiciously at me. She probably remembered all those years that John and I sneaked into the kitchen, snatching so much food that by the time dinner came around, we'd be perched somewhere—full-bellied and snoring— with crumbs on our faces. John's father would lift us up one-by-one and carry us to our beds where we'd sleep it off until morning.

"I promise that John and I will not steal your food," I added with amusement.

"What's that about no food stealing?" John interrupted. "I can't promise that."

"Och, away with the both of ye!" Mrs. Avery exclaimed, swatting at John. She turned around to continue to the kitchen. Right before she moved out of sight, she glanced back at me. "Don't worry, your favorite will be on the table."

John bumped against me once Mrs. Avery was gone. "Remember the year we hid the venison?"

Austin was observing us from the stairs. "Sounds like both of you were capricious as kids."

"Little imps, that's what mother called us," John added. "Always good-natured though. William and I used to have a grand time at Christmas."

Austin quirked his brow and stifled a laugh. "I bet."

Rose peeked out from the drawing room. "What's taking so long? Beth and I are getting ready to decorate the tree."

"We're coming now," John replied. Together, we marched into the drawing room, which now held a tall pine tree. Beth was kneeling on the ground, rifling through a box of homemade ornaments and decorations that Rose and herself had been busy making the past few weeks. Bell shaped ornaments and garlands fashioned out of gold paper and shiny silks. Wreaths of evergreen already decorated the mantelpiece and any other available space on top of furniture, the sprigs of holly, laurel, and rosemary perfuming the room. Rose picked up a bough of mistletoe bearing tons of white berries.

"Can you help me hang this?" she asked. "You're the

tallest." I took the bough from her hands and returned to the doorway.

"Here?" I questioned, holding the mistletoe up against the door frame.

"Perfect," she beamed, handing me a small nail. I pressed it into the woodwork and hung the bough from it.

"Now, you, John, and Austin can all help us decorate the tree."

"Let's do the garlands first," Beth said." Austin and I grabbed a red silk garland and wound it around the tree. John snagged a paper flower and stuck it at the top.

"I love Christmas," Rose murmured as she delicately placed more decorations on the tree, her tongue peeking out from the corner of her mouth in concentration.

John pulled her close and kissed her temple. "And I love you."

"Here," Beth ordered, thrusting more decorations at John. "Less kissing, more decorating."

John let out a rumbling laugh and accepted the decorations. Seeing everyone together, happy, warmed my soul. All my friends were chatting and having fun. Austin was discussing holiday traditions with Beth, Rose was teasing John, and I brought up shared memories. I wished today could last forever.

Clara entered the room with a giant punch bowl filled with wassail, the red liquid sloshing with every step. Rose hurried and cleared some unused decorations from the table in the corner. Clara placed the holiday drink on the side, leaving enough space for the food that would accompany it later.

Dinner would be done "buffet style" as Rose had told us.

Austin had nodded with understanding while the rest of us drew blanks. Once she explained, we understood that it just meant serve yourself, which sounded like a perfect idea, especially since Clara, Hugh, and Mrs. Avery were joining us for Christmas Eve.

"Have a glass," Rose told Clara, pointing at the wassail.

"Later, ma'am," she said, with a belated curtsy. "I've got to help my aunt with dinner."

"Alright," Rose replied. "But come and have fun as soon as you are finished."

"Yes, ma'am," she bobbed, then left.

Beth dusted off her knees and stood. "I asked the Blakeley's to come over," she told John.

"That was kind of you," he said.

Beth nodded. "Yes, from what Anne told me, it didn't seem they were able to afford much of a Christmas. I felt bad at the idea of them sitting at home eating a regular dinner."

"I agree," Rose said. "And we have plenty for all of us."

My mind traveled to Randolph Blakeley. "Is he still gambling?" I asked John.

John's brows furrowed. "Not of late, I don't believe. However, they are still trying to pay off the already incurred debts. It's why I'll be sponsoring Anne this upcoming season, alongside Beth."

Beth looked thoughtful. "Do you think we have something to give them as well when we do our gift exchange?"

"Oh," Rose said. "I'm sure we can think of something."

"I could give Anne the pair of pearl earrings I got from you," Beth told John.

"Are you sure? I thought you loved those."

"I am sure," Beth said. "I think they'd look lovely on Anne." She tapped her finger against the side of her mouth, thinking. "Oh, Mary likes painting..."

"I could give her some brushes and paints," Austin said. He glanced at me and smiled. "William has already given me more than I will use."

"Then, Mrs. Blakeley can be gifted my new silk gloves," Rose said.

"You had been wanting a chance to get rid of those," John huffed.

Rose slid an arm around John's waist. "You know who you married. I'm not a fan of fancy gloves."

"And you remind me every day," he said, nipping at her lip.

I turned to Beth. "I have a scarf still wrapped up and boxed. I was going to give it to John." John cocked his head at me when I mentioned his name. "But Randolph is probably a better destination. John already has enough scarfs."

John shook his head while Beth's grin lit up the room. "I'm so glad we all get to share gifts."

* * *

Hugh and Mrs. Avery brought in the serving dishes laden with food and placed them by the wassail. Clara set a stack of clean plates, napkins, and cutlery next to them. The doorbell rang and Beth hurried to the front door. I could hear Randolph's deep voice thanking Beth for the invitation while Anne and Mary chattered, their voices bright. Fabric rustled as they shrugged out of their coats and then their footsteps headed our way. Clara blushed as she spied Randolph's figure walking through the doorway; her eyes shot up to the mistletoe dangling above him.

"What beautiful decorations," Mary exclaimed as she entered, her eyes fixed on the tree. At the base of it, we had splayed out all the paper wrapped gifts.

Mrs. Avery took a seat in one of the high-backed chairs near the fireplace, after thanking John and Rose for the invitation.

"My pleasure," Rose said. She headed to the table and started pouring glasses of wassail. I joined her and helped hand out the drinks to everyone.

Mrs. Avery and Hugh seemed a bit uncomfortable to be served by us instead of doing the serving, but I smiled deeply and wished them a merry Christmas as I handed them their drinks. Clara also accepted a glass from me, though her eyes still avoided mine. No doubt, she was still feeling embarrassed about what happened with Captain Tremblay.

John, being the master of the house, picked up a small piece of log set aside on top of the bin that held the firewood.

"Since we are all gathered here, a drink in our hand, I think it is time to light the Yule log." Ceremoniously, he placed the small piece of log into the fire. Then, he added another larger log, a bit to the front of the fireplace, halfway out of the fire, so it would smolder slowly and take a long time to burn.

Once the first flames licked at the wood, the entire company clapped and drank from their glass. The fruity drink packed a punch as it slid down my throat. Mrs. Avery had been generous with the brandy. John resumed. "Please, eat as you please and let us celebrate Christmas together."

"Will you play for us?" Beth asked Anne. Anne nodded and slid onto the piano bench, a holiday tune soon starting beneath her fingers. Austin and I headed to the table for some food. I handed him a plate. He picked up some goose and roasted vegetables. The potatoes were looking especially delicious, all golden brown around the edges. My favorite, Mrs. Avery's Christmas pudding, was the center piece of the table. I had to restrain myself to not start with dessert. Instead, I took some venison, potatoes, and bread.

The room was warm and full of laughter. The women took turns playing the piano; the men played rounds of Snapdragon under the watchful eye of Mrs. Avery. Randolph's fingers had to be submerged in a small bowl of water when he took too long to snatch the raisin out of the brandy lit fire.

Eventually, we got around to the gift giving. I could tell that Mrs. Blakeley was fidgeting, having arrived with no gifts to give. But Rose started off the gift giving by handing Mrs. Blakeley the first package. The woman accepted it gratefully, beaming at Rose. She tore away the paper and opened the box, revealing silky blue gloves with a beautiful sheen.

"How lovely," Mrs. Blakeley said, overwhelmed. She took the gloves out of the box and slid them through her palms. "Thank you so much for your kindness. I shall change into them this instant." She pulled off her own white gloves and replaced them with the new pair.

"I'm glad you like them," Rose said softly.

Next was Hugh, who got bonus pay and a bottle of whiskey. He immediately broke it open and offered to share it with us. The women declined but John, Austin, Randolph, and I agreed to a small amount. While Hugh poured us some of his gift, Beth handed her gift to Anne.

"Beth," she choked out. "They are wonderful." Anne's eyes were shining a brightly as she inspected the earrings.

Austin jumped up. "Now for John and Rose," he said. He picked up a larger package from the base of the Christmas tree and handed it to Rose. John joined her and helped tear the paper away.

Rose's eyes grew wide as she held up Austin's gift. She glanced at him with her mouth open. "This is beautiful," she said, her voice low.

"I figured it could hang in your school," Austin said, flushing. He brushed some of his hair behind his ear.

"Show us," Randolph called from the men's table.

Rose turned the painting around and held it higher, showing it to all the guests.

"Mr. Miller is a talented artist," Mrs. Blakeley said to no one in particular. Mary nodded, oohing.

"Thank you so much," Rose told Austin. "I love it."

John clapped Austin on the back. "You couldn't have given her a better gift." I beamed at Austin as his eyes locked on me, a proud smile on his face.

Mrs. Avery, Estelle, and Clara all received extra pay, and while Mrs. Avery got a new apron, Clara received a pretty day dress. Estelle lit up with pleasure as she held her new hairpins up to her face. Mary was happy with her new paint set, and Randolph thanked us for the scarf. Austin was showing off the kerchief he was gifted, and I accepted a polish kit for my boots. Rose returned to the piano, starting an upbeat tune.

All of us—the Blakeley's, Hugh, Clara, and Mrs. Avery, Austin, John, Rose and I— danced and sung carols, bolstered by the brandy in the wassail. Clara managed to steal a kiss from Randolph when they found each other standing underneath the mistletoe. I doubted it was an accident on Clara's part; she looked mighty pleased.

At the end of the night, after we said goodbye to our guests at the front door, I was exhausted and ready for bed, but I had one more thing to do. I returned to the drawing room, bumping into Austin as I tried to turn into the doorway.

"Oops," he said, with a lopsided grin. His eyes glanced up at the white berried mistletoe dangling above us. "It's tradition," he said, slightly slurred. He raised onto his tiptoes and planted a kiss at the edge of my mouth, his breath heavy with the fruity alcoholic concoction. Then he dropped back to the flat of his feet. I hesitated, the spot where he kissed me burning.

"I was coming to look for you," I said, my hand digging into my pant pocket.

"Oh? What for?" Austin said, still standing so close to me that I could count every variation of color in his green eyes.

I pulled a small package out of my pocket. "I wanted to give you this."

Austin's eyes followed my hand. "You didn't have to..."

"I wanted to," I said, handing him the box. Austin opened it, taking out the two silver rounds.

"What are they?" He held them up to his face.

"They are cuff links," I told him. I pointed at one. "This one has my initial. And the other has yours. I figured that if you wore them, whenever you looked at them, you'd always be reminded of me, no matter where you were."

Austin remained silent, a small smile on his face as his eyes remained trained on the cuff links. Then his eyes met mine. "Thank you, William; I will cherish them." I nodded. My skin flushed from his remark, though it could have been the liquor.

"Alright," I stammered. "I'll leave you to it." I turned on my heel, leaving Austin behind me, still standing underneath the mistletoe. I worried that if I stayed even a moment longer, I wouldn't be able to stop myself from kissing him. Not like the chaste peck he had given me but thoroughly, passionately, without a thought of anybody else.

23

Mrs. Ashbrook's Masquerade

"William, will you come with us?" Beth was practically dancing as she, Anne, and Estelle walked down the staircase. The French maid had been busy perfecting the girls' hairstyles. Glancing at their up dos, I had to admit that Estelle was gifted at her job. Beth was fidgeting with her hair, pressing her palms against the pulled-up strands at her temples, ringlets flowing out at the back of her head. "Do you like it?" She seemed equal parts eager and nervous. I grinned at her.

"It must've been difficult, but I suppose that Estelle has managed to make a lady out of you."

Beth swatted at my arm with her fan, "You are such a tease."

"You are often in need of teasing," I replied. "And to answer your question, yes; I'll drive with you and Anne. Austin wanted his costume to be a surprise, so he'll follow along to Mrs. Ashbrook's estate with John and Rose."

Beth nodded and whispered conspiratorially, "I can't believe Anne and I are actually going, without Mrs. Blakeley."

I shook my head at Beth and Anne. "You know John only wants to protect you."

"Protect me from fun is more like it," she huffed.

"But you are going thanks to Rose... and myself." Beth rolled her eyes. "Just promise me that you won't go looking for trouble."

"I would never," she said, appearing as if she was innocence itself.

I snorted. "At least you have Anne by your side to keep you out of trouble."

Anne's mouth was quirked into an amused smile as she witnessed our bantering.

"Who's to say that Anne won't be the trouble?" Beth retorted.

"I won't be trouble as Beth's chaperon," Anne hurried to say; she shot Beth a glance that spoke volumes, one of them being that Beth needed to stop talking. I stifled a laugh before extending both my arms.

"Are you ladies ready for the masquerade?"

* * *

Mrs. Ashbrook's estate had turned into a magical winter wonderland. Someone cleared the driveway of snow, but a layer of white still blanketed everything else, from the hedgerows framing the mansion in evergreen, the Roman statues now topped with white hats, to the roof above the stately home. Candles lined the driveway, illuminating the path to the entrance. Voices mingled with music coming from inside.

The butler opened the door and let us into the warmth. We hadn't been outside for long, but I could tell that Anne and Beth were feeling chilled; their silk gowns offered not much protection from an English winter. But fashion above function, as I'm sure Beth agreed.

The three of us donned our masks. Beth wore a pale blue one that matched her dress, lined with sparkling beads and peacock feathers flaring out above her head. Anne had chosen a more understated creation, rippled silk in a soft lilac above her purple gown. I could have chosen any manner of things to pretend to be today, but I'd chosen a wolf mask. The brown fabric was soft against my face with pointy ears. I'd admired myself in the mirror earlier today, wondering what Austin would think.

I led Anne and Beth further down the foyer, following the sounds of revelry. Couples were standing around in groups, chatting in the hallways leading to the East and West wing. The ballroom was in the west wing, so I made a left turn.

A servant making rounds held out a tray with flutes of champagne towards us. Anne and Beth gladly accepted them. I shook my head and declined. There would be time for alcohol later. The hallway was dimly lit, offering plenty of dark alcoves for masked couples to retreat during the party.

I pulled Anne and Beth along as I spotted a man and woman dressed as a jester and a peacock standing a little closer than propriety required. I didn't mind couples enjoying the freedom that donning masks gave them, but I had two young women with me who knew nothing yet of the world, I hoped. "Perhaps John had been right," I grumbled to myself.

"What were they doing?" Beth asked, confirming my thoughts. Just then, we entered the ballroom, and I was spared the response. Mrs. Ashbrook had outdone herself. The ballroom was resplendent, gold lined wallpaper and frames gleaming with the warm light seeping out of the sconces that lined the walls. Tall standing candelabras were lit in the corners; a wide table decked out in finger foods was set against one side of the room. The floor was filled with masked people dancing and chatting. Laughter rolled from the crowd while an equally dressed up orchestra played from a raised stage.

"Promise me you'll behave," I told Beth, who had the audacity to pretend she had no clue what I was talking about. I turned to Anne. "And you, stay by her side at all times. Don't let some dandy shuffle her off somewhere private." Anne nodded gravely, which I appreciated. "Alright, in that case," I continued, lightening up. "Let's enjoy the masquerade."

I followed Anne and Beth to the table laden with foods. I'd shared a late lunch with Austin earlier today but since we had passed eight o'clock, I was famished. Snatching a cucumber sandwich, I scanned the room.

I hadn't seen Mrs. Ashbrook yet, but as the host, she was sure to be around. Besides, she'd be the one kicking off the games. Rose had managed to bow out of the obligation.

I nibbled at the soft bread and crunchy cucumber. Two men, one with a devil's mask and the other donning rabbits' ears, bee lined straight for Anne and Beth, bowing slightly and extending their hands. Setting aside her champagne,

Anne grasped the devil's hand and was led to the middle of the dance floor; Beth followed with the other. *And so it begins*; I sighed, wishing John was here already to play the watchful older brother.

I straightened, grabbed a glass of champagne, and took a sip of the tart, bubbly alcohol. Taking a turn around the room, while keeping an eye out for Beth and Anne, I spoke to some guests.

I kept my conversation with Mr. Brocklehurst as short as I could, though. He and his wife had decided to join the masquerade, citing it as good fun, though they'd left their daughters behind. I could understand that; once facial features were obscured by masks, the dear people of Westbridge tended to show a bit more of their wild sides. Mr. Brocklehurst was intent to speak to me about what happened at his hunting party.

"I've heard tales of men with similar ailments," he droned on, in a tone that meant to convey sympathy. "Yes. War heart, I've heard it called. All manner of men can be susceptible," he added. "It by no means is a reflection upon your honorable nature." I swallowed my responses, choosing to simply nod as I listened to him. With the airs of a doctor, chest and rather bulging stomach pressed forward, he continued, "Some sea air might do you some good. Blow those bad humors right out of you."

"I'll have to consider that," I replied curtly.

Mrs. Brocklehurst pulled her husband's sleeve. "Darling, this isn't suitable conversation."

"We are simply two men having conversation," Mr.

Brocklehurst said, clapping me on my back. "Isn't that right, Mr. Chambers."

I forced a smile. "Indeed." I pretended to crane my head to someone behind them. "Oh, I believe I see someone I know. It was a pleasure speaking with you," I told Mr. and Mrs. Brocklehurst with a nod of my head then strode toward another corner with purpose. Breathing a sigh of relief, I wound my way through the ever-thickening crowd until I saw that Mr. Brocklehurst had found another person to corner, then I returned to the table of food and picked up a stuffed pastry.

Beth and Anne appeared to be enjoying themselves; they were dancing to the up-tempo songs. Beth's lips turned up into a bright smile, even more sparkling beneath her blue mask. John would have his hands full this coming season in London.

Once I finished the bites of crumbly dough, I decided why not, I liked to dance as well. My eyes fell on a curvy girl, dressed in a pink ruffled gown with a black mask. She stood by herself, clearly watching the other couples. No, not all the other couples, I corrected myself as I continued looking; her eyes were tracking one couple in particular.

I strode over and held out my hand to her. "Would you like this dance?"

The girl's face remained blank. "Why?"

The straight-to-the-point demeanor with an undercurrent of incredulousness made me want to burst out laughing. I had to school my face. Thank heavens for the mask; otherwise, my mirth would have been revealed by the crinkling of me eyes.

"Why what? Why I'd ask you to dance?" I said. "Well, for

one, I quite like dancing and, two, you don't seem to have a partner yet."

Her brow raised above the mask. "I don't want a suitor." She was so bold; I didn't know who she was, but I liked her. I imagined she'd be a good and funny friend to have.

"I promise you, I have no intent to become your suitor. I simply like to dance, and you are unaccompanied."

"You aren't? And you do?" she said, taken aback.

"I do," I nodded.

"Oh."

"So? Will you do me the honor?"

"Umm, I suppose." She took my hand, joining me and the other couples, ready for the quadrille. Beth and Anne nodded at me as we all started dancing in circles, skipping towards and away from one another. The girl smiled as she was dancing about the room.

When the song was over and I deposited her back at the edge of the room, she asked, "What are you supposed to be?"

"You can't tell?"

She shook her head. "No, though I think it looks like some kind of animal."

"A wolf," I supplied.

The girl paused for a moment. "I don't think that suits you. I've met plenty of wolves; you don't appear to be one of them."

"I'll take that as a compliment."

"It is," she smiled then.

Before I left her, I asked, "Can I ask who I had the pleasure of dancing with?"

She looked to the floor before answering. "You can call me Willa."

"Thank you for the dance, Ms. Willa."

Walking away, I found a server and grabbed another flute of champagne. My eyes moved to the hallway; Mrs. Ashbrook was sliding through clusters of guests as she strode into the ballroom. She stopped here and there to speak with masked men and women. I returned my gaze to the dance floor; Anne and Beth had changed dance partners. They clearly were having the time of their lives. I wondered where John, Rose, and Austin were. Judging by Mrs. Ashbrook's advance towards the musicians, the games would be starting soon.

I drained my glass, bubbles tickling my throat, and handed it to another server. Mrs. Ashbrook reached the raised stage and climbed the small steps until she reached the center. The surrounding musicians paused their playing. She waited for her captive audience to glance up and focus on their hostess.

With bated breath, the crowd watched Mrs. Ashbrook. I glanced back and saw Rose and John enter the room. Then I spied Austin behind them, because it could only be Austin. I'd recognize his figure anywhere. Though nothing could have prepared me for the way he looked tonight. He was danger-ously handsome in his tailored suit, the mask sculpted to his face, highlighting his expressive eyes. He noticed me and cocked his head in acknowledgment. I had to force myself to look away and return my attention to Mrs. Ashbrook.

"Thank you all for joining me at my masquerade," the stately older woman said, her powerful voice echoing through the room. All the guests had entered the ballroom, waiting

for her announcement. "I know what you have all been waiting for. Finally, now that we all have had a chance to dance
and eat, it is time to start the games."

24

Hunter and Prey

It was time for the games to start. Mrs. Ashbrook held up a coin, though I was too far away to see the stamp on it.

"Tonight, we are playing the hunter and the prey. One of you shall play the hunter," she said, her eyes gliding across the crowd. "And one of you shall receive this coin; they will be the prey." A man howled at Mrs. Ashbrook's remark, much to the amusement of the other guests. Mrs. Ashbrook waited for the crowd to quiet once more. Then she continued, "The goal of the game is for everyone in this room to hide and not be found. If and when the hunter captures the prey, the game will be over."

A group of girls giggled when one of the men spoke up and said, "I know where'd I go if I was the hunter."

"Who will be the hunter?" a woman near the front of the stage said.

Mrs. Ashbrook seemed to think, her eyes slowly skipping

from guest to guest. I nodded when her eyes made contact with mine before moving on to the next. She smiled.

"I have the perfect hunter in mind. Mrs. Easton, my dear grandniece, is hosting a friend from America. How about we give him the role of honor?" she asked the crowd. Some muttered, disappointed they didn't get chosen, but most clapped. Mrs. Ashbrook pointed at Austin. "Come on up, Mr. Miller," she said. Rose gave him a little push, and he cut through the crowd, taking his spot beside Mrs. Ashbrook.

The older woman turned towards Austin and grasped his arm. "Shortly, I will have you leave this room while I choose the person playing the role of the prey. Once they have been chosen, you'll return and wait for five minutes while everyone finds their hiding place."

Austin nodded. Mrs. Ashbrook let go of his arm and a server stepped up, ushering Austin away from the room.

"Now, everyone, close your eyes while I move amongst you," Mrs. Ashbrook said, her voice lowered. "And don't forget to keep quiet if you receive the coin."

As one, the guests closed their eyes. I could hear the heavy swishing of skirts and steps along the ballroom floor as Mrs. Ashbrook wound and curved her way through clusters of people. Feet shuffled and some coughed quietly, but other than that, the room was silent. Everyone eagerly awaited the brush of their hostess' hand, the drop of a coin in the palms of their hand.

Judging by the footsteps, the stately woman had repeated many circles. Surely, to confuse the guest, to keep them guessing. Then, the steps neared and her skirts brush past me. She continued another circle before coming closer again, until she stopped in front of me. Her gloved hands grasped my fingers, opening them up, and pressing the coin into them. She continued moving while I slipped the coin into my pocket.

A few more rounds across the floor later, she returned to the stage. "You may all open your eyes," she said. I blinked a few times, returning my gaze to Mrs. Ashbrook, as did the others. Many guests were craning their heads, hoping to guess which of them played the prey.

The server returned with Austin by his side. Mrs. Ashbrook motioned her hand for him to join her. She addressed the crowd once more. "You shall have five minutes to find a hiding spot; those found can return to the ballroom. My entire home is open for hiding, so do your best. Happy hunting!"

A few girls squealed as they hurried out of the ballroom, trailed by their beaus. The other guests followed, filing out into the hallway. A few groups headed towards the east wing, probably to hide amongst the artwork in Mrs. Ashbrook's gallery. Others headed towards the servant quarters, which wasn't a bad idea. There would be plenty of pantries and other nooks and crannies to choose from.

A few guests stayed close to the ballroom, choosing one of the adjacent rooms or even curtained alcoves in the hallway. They probably figured that Austin, the hunter, would assume the guests would find a hiding spot as far away from the ballroom as possible.

Rose and John had shot each other amused glances and veered off into a utility closet. Beth and Anne had stuck together, I saw them slip behind a curtained window. I headed towards the foyer, then climbed the stairs to the second floor.

More guests followed me, some racing past me to hide in the guest rooms, giggling as they did so with their companions hot on their tails. By the time Austin found them, I had no doubt they'd be missing some items of clothing.

I headed down the corridor, finding the upstairs library to the left. I sighed when I entered; no one else had taken up hiding there, yet. Soft moonlight cast across the oak furniture and bookcases lining the walls.

I didn't think Mrs. Ashbrook visited this room often. The library was clearly clean, no dust to be found, but it felt un-used, the books too uniformly lined to be pulled out and read. Vacant, they seemed to call. My eyes shot to the large bay window, the thinner cream curtains and thicker navy outer drapes framing the sides of the wide windowsill and glass.

I pulled the curtains close and slipped behind them, seat-ing myself on the sill. Surely, the five minutes had already passed, and Austin had started the hunt. I remained silent, my thoughts veering to that strange man, the time-traveler. To him comforting me during my nightmares, nestling up with me at the inn, and to the kiss he gave me underneath the mistletoe.

Between Christmas and now, we didn't speak much about anything serious. I think we both pretended that nothing happened. Or, at least, I had. I continued my riding lessons with Austin, but whenever our conversation skirted some-thing more personal, we'd quieted, sentences trailing, until we separated. I'd been longing to talk to him, to say anything more. But I hadn't been able to work up the courage.

I leaned my head against the window frame, glancing

out across the snow-covered gardens. I should've taken some champagne with me.

I wasn't sure how long it had been when I heard the door creak. Holding my breath, I drew in my legs even more. It could be one of the guests trying to find a new hiding spot or...Austin.

Steps headed straight for me, then with a swift jerk, the curtains pulled aside, revealing me in front of the window. Austin stood there, a smirk playing on his lips, his eyes bright beneath the glossy black mask.

"I found you."

"I was under the presumption you were looking for the coin. Who's to say that it is in my possession?" I cocked my head at Austin, teasing him. "Perhaps some other lady has it in her pocket."

"Perhaps I should check," he retorted, reaching out his hand. He squeezed my knee before his fingers slid up my thigh until they touched the small round protrusion in my pocket. The sensation sent a shiver down my spine. Austin grinned. "Look what we have here."

"Congratulations," I muttered as I stood, his face mere inches from mine. I was planning to hand him the coin but, before I could, he reached out to me. His hand cupping my cheek.

"Will, you look." He bit his lip. "I couldn't take my eyes off you tonight. I nearly groaned when Mrs. Ashbrook chose me as the hunter because it meant I couldn't stay near you." His fingers skimmed my jaw. "You can stop me," he said, drawing me closer. "But I've been meaning to do this for a while." His eyes raked across my face, looking for an answer.

My breath hitched. All thoughts and words stopped, except for one. "Yes."

Austin jerked forward pressing me against the curtains, crushing his lips against mine. He tasted like dark chocolate with a hint of tartness. His hand moved up along my jawbone until he fisted my hair. My mouth opened and our tongues met, tasting and teasing. Blood rushed through my body like liquid heat. I could scarcely believe this was happening. My arms enveloped Austin, pulling him flush against my chest. Touching him, kissing him, was like heaven. Austin moved trailing kisses along my jaw and neck, teasing the lobe of my ear. The scent of him was intoxicating.

"Austin," I breathed.

"Yes?" He stopped what he was doing to glance at me.

"Don't stop." A deep chuckle escaped his throat before he claimed my mouth once more.

Much too soon, he pulled away, gazing into my eyes. My lips tingled from the lack of pressure. Austin slid his fingers along my cheek, trailing the scar that sliced along the side of my face. I wanted to see all of him, so I reached out and pulled off the mask he was wearing.

I swallowed. "How long have you wanted to do this?"

Austin's eyes burned. "Maybe since you stepped out of the coach that first day or when I shared my candy bar with you."

"That long?" I hadn't realized. Austin pulled me down with him onto the windowsill.

"I knew I shouldn't. That it isn't fair to you. But I can't help being drawn to you. I—"

I silenced him. "I didn't want to admit it either. At first, not to myself, and then I didn't want to jeopardize our friendship." I hung my head for a moment before taking his hand. "I don't deserve you. You are an amazing person, Austin. You are so gentle and caring; all you do is take care of others, of me. I can tell by your voice every time you speak about your sister."

Austin's face turned steely, eyes burning. "Don't ever say you don't deserve me. I don't know how much time we'll get together, but any person would be lucky to be with you, to hold you and care for you. You deserve love."

I clutched his hand tighter and pressed another kiss to his lips. "Let's not speak about futures we may or may not have. We are both here and now, and I want to make the most of it."

Austin's brow quirked up. "I am the hunter and I did catch my prey." He nibbled at my throat.

I laughed. "That reminds me, did you catch any other players, or did you come straight here?"

Austin's tongue trailed a line down to my collarbone. He fluttered a soft kiss on my skin before answering. "I found some. There were a few couples hiding in the alcoves. I caught John and Rose in the utility closet, though I had to close the door pretty quickly."

"It's the masquerade," I said, laughing.

Austin nodded. "I can't say I blame them. Finding you here alone, I want to do all kinds of naughty things." He laughed. "I think it's the masks."

"Definitely the masks." I'd never seen this side of Austin. His assertiveness blew me away. I hadn't known it was possible to be this enamored with a person. Austin was both flawed and perfect at the same time. He was human. He was everything. My breath hitched when his hand slid into my pants pocket. His fingers slipped around the coin that Mrs. Ashbrook had given me. It was a good thing he withdrew his hand, clutching the coin, because every part of me burned for him.

"How'd you know?"

"Where it was?" Austin finished, flipping the coin. "I never wanted to find the coin, I was looking for you."

"Oh."

Austin's grin lit up the room. "I wish we had more time. But we should probably return to the ballroom. Otherwise, I'm worried someone might come and look for me instead. He stood and held out his hand. I grasped his palm. "And I need time to do what I want to do to you."

Fire heated my cheeks. "If you do, I may not let go again," I told him.

His eyes met mine. "I hope so."

Together, we returned to the main ballroom, our kiss a delicious secret between us while we enjoyed the rest of the evening at Mrs. Ashbrook's masquerade, dancing and drinking until we returned to Hawthorne in the late hours of the night.

25

Ice Skates

My second gift for Austin had finally arrived with the post. And it was right in time for the weather. The pond had frozen over solid these past two weeks, with temperatures dropping well below zero. I was excited to give my present to him. Since the masquerade, we'd spent as much time together as possible. I stored the gift in the coat closet and went to find Austin. I found him in the dining room eating a piece of toast.

"Good morning," he said as he saw me enter the room.

"Did you sleep well?" I asked.

Austin yawned. "I did, but I'm still tired apparently." He grabbed a slice of buttered toast from a serving plate and transferred it to a smaller plate. "Here, have some breakfast." He placed the plate of toast in front of the open chair beside him.

John, Rose, and Beth had left this morning. They were

going to be gone for a few days to browse for new furniture for the school. Of course, Beth had opted to come with. She wouldn't pass up an opportunity to go shopping. It was strange being at Hawthorne while they were gone. But it meant I should grasp every opportunity to spend time with Austin without company.

I took my seat beside Austin and took a bite of bread.

"Do you want some tea? Mrs. Avery brought me some mint tea before returning to the kitchen. It's very good."

"I would like some," I said pleasantly. Austin reached for the teapot and poured me a cup. "Thank you," I said as I accepted the tea.

"You're welcome," Austin said. He finished the last bite of his toast and followed it with his tea to swallow away the crumbs.

"So, there was something I wanted to show you," I said.

"Yeah, what's that?"

"Well, if you are finished with breakfast, perhaps you can follow me?"

"Now I am intrigued," Austin said. He grinned at me and stood from his chair.

"It has to do with the weather," I said as we left the dining room and followed the hallway into the foyer.

Austin smirked. "You've built a snowman?"

"No," I laughed. "Is that what you think I was doing this morning?"

"Maybe." Austin shrugged, his eyes twinkling. "If building snowmen is something you like doing."

I gave him a small tap and laughed. "I thought perhaps we could go ice skating."

"I've never skated before," Austin said, hesitantly. "Besides, don't you need skates for that. I don't have any, and I doubt we can rent them around here." Austin looked apologetic, for what it was worth. But I hoped I hadn't made a mistake. I wanted him to enjoy his gift.

"You really have never skated before?" I joked.

"No, never."

"Is there no snow where you grew up? I believe Rose said that where she grew up it was almost always warm, although I believe she used the words scalding."

"Oh, it definitely gets cold where I'm from," Austin emphasized. "I just never went ice skating. I was too young before my family..." he swallowed. "And when I got placed into foster care, it wasn't something my foster family could afford. I guess I could have gone when I was on my own as an adult, but I never did."

"It's never too late to try." Hidden in the closet, I had the pair of skates wrapped and ready for him. "Wait right here," I said, retrieving my gift. Austin looked confused when I grabbed his hand and handed him the package. "This is for you. Open it."

He gently accepted the package and trailed his finger along the string that held the brown paper in place.

"You got this for me?"

I nodded. "I don't see anyone else here."

Austin neatly untied the string and folded the paper as he revealed the brand-new skates. He was so careful and considerate, the opposite of me. I would have ripped the paper up to reveal my gift.

"You shouldn't have. I already got the cuff links."

"I wanted to."

Austin bit his lip. "Thank you. I can't wait to try them out."

I pulled a scarf from the coat hanger and threw it around my neck. "Let's go now."

"Are you sure?" He laughed. "Do you even have ice skates."

"Of course, I couldn't buy you a pair without getting myself some." I grabbed another set of skates from the closet.

"Okay, let's go." Austin pulled on a coat. I grabbed another scarf, a dark gray knitted one, and looped the fabric around Austin's neck, pulling him in for a kiss. His hand brushed mine as he helped me knot it. I let go of the soft knit scarf and shrugged on my own coat. I thrust a pair of gloves at Austin before leaving the warmth of the foyer behind.

Frost nipped at our noses. Winter had well and truly arrived to England. White fluff blanketed everything in sight; it felt like being in a snow globe. Soft flurries trailed their way from the skies to add to the piles on the ground. I glanced back at Austin who was following me, his cheeks a bright pink.

"I wish I had a winter hat," he shouted at me as he trudged through the snow.

"Some activity will warm us up," I yelled back. "And nothing is better than drinking some hot chocolate after having been outside in the snow. I'm sure Mrs. Avery will be so kind to prepare us some when we return."

"I'll hold you to that."

We walked to the edge of the pond. Icicles hung from the roof of the new school building. Rose would still have her hands full dressing up the inside but at least the exterior stood firm. I pulled off one of my shoes and tried to balance on one leg while trying to stick my foot into one of the skates. I almost fell when Austin threw his arm around me.

"Here, lean on me."

"Thank you. I promise you can use me for balance as well."

Once we both wore our ice skates, I stepped on to the clear icy surface. With just a few swipes of my feet, I skated to the middle of the pond. I braked and turned to watch Austin, his movements hesitant. Carefully, he took choppy steps that made him wave his hands around to stay up right.

"How are you so good at this?" he asked, accusingly. His brows furrowed.

"I've had practice." I grinned and skated towards him. "Take my hands." I extended my hands, palms up. Austin grabbed them firmly. "Now, keep your feet on the ice." He glanced up at me with his big green eyes. They had a trace of fear in them before they turned determined.

"Okay, I'm ready."

"Now, I want you to slide your feet forward, one at a time." Austin slowly moved his right leg forward while he squeezed my hand. "And the other one," I encouraged.

"I'm trying," he shot out as he shakily moved his left leg forward. "You make skating seem much easier than it actually is." He let go of one of my hands, but then immediately reconsidered when he lurched backwards.

"Careful." I held on to him and pulled him with me while I skated backwards. "I'm sure you'll get the hang of it." I moved slowly to let Austin get used to the ice and the weight of the skates. The surrounding light was getting darker, more snow falling around us. The sky turned a deep gray, not a hint of blue anywhere. Austin tried some more strides.

"I think I'm getting the hang of it," he said, snowflakes sticking to his eyelashes. He let out an uncharacteristically light giggle as he skated towards me. I moved out of his way, so he could keep going.

"You are doing great." Austin held out his arms as he slid across the ice in a straight line.

"Look at me," he said, glancing back at me. His face was bright. Then his skate hit an uneven patch and he stumbled. "Oh," he grunted as he landed on his behind. I hurried towards Austin.

"Are you hurt?"

"My pride a little, perhaps." He rubbed his back and let out a loud snicker. I grabbed Austin's wrist and pulled him back to standing. Then I held him by his arms to steady him while he found his footing. His face was so close to mine; his hot breath warmed my chilled skin.

While skating, the snow started to fall thicker and faster, covering us and the ice in a fresh layer of white. I peered around us and the rapidly growing snow.

"The snow is really coming down," I said.

"We should probably go, return to the house."

The wind picked up, lashing at our faces. I hadn't anticipated a snowstorm, but now that the weather was changing, I hesitated to make the walk back to Hawthorne. The imprints of our feet when we arrived had long since disappeared. Austin shuddered beneath my hands.

"It might be safer to wait out the storm," I said, raising my voice, so I could be heard over the howling wind.

"Where?"

"Follow me," I said, while I held on to his coat with my

right hand. I cupped my left hand above my eyes to shield them from the elements. I managed to find our shoes but didn't risk taking the time to exchange them for our skates.

We dragged ourselves through the rapidly growing layer of snow, blades sinking deep with every step we took. Once we reached the newly erected schoolhouse, I had to thrust myself repeatedly against the door, until we burst through.

I wobbled around on the blades of my ice skates. They were certainly not meant for wood floors. I untied them as quickly as I could and threw them to the side. After dumping out the snow, I pulled on my regular shoes. Austin did the same beside me. Shivering, I brushed the snow from my hair and off the shoulders of my woolen coat.

"Can you give me a hand," I asked Austin, once he was planted firm in his regular footwear. He added his strength to mine and together we pushed the door closed again.

"It is freezing!" Austin exclaimed. He pulled the collar on his coat up higher, but all that did was slide some cold snow into his shirt. There wasn't much in the school building. Rose was still arranging the furniture. But there was a fireplace, a necessity during English Autumns and Winters, and there was a stack of wood already gathered in a bin. "How long do you think we'll be stuck here?" Austin peeked out the window.

"I'm not sure. By the looks of it, we may very well be here a while. Hopefully only a few hours, but I wouldn't be surprised if it ended up being all night." I moved to the bin with logs and stacked a few in the fireplace. "Don't worry, I'll start a fire. We won't perish from hypothermia."

Austin's eyebrow twitched. "That's a relief. We won't die of the cold; we'll just be starving."

238 - HARMKE BUURSMA

"Well, I can't help with food, but I can offer you a cigarette, if you'd like." I smiled ruefully. I pulled off my kid gloves and stuffed them in my coat pocket. From my inner pocket, I retrieved my tinder box. With a few strikes of the steel against the flint, I managed to light the char cloth. "Can you hold this for a moment?" I said as I handed Austin the flint box. Using one the of the matches, I transferred the fire from the tinder box to some kindling in the fireplace. "You can close the box now. We might need it again later." Austin closed the metal top, extinguishing the flame.

"I've never seen something like this before," he said, turning the tinder box over in his hands. "It's pretty cool."

"I guess the metal would be cold to the touch in this weather," I replied, while fanning the flames until they licked the larger logs. Once I was sure the flames had taken root, I stood.

"No, that's not what I meant. In my time, when we say cool, it means something like interesting or fun." He shook his head. "Being here has been such a strange experience."

"Oh." I walked over to the wall and leaned against the windowsill. The idea of him being from the future always baffled me. Whenever he used strange words and phrases, it reminded me how different our lives were.

Austin stepped towards me. "I don't mean it in a bad way."

"No, I didn't presume."

"It's just that I'm not from here. Everything is new to me. You grew up in this time, while I have to learn everything from scratch."

We had grown closer, but inevitably, I was reminded that

he didn't belong here. That he would leave. I caught Austin's gaze. "You must resent being sent here."

He frowned and hesitated. "No, I don't resent it at all. I'm just," he trailed off.

"You didn't want to be here," I finished.

"William," he said, sighing. He grabbed my hand. "I am so grateful to John and Rose for letting me stay with them." He paused, staring up in to my eyes. "And... You. I would never in my wildest dreams have imagined meeting someone like you. You made this whole strange experience a million times better. I loved what you tried to do for me today. The ice skates were a great gift. But eventually, I'm going to go home. I don't know how or when yet, but I can't stay here. You must see that as well."

I nodded.

"I know you've been avoiding the topic, but we should talk about the masquerade."

"You don't have to say. I understand." I averted my gaze. I was the one who told Austin we shouldn't think about the future.

"No, I don't think you do." His gloved thumb caressed the side of my palm. "Please look at me," Austin said, his voice soft and questioning. I stared into his beautiful green eyes. "That night was special. You are special," he emphasized. "I've loved every minute we've spent together since."

His words lit up my skin.

"But I don't want to start something just to hurt you. That wouldn't be fair to you. If I were from here, if I had all the time in the world, we could have seen where this would lead.

But I can't do that to you when I know that when the time comes, I'll return home."

Heartache blossomed in my chest, a pain all too familiar. But one thing I had learned from James' loss was that no one knew how much time they had. And love or even its starting branches were too important and precious to waste.

"I know our time together will be short," I said, drawing Austin closer to me. "Which means we should make every moment count while we can."

"I don't want to hurt you."

"Then don't. You don't have to borrow trouble from the future. As far as I can see it, right now, we are stuck in this room with no other place to be or other things to do besides keep each other company. And I," I said, lifting my palm to cup his cheek, "like your company."

Austin pressed forward and crushed his lips against mine. He tasted like the mint tea we had for breakfast. The snowflakes in his hair melted, leaving it shiny and wet as I raked my fingers through it.

"We should take some of these clothes off," he said as he came up for air. I grinned against his mouth.

"I think so too." At that moment, blocked in by the snow, it felt like the universe was giving us our own private place to be undisturbed. It wasn't what I'd foreseen or even imagined when I gave Austin the skates, but I sure was grateful. Austin unbuttoned my coat and peeled the layer back while I pulled off his scarf.

"We should get closer to the fire," I breathed in between our kisses. Austin nodded while I helped him shrug out of his coat. I didn't want to break the spell I was under. Being so close to Austin was intoxicating. But I wanted us to be comfortable while we were here. "Just a moment," I said as I pulled back from his embrace. I clutched his fingers and kissed the top of his hand.

Austin smiled widely. "You are such a gentleman. I could get used to that. But you'd better hurry."

"I'll do my best." I splayed our coats in front of the fireplace, the embers spitting up as the flames licked the dry wood. The heat from the fire warmed my skin and left it pleasantly tingling. I pulled Austin down to the makeshift bed, angling my head to taste his skin. Something inside me ignited, as my hands scoured the sleek planes of his chest. Austin moved against me, hungry for more.

After, when he laid nestled into my arms, I asked him, "What is it like in your time?"

"For people like us?" he asked.

I nodded, brushing my lips against his temple.

He paused, briefly. "There are still plenty of hateful people -my foster family couldn't accept me for who I was."

"Is that why you moved out and why your sister lives with you?"

"It is. My foster family kicked me out." Austin swallowed. "I'm sad about losing them but grateful that I still have the support of my sister. However, overall, my time is a lot more open and accepting. You are free to be who you are, love whomever you want. We could walk down the street holding hands without worrying about what anyone would think."

"That sounds wonderful," I breathed. "I can understand why you'd want to return."

Austin kissed me. "How about we talk about the future some other time. For now, let's just snuggle."

Outside, the wind howled and snow whipped against the windows and boards. I hardly even noticed what happened around me with Austin's body pressed against my own.

26

Strangers at the Door

Every moment I spent with Austin felt like a gift. We gravitated towards each other, craving each other's touch. Our hands met as we passed in the hall; we stole kisses when we were alone, and he nestled into me when we spent time in the stables. The one thing I regretted was not being able to take him out for another ride, the snow still too deep for the horses.

Late at night, when I was alone, it was a different story. Then, my mind raced as questions bombarded me. How long could what we have last? When would he leave? Did he have to leave? Was it fair to Austin? What if he never left?

I pushed the questions away whenever possible. For some reason, I had been given a chance for momentary happiness, and I was going to grasp it with both hands. And if it crashes and burns, leaving me wrecked in the process, so be it. I wanted Austin for however long he wanted me.

It was a lazy day; John, Rose, and Beth were already gathered in the drawing room for tea time. I found my way to one of the chairs, sinking in and crossing my legs.

"What are you making now?" I asked Beth. Her blonde hair was loose and trailing forward over her shoulder. She looked up from the stretched frame in her hands, holding a white cloth between the wood.

"I'm stitching lavender decorations on a napkin," she said, flipping her handiwork. "See. The pattern is almost finished."

"Nearly the real thing," I praised as Mrs. Avery entered with the tea. Austin followed the housekeeper in and helped her place it on the table. Then he took a seat beside Beth.

"I can't believe it's a new year already," Rose said, scratching behind her ear. "Soon, we'll have to prepare to go to London for Beth's season." She smiled in disbelief. "Season...listen to me, as if I've always lived in this time."

John chuckled. "Don't fret, you're still my wife from the future."

Rose shook her head. "It's crazy sometimes how normal it feels. This. Us. To think that a year ago, I was back home, going to work, driving a car." She paused briefly, glancing at her husband. "I wouldn't trade you and our life together for the world. Though, I do miss fast food, sometimes." She let out a small sigh. "What I wouldn't do for a plain old burger and fries."

Austin nodded. "I miss take-out Chinese food and going to the grocery store at night to pick up something precooked, all the different flavors of ice-cream, stopping at Sonic for drinks and slushies at the start of a road trip." Austin ticked each item off on his fingers.

Mrs. Avery finished pouring our tea and returned to the kitchen.

"I forgot about Sonic," Rose told Austin. "I do miss car rides. An ice-cold drink in your hand, AC blasting straight in your face, singing along to the radio." Her eyes moved from John, to Beth, to me. "Sometimes, I wish you all could've experienced a bit of my life too."

"At least we have you to tell us about it," John said. He bent forward, lifted a cup of tea and handed it to Rose. She blew him a kiss as she accepted it.

Beth set aside her embroidery piece and took a sip of the hot drink. "I'm excited to visit the London modistes; Rose said we'd get some special outfits designed— lady trousers. Mind, only for when we are at Hawthorne."

Rose grinned. "I need something to wear beside dresses."

Lady trousers, that was so like Rose. "I wonder what the dressmakers in London will say about that," I told Rose. "You might cause a scandal."

John shrugged his shoulders and kept his face blank. "You know my wife. If someone somewhere isn't shocked by what she's doing, she's done it wrong."

Rose raised a brow and glared at her husband. "Is that so?"

John nodded. "And I wouldn't want it any other way."

I laughed. "To modern apparel and—"

Heavy knocking on the front door interrupted what I was about to say.

Rising out of his chair, John muttered, "I wonder who that is." I motioned to stand as well, but John waved me off. "Please, stay seated. I'll find out who it is and return shortly."

I returned to my tea, finishing the last dregs. Austin did the same across from me.

In the distance, the heavy front door opened with a creak that always remained, despite Hugh oiling the hinges often. Softly, I could make out John's voice.

"What's the matter?" I believe he said.

Louder, a booming voice answered. "We're here for William Raphe Chambers and an Austin Miller; they are said to be guests here?"

"By whom?" John's voice raised.

"I'm afraid I can't disclose that. Now, sir, if you can let me pass."

I didn't hear John's answer, so I took it that the constable, for that surely had to be who was at the door, was now headed our way.

I jumped out of my chair. "Hide," I hissed at Austin. His eyes grew large, stumbling as he stood.

"Where?" He looked around for a spot that would fit him.

Rose, remaining level-headed, pointed at the settee. "If you lay flat, you can fit under there."

Austin hesitated. "I'm not so sure."

"Try," Rose ordered. "And Beth, you join me on the settee. Grab your embroidery piece and your other fabrics and lay them down next to you, draping them to cover the gap between the floor and the start of the couch."

Austin lowered himself to the floor, crawling underneath the padded love seat. "But... What about you?" he whispered.

I shook my head. "Don't worry about me."

We had only moments now; John and the constable were closing in. I helped Rose push in two side tables, hiding the sides of the settee. Then she planted herself firmly on the seat, her and Beth's feet obscuring Austin's body. I returned to my own seat, slipping my face into a mask of unconcerned pleasantry. I almost broke out of it when I caught sight of Austin's empty teacup. I managed to snatch and hide it underneath a pillow right before the constable entered.

The constable, a barrel-chested man with a small mustache, immediately homed in on me.

John stepped next to him. "Can you tell me what's going on?"

Without taking his eyes off me, the man answered, "I'm not at liberty to say." His tone curt. "Are you the man known as William Raphe Chambers?" he questioned me.

"I am." I did my best to remain calm and keep an unaffected tone, though I felt like I was failing. The hair at the back of my neck raised; I wanted to flee. A constable at the door never meant good news. I could guess at why the constable wanted Austin and myself. But how had the news spread? Had we not been careful enough during the masquerade? Had there been someone else at the pond?

No, surely not. The snowstorm had been too heavy. Even if anyone had been outside, they wouldn't have been able to see a thing. Then who? I didn't get a chance to continue my train of thought because the constable gripped my arm and pulled me out of my chair. At least it was only me. I hoped Austin would remain hidden.

"Hands behind your back," he ordered, much to Rose's discontent.

"Now wait a minute," she started.

"Just doing my job, Mrs.," he said as he slipped heavy iron

handcuffs around my wrists and tightened them, the metal biting into my skin.

John stepped around. "Can't we discuss this like civilized people?"

The constable ignored him. "I was told there were two guests. Where is Mr. Austin Miller?"

John swallowed. "He's left already."

The constable whistled. "Is that so?" He turned his eye on Rose. "Do you agree, Mrs. Easton?"

Rose nodded. "Yes, he left for London a few days ago. From there, he was going to travel south and take the ferry to France."

"Does one often travel abroad during winter?" the constable said to Rose. Beth remained stone faced.

"Not usually. But he was in a rush to meet other acquaintances of ours."

"What fortunate timing," the constable said, staring down Rose. "Who are these acquaintances in France?"

"You can stop questioning my wife," John cut in. "We haven't done anything wrong."

"That remains to be seen," the constable intoned. "I'll have to search your home of course."

"Why? We've told you that Mr. Miller isn't here." John frowned, folding his arms.

"I'm afraid I can't take your word for it," the constable said, sounding not a bit sorry. He dragged me into the hallway, the iron cuffs cold against my skin. Already, the weight of them bruised my wrists.

Please, let Austin remain hidden, I prayed. Hopefully catching me would prove enough of a distraction. It's why I didn't even bother trying to hide. First, there wasn't any space; I was bigger than Austin and the drawing room only had limited hiding spots. Second, perhaps if I let myself be caught, pretending to not know what was coming, the constable wouldn't search as thoroughly.

I hoped my assumptions were right. I kept catching my breath as the constable dragged me through every room at Hawthorne, from the guest rooms and private chambers to the servants' quarter and even John's hot house. Of course, the constable returned from all those locations empty-handed. All the while, I worried that he'd decide to take a closer look at the drawing room.

Pushing me in front of him, he led us back to the hallway where John stood half-blocking the doorway into the drawing room. I worried that John's stance would be suspicious. Thankfully, however, the constable didn't seem to notice the tightness in John's jaw or the way he angled his body, hiding his wife and sister as they perched stiffly on the settee.

"It seems you've spoken the truth," the constable said. "Mr. Miller isn't here."

"I told you." John uncrossed his arms and stepped into the hallway. "The search was a waste of time."

I shot John a pointed look, hoping he'd understand the meaning and tone his hostility down.

"What now?" John asked.

"I'm taking the prisoner to our jail. There, he'll await his sentence. Depending on the courts, he could either be tried in our own parish or he may get diverted to the county jail to be sentenced in court."

"Tried for what?" John asked again.

The constable sighed, annoyed. "As I've said before, I'm not at liberty to say, sir."

John frowned. "Then who can I speak with? Who can clear this up?"

"That would be the court, sir. Now, if you'll show me out, it is high time I return with the prisoner." Worry etched on John's face as he led the constable and myself to the front door.

"Do send word if Mr. Miller returns," the constable told John as he pushed me out the door.

Walking down the front steps and across the gravel, he led me to an enclosed carriage made of polished black wood with bars on the windows. Shoving me inside, he closed and locked the door behind me. I groaned as I righted myself. The bonds rubbed my tender skin.

Sitting askew on the small hard bench, I wondered what was going to happen to me. If I was lucky, I'd end up on the pillory for a few days. *Lucky*, I snorted as the carriage started forward with a jolt. I could hardly call being put on display at the pillory lucky. Ridiculed by every passer-by, beaten, and thrown rotten food at. No, that wouldn't be lucky. But it would be better than the alternative. The alternative being...

No. I couldn't think like that. Sure, I was caught, but Austin remained hidden. And I trusted John with my life. I had faith that he would try everything in his power to get me out of this.

But I couldn't help that my mind returned to the stories I'd been told at The Waddling Duck. Men wasting away at the Tower of London or being sentenced to hang without a chance to defend themselves. Even the pillory sometimes had an everlasting ending when a poor soul got stoned to death by drunk men.

I didn't know what awaited me after today. At least I could rest easy that Austin was safe. John and Rose would make sure of that. Though, for the first time, I hoped that witch would return and whisk him away to his own time.

27

Kingswood County Jail

I was cold and uncomfortable, sitting in a small cell with my back leaned against the rough stone wall. The only source of light was the small amount of sun that shone through a high, barred window. The only kindness the constable had shown was when he threw an itchy, patched-up blanket into the cell. I'd scrambled forward, snatching it up and throwing it around my shoulders. My teeth were shattering so loudly that I didn't even mind that the blanket reeked like stale liquor, unwashed body odor, and a touch of other unmentionable things.

The skin on my wrist stung, rubbed raw by the cuffs. I didn't really want to ruin my clothing but the shoot of pain I felt every time I moved my arms told me I needed to do something. I raised my hands, until the edge of my sleeve rested against my lips. I bit into the shirt and ripped and tore until I had a loose piece of fabric. Opening my mouth, I let the torn piece of cloth fall into my lap. Then I repeated the same with my other sleeve.

Finally, I had two pieces of fabric I could use as a buffer between the cold iron and my raw skin, though, the tugging had hurt my wrists even more. I wriggled my fingers, using the little space I had to move to tuck the cloth between the metal and my skin. I let out a pained breath. At least this should protect them for a while.

I wondered if and when I'd be able to speak to John. By my count, I'd been here nearly a full day. The constable deposited me into the cell without preamble the previous day. I'd asked what I was accused of, but he'd told me nothing. He'd brusquely walked off, only to return a few hours later with water, some kind of stew, and a stale piece of bread. My stomach gnawed. I hadn't had a bite to eat since. Pulling up the scratchy blanket, I tucked my knees in more to preserve my body heat.

I dozed off a few times when eventually, I heard a door open. Light filtered in through the open doorway as the constable strode towards me. He unlocked the cell door and bending over, set a fresh bowl of slop on the dirty floor.

"Is there any news?" I asked. "What's going to happen to me?"

The constable picked up yesterday's bowl. "You're being transferred to the county jail in the morning."

"Has John—Mr. Easton— asked about me? When can I see him?"

Shoving the fresh bowl closer to me, the constable said, "He hasn't reached out. Why? Was he part of your little group?" The sneer on his face made it clear what he thought of me.

"Little group?"

"Mollies," the constable answered, disgust dripping off every syllable. I remained silent; if I wanted a chance to defend myself in court, I couldn't react. I had to hope John would figure out a plan.

Playing dumb, I picked up the bowl of stew and started eating. The constable huffed and re-locked the cell, leaving me by myself once again.

* * *

The next morning, I was roughly hauled out of the cell, my eyes blinking at the sudden brightness.

"Time for the transfer to the county jail," the constable said, roughly pushing me ahead of himself.

"And then?" I questioned, glancing around. A different carriage was waiting outside, two guards from the county jail already positioned at the driver's seat.

"You'll wait to say your peace in court."

"When will that be?" I flinched as the cuffs rubbed my raw skin.

The constable jerked open the carriage door. "You are asking a lot of questions. You'll find out at Kingswood." His hand pressed down on my head to lower it as he led me into the prison wagon, then he locked the door behind me.

Would John show up at the county jail? Would I have a chance to speak with him? I hated that I got my friend involved in this. Everyone at Hawthorne had to be worried about me. I missed Austin. However, I was glad he wasn't here to witness this—me.

It was much of the same once we reached Kingswood County jail. I was pulled out of the police wagon and dragged up the steps to the jailhouse. There, the two guards confirmed my arrival with the chief constable and dropped me in another cell. This one was larger than the small parish jail cell.

I wouldn't be alone this time. The cell was already occupied by some kind of vagrant sitting wide legged on the floor, dressed in unwashed clothes with long greasy hair. I could smell his stench from outside the cell. It had to be more overwhelming up close. In the other corner, another man sat on a small stool. He was an unassuming fellow— dark hair, dark eyes.

"Watch out for that one," one of the guards said as he finally removed the cuffs from my arms. "He's a wily one." I rubbed my raw wrists and glanced at the man on the stool. I wondered what the warning from the guard meant. That particular cell mate looked more harmless than the vagrant who was lewdly grinning at me. I shrugged and found a spot to sit where I hopefully wouldn't be bothered and leaned my head against the bars.

Closing my eyes, I tried to block out what was happening to me. However, it seemed I wasn't allowed a moment to myself.

"Psst. Hey. Hey," the vagrant called, his deep-set eyes staring me down. "You over there. What they nab you for?" Did I detect a hint of alcohol? Perhaps he'd been arrested for public alcoholism and indecency. I ignored him. The vagrant moved, inching closer. "Don't want to talk to me. You a fancy lord?" he spat. I rolled my eyes at his attempt to goad me into a reaction.

"Leave 'im alone," the man on the stool said. "'e's in the same boat as the rest 'o us. Lord or no Lord." His eyes swept sideways, resting on the vagrant, while he picked dirt from underneath his fingernails.

The vagrant didn't listen. He inched closer until his filthy hands touched the top of my shoe. I pulled my foot back. The scent of alcohol, buried under a layer of piss and shit, wafted off him. "You a thief?" he suggested. "Owe money to someone?"

The man on the stool stopped picking at his nails. "What did I just tell ye?"

"We're juz' having a bit of fun," the vagrant responded. "Aren't we?" His eyes trailed my face. "How'd you get the scar?" His dirty crusted hand reached for my cheek, but I slapped his arm away.

"Leave me alone," I said firmly.

The vagrant snickered. "Ooh. He has a bit of fight in him. I like that. Makes it more fun when their sentence comes around." He scuttled back to his own corner and turned to the man on the stool. "You reckon he's going to hang?"

I swallowed, a lump stuck in my throat.

"I reckon *you* might be if ye don't shut yer gob fer once," the man on the stool said. The vagrant glared but stayed quiet.

I nodded at the man, thanking him for calling off the vagrant. He returned the gesture.

"Harry," he said.

"Will," I replied. Then, deciding I had nothing to lose, I asked, "How long does it usually take to get your hearing?"

"No more than a couple 'o days. A week, if the court is busy."

I mulled the information over. Within a week, I could be standing in front of the county court, getting sentenced to who knows what. My hand traced along my neck as I replayed the vagrant's words in my head. As soon as I noticed what I was doing, I dropped my hand into my lap. There was no point in letting that comment scare me. The vagrant didn't know what he was talking about.

I sat there, leaning against the bars, for hours when a guard returned, a thick-necked bald man.

"You've a visitor," he said, tapping against the bar my head rested against.

I scrambled up. "Who is it?"

"A Mr. Easton. You want to speak to him or not?"

"Yes, please send him in." The guard walked off.

The vagrant cackled lasciviously. "Who's that, your lover?" I ignored him, craning my head to see who was heading towards my cell.

John strode in, nose crinkled and brows raised. "Will," he said, looking me over. "God's man, are they treating you well?"

"As well as can be expected." I shrugged. I grabbed hold of the bars, getting as close as I could. "Is he safe?" I whispered. John's eyes slid down my body, taking in my dirtied state, stopping at my wrists.

He frowned. "What happened?"

"The parish constable left the cuffs on too tight." John

reached out his hand to give my palm a quick squeeze before returning to his regular stance. I looked him in the eye. "Now...what about Austin?" I made sure to keep my voice lowered. Neither my cell mates nor the guards needed to over-hear us. I knew the vagrant was interested in our conversation by the way he kept angling his scruffy face towards us.

"He's safe, staying indoors of course. But... Well. He's worried about you."

I swallowed. "Tell him not to be. I'll be fine." My heart danced a jig. Austin was still here.

"You will be. I promise. I've reached out to some acquain-tances."

"And?"

"Captain Tremblay reported you." John looked angry. "I can't believe that little weasel stayed the night in my home, under my roof, and is now dragging your name through the mud."

Captain Tremblay. That arrogant bastard. He made sense. I had hoped we were finished with that man when he'd failed to blackmail me, but I supposed his bruised ego propelled him to lash out. What did he hope to achieve? My death? Or merely humiliation? Or was he hoping to find another way to blackmail me? If that was the case, then this had to be his stupidest idea; it's not like he could wring money from a dead man. I let out a dark chuckle.

John furrowed his brow in worry. "We are going to sort this. They will release you," he urged.

"Thank you," I said, even if I didn't fully believe his words.. "Thank you for trying."

John pursed his lips and hesitated. "I'm going to have to

go. I was told that your case would go in front of the court in two days."

"I'll see you then," I said. Before he turned, I grabbed his hand. "You are my best friend. If I don't find another chance to say it, remember that. And tell Austin... Tell him I love him and that it will be alright. Tell him that he should go back to his own time if he gets the chance. I-I." My voice broke. "I'm so glad I got to meet him."

"I know. And you are coming back with me, Will. Two days. That's it. Two days and you'll be back at Hawthorne. You've trusted me before; trust me when I say this: I'll make it right."

"I trust you. You know I do. You're not just my best friend; you're my brother."

John nodded, face serious. "I have to go but Rose, Beth, and I will be at the court hearing. Please, rest. At least, as much as you can manage. Austin would want you to take care of yourself."

Once my friend left, I sank back to the ground. Two days. I'd be standing up in court in two days. No matter what happened, at least Austin was safe.

28

Sentencing

Standing at attention in the stands of the Kingswood County courthouse, all I wanted to do was shiver and hide. Instead, I forced myself to remain calm and collected. I had to keep faith in John, and in myself. All I could do at the moment was appear as if I had nothing to fear because I had done nothing wrong.

However, with the magistrate's eyes periodically sweeping over me while I waited for my case to come up, I worried he'd be able to see the nervous sweat beading my brow. The magistrate was currently sentencing a woman accused of stealing food—she'd been locked up in a different cell at the Kingswood County jail— while the judges leered and whispered.

My cell mates stood beside me, waiting their turns as well, chained together and watched over by the bald guard. The vagrant still stank to high heavens, but I at least had been able to change into a cleaner set of clothing.

John and Rose had dropped by the jail to hand me a clean shirt, pants, and jacket before I was transferred to the courthouse—to make sure I'd appear like a decent upstanding citizen. However, nothing could be done about my growing beard. I wasn't allowed access to a razor.

The court must deal with many unwashed prisoners because the wooden benches were lined with small hanging sachets of potpourri. The magistrate even had a fresh bundle of flowers at his stand. I glanced behind me. John, Rose, and Beth had slipped into one of the spectators stands. I was glad for the show of support.

I focused on the court hearing. "—since you are of the gentle persuasion, and because this is indeed your first offense, I am inclined to be merciful," the magistrate intoned. The rail thin woman's face brightened at his words.

She stumbled forward, her cuffed hands outstretched. "Please, sir, have mercy, I'll never do it again. I was hungry, sir."

"That may be so," the magistrate answered. "But hunger is no excuse for thievery. Had it not been your first offense, I might have sentenced you to be hanged, or perhaps to be shipped out to the colonies in Australia. But as it stands, I shall be merciful in my verdict."

"Oh, thank you kindly, sir." The woman clasped her hands together.

"Take her away to be flogged," he ordered another guard standing in the corner of the room.

The woman's face blanched. "Wait, no," she shouted, as the

guard stepped up and grasped her arm. "Where's the mercy?" she cried, as he dragged her away through a side door. The judges looked bored. I agreed with the woman. Sentencing her to be flogged when she looked about a week away from starvation was not mercy in my eyes.

Next up, was the vagrant. He'd gotten away rather easily in my opinion— banishment from Kingswood County. No laws against vagrancy, I supposed, merely a dislike.

Then, my name was called. The bald guard unlocked me from the chain that connected me to the other prisoner, Harry, and led me in front of the magistrate.

"Can you confirm that you are indeed William Raphe Chambers?

My chin held high, I answered, "I can." The magistrate pressed his glasses up his nose and glanced at the sheet of paper in his hand.

"It says here that you are accused of," the man paused for effect, looking down at me. "The act of sodomy. How do you plead?"

"Not guilty," I said, keeping firm eye contact. The magistrate coughed and glanced at the judges when the door to the courtroom opened and in strode Captain Tremblay, his face smug as he joined the spectators. I seethed. That bastard had come to gloat.

"Your Honor," John spoke loudly, drowning out the mumbling crowd. "I have some evidence to submit to prove this man's innocence."

The magistrate scowled. "This is highly irregular."

"Be that as it may," John cut in, "this man is being falsely accused by that man over there." He pointed at Captain Tremblay. Voices rose as spectators voiced their shock at the turn of events. Tremblay seemed livid. My eyes grew wide when I noticed Mrs. Avery and Clara enter the room during the commotion.

"That is quite an accusation," the magistrate said. "Can you prove it to the court?"

"If you'll let me, Your Honor," John said.

The magistrate motioned for John to step forward. A guard opened a small gate to let him pass. John carried a folder which he slid on top of the magistrate's stand, opening it to the first page. He waited for the magistrate to read. I stood there, heart beating in my chest, as John shot me a quick nod. Then the magistrate glanced up from the paper.

"You may proceed," the magistrate told John. "Please state your full name for the court."

John angled his body so he could be seen by the magistrate and judges as well as the spectators while he spoke his part. "My name is John Easton; I'm the owner of the Hawthorne estate in Westbridge. I have been a friend of Mr. Chambers since childhood and can vouch for his moral upstanding. He is a veteran who fought in the war against Napoleon and who is a part of the social elite. The allegation brought against him is made under falsehoods by Captain Tremblay, the man standing with you in the stands today." John let his eyes sweep across the judges and magistrate, then, pointing at the folder on the magistrate's stand, he continued. "I brought with me today, letters which prove Captain Tremblay's duplicity. The top letter is written by a Mr. Glencoe, owner of the Sterling bank; he states that Captain Tremblay owes him a rather sizable sum of money. It appears Captain Tremblay has a penchant for gambling and no talent to back him up."

"My financial situation has nothing to do with this," Captain Tremblay spat, his fingers clenching the wooden stand. The spectators roared behind him.

The Magistrate slammed his hammer against the wooden stand, silencing the crowd. "I'll only warn you once," he told Captain Tremblay. "Let Mr. Easton make his case."

John's lip lifted. "As I said, Captain Tremblay has accumulated massive amounts of debts, debts he'd never be able to repay on his own. Mr. Glencoe isn't the only person he owes money to. Below that letter are three more just like it from other money lenders."

"Get to the point Mr. Easton," the magistrate said as he handed the other evidence to the judges to review.

"My point is that in November, at a hunting party at a mutual acquaintance's place, Captain Tremblay ran into Mr. Chambers and decided that my friend would be a good, rich target for extortion. Merely days later, he stopped by Hawthorne, under the guise of being a friend, and threatened Mr. Chambers. He told him that he would go to a constable and tell the whole world he was a molly, if he didn't give him money. Mr. Chambers, of course, disagreed. Captain Tremblay then had the nerve to accuse my friend in front of me. I turned him out with a few unkind words. This whole accusation is a farce, merely to satisfy the inflated ego of a blackmailer. Captain Tremblay should be the one arrested."

"Is this true?" the magistrate asked me.

"Every word of it."

The magistrate pointed. "Guards, grab that man." A guard in the back of the courtroom, near the entrance, made his way past the stands to grab Captain Tremblay's arm. Captain Tremblay, wild-eyed and red-faced, was glancing around the room. He caught sight of Clara, huddled halfway behind her plump aunt, trying to shrink even smaller.

"I've got a witness. I've got a witness," he yelled. "That girl witnessed it. Call her to the stand."

"I don't think—" the magistrate started. But the crowd jeered. He sighed, scratching underneath the powdered wig. "Girl, will you join us?"

Clara paled as she walked to the front, moving through the crowd, joining John, myself, and Captain Tremblay who was being held in place by the guard.

The magistrate glanced down at her. "Who are you, girl?"

Softly, she said, "Clara, sir, Clara Collins."

"Speak up, girl. How do you know the accused?"

A little louder, Clara continued, "I work as a maid, sir, for Mr. Easton."

"And how do you know this man over here?" the magistrate said, pointing at Tremblay.

"He spent one night at Hawthorne, said he was a friend of Mr. Chambers."

"Tell the magistrate what you witnessed," Captain Tremblay ordered Clara.

The magistrate shot him a pointed look. He turned his gaze back to Clara. "Go on, girl. What did you witness?"

Clara, slightly trembling, kept her eyes focused on the wooden stand with the small bunch of flowers. "Captain Tremblay came to my room in the middle of the night. He promised me a prosperous future if I'd help him. He told me about his plans to blackmail Mr. Chambers."

Captain Tremblay pulled at the guard, growling. "She's lying."

Clara ignored him, continuing with her story, "At first, I agreed. I thought he liked me. But I figured out soon enough that he just tried to use me. Please, let Mr. Chambers free. He is a good man. He's valued by everyone at Hawthorne."

Captain Tremblay fought the guard. "They're all lying. He should be going to the pillory."

"Restrain him," the magistrate ordered the guard. The bald guard joined him, and together they handcuffed Captain Tremblay as he bucked and thrashed against them. Then, the first guard led him out the side door while the bald guard returned to my former cellmate's side.

"It seems it is time to come to a verdict," the magistrate remarked dryly. I stiffened as the magistrate raised his voice. "Mr. Chambers, the Kingswood County courthouse finds you not guilty. You are hereby released." I released a breath. I was free.

Beth, Rose, and Mrs. Avery applauded along with other spectators. John clapped his hand against my shoulder. I stepped back, relieved, and turned to the bald guard, so I could be freed from the handcuffs. Once my wrists were once again bare, I crossed through the crowd, heading straight for the exit. Clara and John followed me out. Rose, Beth and Mrs. Avery joined us outside the courthouse only a moment later.

I sank down on a bench. "I'm so glad that is over." I felt a bit numb, still processing everything that had happened.

John sat down next to me. "I promised we'd find a way to release you."

"You did." I glanced up at him. "What do you think will happen to Tremblay?"

"He'll get his own day in court," John said darkly. "With all the proof we just handed the magistrate, I doubt he'd be able to talk his way out of it. He'll probably be sent to debtors' prison. Either way, he's not our problem anymore."

I rubbed my sore wrists. "How did you find proof so fast?"

"I called in a favor with everyone I knew. His gambling was a not so secret, secret, in London. Many other members of society have been burned by him cheating at cards. An old friend led me to the banker who provided the other names. The banker and the other moneylenders were already planning to sue Captain Tremblay; I just sped things along, combining our efforts.

Mrs. Avery scooted closer. "John told me about your wrists. Here, let me soothe them a bit. I brought a balm." John stood, providing space for Mrs. Avery to sit.

"I'll fetch Hugh," he said.

Hawthorne's cook pulled a small jar from her apron. She took off the lid and scooped out a thick glob of white paste with two fingers. I held out my wrists. Carefully, she tapped the white paste against my raw skin until both my wrists were circled. The paste felt cool against my tender skin.

"Thank you," I told Mrs. Avery.

She wiped the excess off on her apron and rumpled my hair with her right hand, the gesture motherly. She had always been a bit of a mother hen with John and I. "I've got more back at Hawthorne. I am so glad you are returning to us. What that bad man put you through..." She tutted. "I hope he gets his comeuppance."

"By the sounds of it, he will," I told Mrs. Avery.

"I knew John would find a way to free you. I baked tarts to celebrate. I had a feeling you'd have need of my cooking. It doesn't seem that you've been fed."

"Not a day goes by when I don't need your cooking," I told Mrs. Avery. She smiled brightly, ruffling my hair once more.

29

A Tub in front of a Fire

"Austin? We've returned," John called as we entered the house.

"William?" His voice came from upstairs. I looked up to see his face peeking over the banister. He ran down the steps as fast as he could and flung himself around me. I grunted at the impact. "Oh, sorry. That was harder than I meant it. I was just so—" he stopped, shaking his head. "Will, you got arrested. I was so worried." He squeezed his arms, pulling me in tighter.

"I was worried about you too," I breathed in his ear. Clara and Mrs. Avery had already sneaked off, presumably to the kitchen, and John, Rose, and Beth were also currently backing away to give us some privacy.

"But I wasn't arrested by a constable."

"Perhaps not, but I worried they'd find you too, or that you'd return to your own time while I was gone and I would never get to say goodbye."

"I would never leave without seeing you." Austin kissed my cheek.

"What if you had no choice?"

Austin rested his chin on my shoulder. "I don't know," he said, when he pulled back. "But we are both still here. Let's not worry about things that didn't happen. I just need to hold you right now." He pressed his lips against mine. I kissed him back, savoring the taste.

When we broke apart again, he said, "I can't believe that asshole reported you. What happened at the courthouse?"

"John swooped in to save the day." I grinned then. The knowledge that I was free, that I was back at Hawthorne, that I was holding Austin, settled in my bones. I grabbed Austin's hand and led him to the first step of the staircase. I sat down on the padded runner, Austin sliding in next to me.

"What happened to your wrists?" he asked, tracing his finger along my skin, stopping short of the damaged area.

"Handcuffs. The first constable didn't take them off at all. Mrs. Avery put on some soothing balm which is helping."

Austin frowned. "Unbelievable. I am so glad you're back." He clasped my hand and lifted it to his mouth.

I told Austin about how John swooped in with his evidence. How Captain Tremblay had stood in the stands, gloating. But the evidence was overwhelming, and Clara's confession had been even more damning.

"The nerve," Austin hissed through his teeth. He pulled me in, resting his forehead against mine. "Screw him; you've won."

"I've won," I agreed and kissed Austin again. Then I sighed. "I can't believe you are even hugging me. I stink." My nose crinkled. Days spent in two different cells had not been kind on my hygiene.

"None of that matters," Austin muttered.

A smile tugged at my lips. "Still, I'd like to wash all this filth off me."

Austin planted a kiss on my cheek. "You go upstairs, and I'll head to the kitchen to help Mrs. Avery ready some warm water for you."

"And you'll join me?"

Austin's brow quirked suggestively. "If you want."

I didn't have to think twice about it. "Always."

Trudging up the stairs, I smiled. I was weary, but a hot bath would do me some good. My muscles could use the heat. Once I entered my own room, I closed my eyes and breathed deeply, taking in the familiar scents. I was back. I pulled off my shirt and dropped it next to the bed, wondering if I should've helped Austin bring up the tub.

I didn't need to worry because he brought in the metal tub a while later, lifting it over his head as he kicked the door open with one foot. I was sitting in a chair, dozing off, not wanting to dirty the bed.

"Where should I put it?" he asked. I directed him to the fireplace. Austin set it down a few feet from the fire. "I'll be right back. Mrs. Avery and Clara are getting the buckets of water ready."

"I can come down and help—" I moved to join him.

"No, you've dealt with enough today." He kissed my forehead gently and smiled. "I'll be right back, with water. You take it easy."

"Alright," I acquiesced. While Austin left to go back to the kitchen, I stoked up the fire and pulled out the privacy screen. The fire roared, taking with it most of the chill that always remained in stately mansions.

Clara, Mrs. Avery, and Austin each heaved two full buckets of water into the room, depositing them into the tub. They left, except for Austin, who prowled towards me, towels and washing cloths slung across his right shoulder. He dropped the towels by the foot of the tub and grabbed me.

"It's a good thing you asked me to stay because I don't want to let you out of my sight." He nuzzled the side of my face. "There are so many things I want to do to you. But right now, is not about me, it's about you." His lips trailed down my jawline, scattering kisses along my skin. "I must confess, though, that I kind of like you with facial hair."

A laugh bubbled up inside of me, and I touched my hairy chin. "Oh? So, you're telling me I shouldn't shave?"

Austin hooked his finger around the band of my pants. "You can do what you want. But I like the sensation of it when you kiss me, rugged."

"Like this?" I pressed my mouth against his, our lips and tongues moving in tandem. I suckled his plump upper lip.

"Just like that," he purred. "But I think it's time for a bath." He unhooked his finger and slid his hand lower, rubbing me over the fabric of my clothes.

My manhood strained against the tight weave. "Austin," I whispered. My skin flushed. His touch inflamed me, the sight and feel of him so intoxicating I could scarcely believe he was real. But Austin was real, time-travel and all. And he wanted me as badly as I wanted him. There was no doubt about it by the way he licked his lips and stared at me, as if I was a present he couldn't wait to unwrap. Unfortunately, he had more self-restraint than I did that moment.

"Later," he shushed. "I can tell you are tired. First, let's get you clean. It was a lot of work dragging those buckets of water up the stairs. It would be a shame if it went to waste." Tortuously slow, he unbuttoned my pants, rolling the fabric down until I could step out of them. His eyes darkened when they swept across my naked body.

"Get in the tub," he ordered, his voice deep and sultry.

"Yes, sir," I said, winking, eliciting a groan from him.

"You don't know what you make me want to do to you when you say that."

I played innocent. "What? By saying sir?"

"You understand exactly what I mean. But I wouldn't feel right until you had some time to recover." His eyes flashed to my wrists.

"I'll be fine, Austin. But you are right. I do need a bath and hot water is a luxury I shouldn't waste." I lifted my leg and stepped into the tub, groaning as the hot water soothed my muscles. Slowly, I slid down until I was seated. The days spent on a hard floor in a jail cell had wreaked havoc on my muscles. They strained as I flexed my shoulder blades. The water felt amazing. I sighed.

Austin moved to the washing bowl on the side table and grabbed a bar of soap. Then he pulled up a stool to the side of the tub and sat down. He dipped the washing cloth in my bath water and started lathering the soap, a pleasant lavender scent rising up.

"You don't have to wash me," I said, stopping his hand.

"I know," he breathed behind me. "But I want to." I dropped my arm, letting Austin lather my neck and shoulders. "Can you bend forward?" he asked, as he was circling the soap along my shoulders in varying pressure.

I moved, providing him access to my lower back. I hissed as his hand pushed along a particularly tight spot.

"Sore?"

I nodded and he softened his hold. Austin kneaded and rolled my muscles until I felt like I wouldn't be able to stand, soaping up every part of my skin. Then, he took the washcloth and started wiping away the lather.

I turned towards him. "Will you join me?"

Austin laughed. "I am here with you."

I glanced between him and the tub.

He quirked his brow and shook his head. "There's no space. I wouldn't fit in the tub with you."

"Are you sure? I think the tub has plenty of space." I stood and grabbed him, pulling him into the tub." Water sloshed over the edge as he landed in my lap.

"What about my clothes?" He laughed.

"What about your clothes?" I said as I cradled him and kissed his ear, his pants and shirt drenched and translucent. "Fine, I can get rid of them for you." I pulled up his wet shirt and shimmied it off over his head. Then, I helped him out of his pants, which was a bit of an undertaking in the tub.

"You are so beautiful," I told him as he leaned back against my chest, his head resting against my cheek.

Austin turned his face to kiss me. "You are not so bad yourself." Lazily, I traced the curve of his neck and chest.

Then, I followed the intricate lines of his tattoo. More and more I realized that it wasn't necessarily Hawthorne that felt like home. It was Austin; he felt like home.

* * *

Eventually, after we had well and truly bathed, Austin and I headed to the drawing room where John, Beth, and Rose were gathered.

"You didn't have to give us space," I told them, wet hair combed back but my facial hair still there. I didn't have the heart to shave after Austin's comment earlier. I already planned to brush my face along his skin later when we were alone once more. Then, I wouldn't give him the chance to tell me I needed to rest.

Rose jumped up and hugged me. "We all figured you could use it." She shot me a sly wink before she let me go. I coughed and moved to the settee. Austin smirked into his hand as he joined me.

"At least you smell better," John remarked. "That stench at the Courthouse, frankly, was a bit overwhelming." I had a mind to throw something at his face.

"See how you'd do locked in a cell."

John grinned. "Not much better, I reckon." He pointed at a platter of pastries and meats. "Please, eat something. I saw what they fed you at the jail, so I'm sure you're starving."

I nodded and grabbed a rolled-up slice of ham and an apple pastry. Within seconds, I wolfed them down and reached for another round.

"Mrs. Avery is already preparing dinner, so you'll receive a warm meal as well," Rose said.

"Thank you," I muttered in between bites, sighing as the food hit my stomach. When I filled up a bit more, I continued. "Really, thank you, John. I mean it. This. Me. It could have been so much worse."

Rose gazed at her husband before speaking. "The first thing John did when you were taken away, was head straight to London. He reached out to all his acquaintances on your behalf."

"I am incredibly grateful."

John shook his head. "I did the same thing that you would've done for any of us. Didn't I send you on many fools' errands when it involved Rose and that blasted Danby? Besides, I may have reached out, but you are just as well-known and respected in our circles. Our peers were merely assisting me in a task to help our friend. Sometimes, I think you doubt how many people care about you."

I swallowed. "You are right. And I am so lucky to have such wonderful friends. I have to admit that it felt like justice to see Captain Tremblay go down in front of the magistrate. His eyes nearly bulged out of his skull when Clara outed his deception." My mind wandered to my strange cell mate. I knew what happened to the vagrant but had already left before Harry's sentencing would start. "Do you know what happened to the other accused? Harry, was his name, or something."

"You don't know?"

I cocked my head. "Should I?"

"Well. Most of the crowd in the stands had been there to

witness him. That's why he was saved for last. You didn't spot the poster pasted on the outside of the courthouse?"

"My mind was a tad preoccupied," I said dryly.

"You were sharing a cell with Harry Doyle, the gentleman thief." Now that John said it, I had heard of him. The gentleman thief had been stealing from the beau monde all over Britain, inveigling himself into the lives of his target.

"What was he like?" Beth asked eagerly.

"Seemed like a decent enough chap." There wasn't much more to say about him really. He wasn't what I'd imagine a thief to look like. Beth seemed a bit disappointed.

"I think Will has had enough excitement," Austin said, handing me another pastry. That I had.

30

The Bookshop Owner

Austin and I woke up together in a tangle of limbs and sheets. His hair was adorably ruffled, a lazy smile plastered on his face.

"Morning," he mumbled, sleepily. His green eyes peeked up at me from beneath thick lashes. Gods, I loved him. I tensed. Besides when I told John at the prison, that was the first time I'd truly acknowledged it ,and I realized how true it was. I loved him.

I loved his dimples when he smiled, how he grinned self-consciously when I sneaked up on him to peek at what he was drawing, the sounds he made when I touched him. I loved every little thing about him. He was brave and kind. I didn't deserve him, but I'd try. I would try for as long as I could.

"Austin." I said.

He smiled. "Hmm?"

"I love you." He didn't even have to think about what I said. His face lit up and he kissed me hard.

"I love you, too."

I snuggled into him, breathing in his heady scent. "What do you want to do today?" My heart felt like it glowed.

"Whatever you'd like," he said.

"Well, we could go ice-skating again, though, I wouldn't mind a stop at Rose's school house. We had such a good time there during the snowstorm."

"Scandalous. In a school?" Austin laughed. "It's supposed to be a place of learning." Then he added, "I might be agreeable." I snorted.

"Or... I can finally take you out horseback riding? We'd have to stick to the driveway and the roads that have been plowed. But you might like the scenery."

"I don't doubt I'd like the scenery," Austin said, a smile playing on his lips. "I'm just not sure I'd have the patience to get past the stables."

I grinned. "We can't possibly confine ourselves to the bedroom. What would the others think?"

"Try me," he said, nipping at my earlobe. "Besides, I'm pretty sure Rose would high-five me if I keep you with me all day. Let them imagine all the naughty things we'd get up to."

"High-five?" I stared at him, amused.

Austin shook his head. "I really had to go and fall in love with someone from a different time, didn't I?" he raised his hand. "Slap your palm against mine," he ordered. I did, softly. "Next time, you can do it a bit harder, but, that's a high-five. Now, you are officially modern. We do it to congratulate someone for doing or getting something."

"Oh, so what you are saying is that I'm a conquest? And that Rose would congratulate you for winning me?"

"When you put it like that... Yes," he laughed, kissing me.

"Never in my life did I expect to feel like one of the socialites entering the marriage mart. But I'm not the only prize. If you get congratulated for conquests, I expect a high-five as well." I swept my arm around him and pulled him on top of me.

Austin smiled against my mouth. "I'll be sure to let Rose know."

"You better," I growled as I slid my hands down the length of his back until I cupped his behind.

"While I like where your mind is going," Austin said in between kisses, "I am starving. How about we get some breakfast and..." He quirked a brow. "Revisit this later."

"If we must," I said, squeezing his bottom.

"We must. Your conquest is hungry." He winked.

"Then we shall fetch him some breakfast." Austin rolled off me as I untangled myself. I stood and pulled on a shirt and pants. Once dressed, I handed Austin his clothing.

Downstairs, we each grabbed some toasted bread, eggs, and rashers of bacon. Mrs. Avery always seemed to know when we were in need of food. I poured him and myself a cup of tea.

"So, horse-back riding?" I suggested again.

"I'm not sure if I trust myself to ride yet," Austin said after he finished chewing a bite of bacon and bread.

"We could double up again? I'd steer while you sit in front of me?"

He raised his brows and chuckled. "Alright, I'll go riding with you." We finished our breakfast and drank our tea. On the way out, already wrapped in our winter gear, we ran into John and Rose.

"Where are you both headed?" Rose asked.

"I'm taking Austin riding."

"Have fun," she told me. "And good luck," she added to Austin.

Austin bumped against me when we exited the front door. "Should I have asked her for the high-five," he whispered, grinning mischievously. I laughed.

"You wouldn't dare."

I froze. Heart sinking.

"Will, what's wrong?" Austin asked. He followed my stare straight to the plump middle-aged woman now standing in the middle of the driveway, shivering without a coat. "Who's th..." But then it clicked. "The bookshop owner."

She strode towards us. "I'd forgotten it was winter here," she said, as if it was the most normal conversation. "Let us take it inside before I freeze to death." Her curly hair bobbed as she brushed past us into the foyer.

"Melinda?" Rose exclaimed.

"Hello, dear," the witch said. "How have you been? Still happy?"

Rose nodded. "Very much so. But," her eyes flashed to me. "Why return now? Austin has been here a long time already?"

Melinda shrugged. "It's the right time."

"The right time for what?" Austin asked, stepping forward. I wanted to reach out and pull him back to me. Hold him, so he couldn't leave. But that wouldn't be fair to him. I bit my lip to stop myself from speaking, my heart shattering with every inch Austin moved away from me.

Melinda ignored his question. "Rose probably has told you some things about me. I'll give you the same choice that she had. You can choose to return to your own time, or you can stay here. I can give you a few moments think about it, so I'd recommend you weigh the options carefully. Rose's choice to return was a one-time favor. If you choose to return to your own time and find out that you chose wrong, you won't be able to change your decision."

Austin swallowed. "I-I need to talk to William." He turned to me, his eyes sad.

"Of course," Melinda said. "I'll wait. Rose and I can catch up."

Austin pulled me into the hallway. He kissed me hungrily, passionately, as if it was the last time. I didn't need to guess what his decision would be.

"I understand," I told him. I looked at him, really looked at him, trying to memorize every angle of his face.

"I just... I need you to understand," Austin said, his eyes red. "I want so badly to stay with you. I love you. Every word of that is true. You must remember that, William. You are amazing. But I have my sister to think of. I've got a life, a job I like."

I lowered my head, resting it against his forehead. "I understand."

"And what happened to you, it scared me. I didn't know what would happen to you, if you'd be hurt or killed. I couldn't bear it if anything happened to you. But I want to be free to love the way I want. To be out in the open." A tear slipped down his cheek. "Since the masquerade, all I have wanted to do is shout it from the roof tops. Show you to the world and tell everyone that handsome man is with me. But I can't. Not here."

I brushed the wetness from his face and kissed him. "I love you too, and you must go. I want you to go." Austin moved his lips as if he was trying to say something but seemed to change his mind. "What are you thinking?" I said, softly, gazing into his green eyes.

"I just wished it was different." He sighed. "I don't know how to do this, how to say goodbye."

"Then don't. It's not goodbye." I placed a finger under his chin, tipping his face up and crushed my lips against his. I let my hands rove across his body, our tongues clashing as they met. When we broke apart, panting, I said, "You'll be with me every time I think of you. As long as we have our memories, we won't truly have left each other."

"I hope so." Austin's voice broke as he said this. It took every shred of strength I had in me to not break down. But I didn't want to make this harder for Austin. He had to go to his own time. A time where he was safe, where he could love.

I clasped his hand, fingers twined. "Let's go."

"Have you made your decision?" Melinda asked when we returned to the foyer.

Austin nodded.

I noticed that Rose had disappeared. "Wait, wait," she shouted from upstairs. Holding Austin's drawing, she walked down the grand staircase. Once she reached the floor, she handed it to Austin.

"My drawing?" he asked, confused.

"I love it, but I spoke with John, and we both thought you might be able to take it with you to your time. I asked Melinda to make sure."

"And I said yes," Melinda said.

"Would you give it to my parents? I tacked a letter on the back with their address. It might be a lot to ask... but would you visit them? Tell them about me and John. Tell them about my life here?"

Austin flashed her a watery smile. "I will."

"Thank you. It was fun to have you around." John and Beth echoed Rose's sentiments.

Melinda pulled a pale blue cloth-covered book out of a pocket in her skirt. "Are you ready to leave?"

Austin hesitated. "One moment." He pulled me in for a kiss. Our last kiss. "I love you," he whispered, finishing with another small peck on the tip of my nose.

"I love you," I replied, forcing myself to stay still. I watched as he turned to the time-traveling witch. Melinda flipped open the book. Austin gripped the drawing tighter and lifted his hand.

"Just touch the book," she said. Austin's finger lowered. I couldn't breathe.

"Wait," I cried out. I rushed forward, grabbing his shoulders, kissing him. When we broke apart, I turned to Melinda. "What about me? Why can't I join Austin in the future?"

Austin gazed at me. "You'd do that?"

"How can you even ask that?" I said. "I'd follow you anywhere. I'd follow you to the ends of the earth."

Austin looked at Melinda, waiting.

"If you are certain, then, yes. William can join you."

Austin's face brightened. "I am," he answered immediately. "Yes. I want him with me."

I glanced back to John. He smiled at me. "Go," he muttered. "Be happy."

"You can't tell me to go like that," I told him. "I need a hug from my best friend." I stepped towards him and pulled him into an embrace. "And you too," I said to Beth, who joined in the hug, fully crying. I rumpled her hair. "Be a menace to John during your season. And remember, none of the men attending are worthy of you."

"I already know that," she laughed in between her tears.

"Good." I flashed them all a bright smile. "Don't worry about me. I'll be with Austin."

I returned to my lover's side; he clasped my hand and kissed it.

Melinda held out the book once more. "Now, keep a tight hold of each other and touch the book."

Gazing into each other's eyes, we lowered our clasped hands to the pages. First, we stood in the foyer, but the next moment, I blinked and opened my eyes to a busy street. But not a street like I had ever seen before. There were loud noises and honking all around us. Everywhere I turned my head, I saw bright signs and strange buildings. I glanced down; on the ground in front of us lay the pale blue book.

Austin grinned. "Welcome home."

31

Welcome Home

"What do you want?" Austin asked, glancing in the rear-view mirror.

"A cherry slushie," his sister, Alyssa, said from the back seat. She was leaning forward, focused on her phone.

Austin turned his gaze to me. "And you?"

"What do you recommend?" He considered for a moment before rolling down the window and pressing a button on some weird stand.

"What can I get ya," a tinny voice from the stand said.

"A cherry slushie, and two Strawberry slushies. Oh, I'd also like an order of onion rings."

"Coming right up," the tin voice replied. A short while later, a young man brought up a small bag and a cup holder with three giant drinks.

Austin accepted the drinks and food, and thanked the man.

"Here," Austin said as he doled out the drinks. "Everybody ready for a road trip?"

I nodded, staring out the side window. "How long was it again?"

"About fifteen hours. We'll stop and spend the night in Reno. I booked us two rooms."

"And I arranged snacks," Alyssa said, patting the bags in the passenger's seat next to her. "Oh, and I've created a road trip play list."

Austin chuckled. "It's usually the driver who chooses the music."

"But I've got the perfect mix of songs— oldies and hits."

"Or we can let William pick the songs."

Alyssa rolled her eyes. "But he doesn't know any songs. No offense," she added.

I snorted and took a sip of the ice-cold drink. It was very sweet but refreshing. "None taken," I told Alyssa. I liked Austin's sister; she reminded me a little of Beth. Perhaps an even more outspoken version, if that was possible. I could see why Austin loved her. The drink left my hand clammy from the condensation; I wiped it on the pair of jeans Austin had bought me.

"Fine, you can pick the music," Austin relented. Then he placed his drink into the cup holder, took a hold of my hand, and said, "Who's ready to meet Rose's parents?"

Afterword

One thing I love about writing stories set in past times is the research. With Rose Through Time I delved into historical accounts on clothing and accessories, to period accurate flowers for the greenhouse -or orangeries as they were often called-, to the dishes that Mrs. Ashbrook would cook and serve to the Eastons.

Though I do my research to understand the particulars of that time frame, since it is a time-travel story I do give it my own twist.

Writing William Through Time was a pleasure especially with the interesting topic of sexuality during the Regency era and also the experiences for a soldier during the Napoleonic Wars. If you are interested in reading about Molly houses and homosexuality in Britain during that time frame, I've added references at the bottom. I also included a link to personal accounts of the Napoleonic war if you'd like to read up on that and compare it to William's story.

A lot of touches and anecdotes that I've added to the story did indeed happen, though, not exactly as I have written it. At one instance, William is speaking with James' father about a fellow soldier who "found" a pig, which we come to find out was supposed to be dinner for the officers. A version of that story actually happened. Instead of a British group of soldiers they were French soldiers. One of them, a man named Jean-Roch Coignet, tells the story in which during a long march he and his men caught and butchered a pig. They found out later that the pig had belonged to Napoleon and was supposed to be served to his generals.

Reading personal accounts of the war helps bring perspective to something that happened so long ago and in turn makes it more real. To know what he might have gone through helped bring William and his experiences to life.

Anyway, here I've been rambling on. I hope you liked reading William Through Time, and if you are interested in the topics that came up; check out some of the references below.

https://www.atlasobscura.com/articles/regency-gay-bar-molly-houses.amp

http://rictornorton.co.uk/index.htm

https://archive.org/details/aclassicaldictio1grosgoog/page/n112/mode/2up

http://www.bl.uk/learning/timeline/item126767.html

Acknowledgments

I want to thank everyone of you for choosing to pick up and read William Through Time all the way until the end. It means the world to me. A book that isn't being read is a tragic thing. There are so many things that make up a novel besides the author, that's me, typing away furiously at a keyboard.

Without the support of my husband, Matthew, I wouldn't have the freedom to dedicate my time to writing. Next in the process of writing are my friends and family; you all know who you are. To give me support and guidance, to listen to me drone on about my book plots and characters, pushing me to write because they want to read what's coming next.

Then comes my editor, Megan. She is the hero that swoops in and polishes my manuscript until it gleams. So you, the reader, can enjoy the best version, a version where my characters shine.

Ashley from Patterson Photography provided the author photo to give you all a glimpse into my life. And last, but not least, there's my cover designer, they take the story and condenses it into a gorgeous cover that attracts readers. Then, finally, it's ready to be sent out into the world, ultimately landing in your hands.

If you enjoyed what you read, I would love it if you left a review at a site of your choosing. As an indie author, reviews are one of the most important ways to get my novel out into the world.

About the Author

Harmke Buursma is a writer, and author of the book Rose Through Time. She uses her background in Journalism to help bring her fictional characters and worlds to life. When she isn't writing, she likes to read as many books as she can get her hands on. Originally born and raised in The Netherlands, Harmke now lives in Las Vegas with her husband Matthew and two dogs.

Harmke Buursma
Photo by Patterson Photography

For more information about Harmke and her books, visit www.harmkebuursma.com.

Books by this Author

ROSE THROUGH TIME

WILLIAM THROUGH TIME

BETH THROUGH TIME

Coming soon